'Til St. Patrick's Day

Holly Gilliatt

Turquoise Morning, LLC
P.O. Box 43958
Louisville, KY 40253-0958

'TIL ST. PATRICK'S DAY
Copyright © 2013, Holly Gilliatt
Trade Paperback ISBN: 978-1-62237-153-2

Cover Art Design by KJ Jacobs
Editor, Judy Alter

Digital Release, March, 2013
Trade Paperback Release, May, 2013

Dedication

For all the teachers who encouraged my writing: you forever changed my life.

And most of all, for my mom, LouAnn Schnider—the one person that always believed in me, even when I doubted myself. You are my first reader, my sounding board, my cheerleader. For all these things and so many more than I could ever say, I love you.

This is for you.

Acknowledgments

Writing is a solitary act, but much like a puppet show, there is a whole lot going on behind the curtain. Many thanks to:

Angie Linan, Kara Mathes and Leigh Cook—the three best friends a girl could ever ask for. Period.

My fearless readers for taking the time to read and critique this story: LouAnn Schnider, Troy Schnider (even though this was *so* not your genre of choice) and Kathy Kelley.

Christie Ashabranner for her constant encouragement, words that lifted me up and patience when reading query after query ("Do you like this one or this one better?").

Turquoise Morning Press for taking a chance on a new writer and making a lifelong dream come true.

Judy Alter, my editor, for putting up with this newbie (who most likely drove you insane), remaining kind and gracious through the process of guiding me toward a better story.

Sherry Rosenberger and Craig Taggart for leading by example and showing me that you really can follow your heart and be what you want to be when you grow up. Does this mean I'm a grown up now? (Props Crew Rules!)

Ryan Knighton for reminding me how delightful the English language can be with your wickedly awe-inspiring choices of phrase. And (even though you probably don't remember it) thanks for responding to my emails and giving great advice and encouragement to a fledgling writer. When you, one of my favorite authors, re-tweeted my smart-ass comment…it felt like winning the Nobel Prize for Literature.

John Mayer for writing a beautiful song that captured my imagination (you are by far my favorite living singer-songwriter—Go Local 83!) and his team (Michael McDonald, Reid Hunter, and Sarah McKemie) for allowing the use of *St. Patrick's Day.*

Andy Grammer for the songs *Lunatic* and *Keep Your Head Up,* along with the late beloved Dan Fogelberg for *Icarus Ascending.* These songs were on heavy rotation and kept me going when I didn't always believe in myself and made me think that I *could* do this.

My kids—Tressa, Emily and Nate—for living in a messy house while I write and putting up with Mommy's face staring at a screen for far too many hours. But I hope you now see that if you want something, and you work hard enough…dreams really can come true. I hope you each find something in your life that fills you with as much joy as writing does for me. Never forget you are my three favorite people in the world—I love you even more than chocolate. And that's a lot.

Jay. My love, my husband, my friend…the man that makes me laugh like no one else can and still makes my heart go pitter-patter. I know my writing has stolen time away from you, so thank you for not complaining. And even if you weren't exactly dying to read what I wrote, I felt your love every step of the way. You have made me a stronger and more confident woman. Your love has made everything possible.

And Emily, you kept asking when my book was going to get published. The answer is now, sweetie.

'TIL ST. PATRICK'S DAY

For three best friends, one winter will change everything.

Chronically optimistic Jayne is surprised she's still single at twenty-eight. But as always for Jayne, there's hope. This time his name is Gray—a successful, gorgeous marketing VP that she can't believe is going out with her. She's never given up on the belief that the right man for her is out there. Maybe Gray could be the one…if she just works hard enough to make it happen.

Her cynical friend Karen is suspicious of Jayne's new guy with his model looks and over-inflated ego. She's concerned for Jayne, but has her own relationship to worry about. Not that anything's wrong with her boyfriend. He's actually perfect for her, which is why she's terrified. Not sure she can ever fully trust a man again, she considers bailing on yet another relationship.

Claudia is always there for her friends, mothering them like the children she craves to have. Happily married, Claudia anxiously awaits the day her husband finally agrees it's time to start a family.

'Til St. Patrick's Day is a novel about the depths of friendship and what happens when love doesn't go according to plan.

November

Chapter One

Jayne closed the door behind her and leaned against it, afraid to even move. She was pretty certain the last four hours had just been a dream, and if she dared to move or speak or even breathe too deeply—it might all go away. So she stood silently, desperately still.

When her cell phone blared from inside her purse, she jumped back, startled. Her heart started pulsating quickly, and she was relieved that so far, her night seemed perhaps to be real. She dug around in her oversized purse and grabbed her phone.

"Hello?"

"Hey, it's me." Karen. Relief again. It wasn't some dream fairy about to snatch away one of the best nights of her life. "Are you home yet?"

"Yeah, I just walked in the door." Breathe, she reminded herself. Jayne pulled off the coat she'd worn to keep out the autumn cold that had begun to creep into St. Louis. She threw it over the arm of her couch before she plopped down.

"And? How'd it go?"

"Oh, he's just…dreamy…" Her voice tapered off as a stupid grin flooded her face.

"So I take that to mean it was good."

"No, it was fabulous." She closed her eyes, visions of the night running through her mind.

"Give me the rundown." Karen was always to the point, one of the things Jayne loved best about her.

"Okay, well, first he took me to dinner in the city. That new trendy place in Lafayette Square. It was really great inside, and the food...well, you know how I love food. And it was delish."

"Did he open doors for you and all that?

"Yeah, yeah he did. It was nice." All night long, and now too, she couldn't believe that Gray Brandt had asked her out. He was impossibly attractive—wavy black hair, dimples, a ridiculously bright white smile, and perfectly toned body. She wasn't sure what she'd noticed about him first...his captivating bright blue eyes or his six-foot-two Adonis-like body.

"Then what?"

"Then we went to a movie, and afterwards we went downtown and actually went for a horse-drawn carriage ride."

Karen groaned. "How cheesy."

"You are so jaded. It wasn't cheesy. It was romantic."

"He was just trying to get laid. Did he?"

"No, but he got a goodnight kiss." Jayne giggled. "But I would have done it if he wanted."

"Well, I guess there's nothing wrong with a little hot sex from time to time." Karen sighed. "But a carriage ride?"

"I liked it. I thought it was sweet and romantic and touching."

"Yeah, if it's your senior prom and you're wearing a corsage."

"Oh, stop. Next time I won't give you all the details if you're going to just belittle them."

"But it's so much fun," Karen said, laughing. "I'm sorry. I know you like all that shit."

"Yes, I do. I still can't believe he actually went out with me!"

"I can't wait to see this guy. I mean, he sounds like the love child of Johnny Depp and Maks from Dancing with the Stars. If they were gay lovers, and if gay men could procreate together, that is."

Jayne couldn't help but laugh. "That's actually a pretty good assessment. And did I ever mention to you that he has the most beautiful deep blue eyes I've ever seen?"

"Only a dozen times or so."

"Well, he does," she said, grinning. "So he said he'd call me tomorrow to make some plans for the weekend."

"That sounds promising. If you actually hear from him."

"He'll call."

"I hope for your sake that he does. Well, it sounds like you had a great time."

"We really did." Jayne yawned. "I better get to bed…it's late and I have to work in the morning. Some of us have real jobs, you know."

"I have a real job. I just make my own hours. Jealous, eh?"

"Completely."

"Well don't be. I worked my ass off on a proposal all day yesterday and presented it to the potential client today. And I could absolutely tell he's not going to do business with me."

"Why do you say that?"

"I can just tell. He was disinterested, polite but not friendly, and he didn't really ask any questions."

"Well that sucks. Was it a big customer?"

"Decent." Karen sighed. "But in this economy I'll take whatever I can get."

"You are good at what you do, you're smart and tough. Don't give up—you never know."

"You're an eternal optimist, Jayne. It's what makes you so lovable and irritating all at the same time."

"Not sure if I should say thank you or call you a bitch for that," Jayne said with a chuckle.

"How about, 'Thanks, bitch'?" They both laughed. "Well, I'll let you go…are we still on for Saturday lunch with Claudia?"

"Of course. See you then, if we don't talk before."

"Okay. G'night."

"'Night." Jayne hung up the phone, put it on the charger, and sauntered to her bedroom. Yawning as she pulled off her clothes and slid a sleep shirt over her head, she crawled into bed without so much as brushing her teeth. The incessant dripping sound from the bathroom faucet that normally drove her insane didn't bother her at all. Unlike most nights, she barely noticed it.

She was tired and wanted nothing more than to fall asleep and have dreams of Gray.

****

The next day, Jayne was still in her post-date glow. A smile danced at her lips while she sat in front of her computer at work; it was still there while she went to grab a coffee, and she couldn't seem to lose it while she ate lunch at her desk to meet a deadline.

"Jayne, bring those reports in my office please," her supervisor, Kelly, said as she walked past Jayne's cubicle.

"I'll be right there," Jayne said, pulling the files out of the bin on her immaculate, organized desk. She practically skipped into Kelly's office. "Here they are."

Kelly flipped through them and looked up at Jayne with a smile. "They look great, very detailed. I'll let you know if I need any tweaking once I have a chance to dig into them a bit more. Why can't I have an office full of Jaynes? My life would be so much easier."

Jayne smiled. "Oh, but that would be boring."

"I'll take boring all day long if it means the work is accurate and on time."

"Well maybe someday you'll figure out how to clone me. Maybe R&D could work on that for you." They both laughed.

"You seem awful chipper today. I mean, even more than normal."

"I am," Jayne said, grinning.

"Does this involve a new man?"

"Yep." Jayne couldn't contain the joy that involuntarily spilled onto her face.

"Do I know him?"

14

Jayne felt her face flush, providing the answer to Kelly.

"I do. Well, spill it...who is he? Jonathan in accounting?"

"No." Jayne giggled.

"Well don't keep me guessing."

"Gray Brandt."

Kelly's jaw dropped. "As in, fifth floor, marketing executive, best looking guy in the building?"

Jayne nodded. "It was just one date. But he's supposed to call me today."

"Well that would certainly put a smile on my face," Kelly said with a chuckle. She pointed to the picture of her family on the desk. "I mean, my husband is a nice looking guy, but Gray Brandt is like a whole different species."

"Yeah, well, maybe nothing will come of it. I'm sure he can have any woman he wants."

"Probably. But you're so cute. I bet you'd make a good-looking couple. By the way, I like your hair like that—makes you look like a cheerleader."

"Thanks," Jayne said, tugging at her auburn locks that she'd straightened and pulled back in a sleek ponytail.

"I bet you were a cheerleader, weren't you?"

"No, I wasn't a cheerleader," Jayne said, rolling her eyes in embarrassment. Pom-pom girl.

"Okay, well good luck with Gray, and thanks once again for the good work."

"You're welcome."

As Jayne walked back to her desk, she thought, Kelly said that we'd make a cute couple. We would, wouldn't we?

Jayne was no stranger to relationships—she seemed to have no trouble finding one. Her problem had always been finding the right guy to have a relationship with and never knowing when to throw in the towel. Her last serious relationship had lasted two years but should have only been two months. That's about how long it took her to figure out that Joe was a great companion, sweet, and they had a lot in common—except there was no passion.

Kissing Joe had been like kissing her brother. Nothing there and actually a little repulsive. But she'd stayed anyway, sure she could make it work...for two years.

She knew she shouldn't have stayed, but she always tried to look on the bright side. Whether it was relationships, or work, or life in general...she was the glass-half-full poster girl. Always had been. People made fun of her rose-colored glasses all the time, but she didn't care. When Karen teased Jayne about her positive outlook, Jayne knew it was just her defense mechanism. Karen was too jaded and afraid to be hopeful.

Not Jayne. She was hopeful, a romantic, a dreamer. She wasn't afraid to throw her whole heart and soul out there, because she just knew life had great loves and happiness in store for her, and she was willing to do her part to make that happen. Optimism was not only part of her disposition, it was critical to her life's plan.

But what she didn't dare admit or tell anyone was that there was a part of her that was beginning to wonder if she was being unrealistic, if maybe she was just expecting too much. She'd been on the search for the man of her dreams for nearly a decade but worried that maybe she'd set her sights too high.

And when she considered leaving Joe or whomever else she was with, she was gripped with a nagging fear that she wouldn't find anyone else to love her. Although she was confident of her abilities at work and knew she was a good and loyal friend...when it came to men, she was like a whole different woman. She worried; she felt she wasn't worthy...so she tried to make whatever relationship she was in work.

Which wasn't always possible.

Now here was Gray, and she felt like she had won the jackpot with someone as gorgeous and successful as him. But along with that excitement came an overwhelming sense of fear and uncertainty. Why does he want to be with me, when he could be with anyone? These thoughts were tumbling through her mind when her cell phone rang and Gray's name flashed on the phone.

"I knew he'd call," she whispered to herself as she picked up the phone. "Hello?"

"Hey, Jayne," his smooth, deep voice came across the line.

"Hi, Gray," she said, trying her absolute best not to sound like a swooning moron. He was way out of her league, and she certainly didn't want to scare him away by acting like a stalker.

"Did you have a good time last night?"

"I had a great time. Thank you so much for the lovely date."

"Well, you're welcome." He chuckled. "I know the carriage ride was a little corny, but I thought it would be fun."

"I don't think it was corny at all. I love that stuff." So there, Karen.

"Well, good. How's your day going? I glanced around at lunch time but didn't see you anywhere in the cafeteria."

"I just ate at my desk today. Trying to get a report wrapped up."

"That's my girl, working hard."

Jayne's heart nearly beat out of her chest. He called me "my girl." Keep calm, Jayne. Focus. "So how's your day?"

"Fine, just fine. Meetings nearly back to back today. Some nice opportunities to kiss ass, though." Gray was a rising young executive at the pharmaceutical company where they both worked. At twenty-eight, he'd already managed to make quite a name for himself. He was known for being aggressive, smart, and career-driven. And to most of the women that saw him, he was simply known as hot. A fact which he was definitely aware of. "So, Jaynie, what do you want to do this weekend?"

"I don't know…did you have anything in mind?"

"Well, one of my colleagues is having a house-warming party Saturday night. We could stop by there for a bit."

"That sounds good."

"And there's a local band I like that's playing at a club nearby. We could catch them if you want after we swing by the party."

"I love music. That would be great."

"Okay, how about if I pick you up around six-thirty? We can grab a bite before."

"I'll be ready at six-thirty then." She knew the smile on her face was ridiculous, but she couldn't seem to stop it.

"Well, you're easy," he said, chuckling. She loved his deep, infectious laugh.

"I try to be laid back." *And I'm trying not to completely hyperventilate.* She'd never been with anyone that made her so nervous and so exhilarated at the same time.

"I like that about you. Some women make things so complicated."

No complications here. Unless you think someone worshipping you is a bad thing. "Thank you. I like you, too." She was so glad he couldn't see the blush that was heating up her cheeks.

"Well, okay, Jaynie...I'll see you Saturday night."

She hung up, thrilled that in just two days the fantasy would continue. She glanced at the clock on her computer. Roughly fifty hours to find the perfect outfit, get her nails done, and color her roots.

****

"So, you think that will look nice?" Jayne asked her friends as they stopped on the sidewalk to look at the picture on her phone.

"You took a picture of your outfit to show us?" Karen asked, chuckling.

"I think it's a great idea," Claudia defended. "And I think the outfit is great. Maybe rethink the shoes, though."

"You know, I was wondering about that myself," Jayne said, deep in thought. "I've got a pair of high heeled black peep-toe ankle boots."

"Yes—perfect." Claudia smiled at Jayne in her warm, calming way. Her smile was by far her best feature, although for someone as beautiful as Claudia, it was hard to pick what's best. Jayne always thought she looked classy and polished...like a modern-day, Midwestern Jackie O.

"Okay, good. Now I can relax."

They continued down the cobblestone streets of historic old town in St. Charles, Missouri. It was brisk outside but mild for early November. Temperatures in the upper fifties were welcome as they sauntered down Main Street, window shopping and ducking into shops when something caught their eye.

The street was lined with buildings from the 1800s that were now converted into craft shops, bookstores, restaurants, bars, ice cream parlors, cafés, clothing stores, and boutiques. Walking down Main Street, they caught glimpses in between buildings of the Missouri River a couple of blocks east. Many stores were already decked out for Christmastime, making the district even more festive and fun than normal. The sidewalks teemed with shoppers and sightseers, many with their dogs tagging along on the sunny day.

"I am so full," Karen groaned. "I can't believe I ate that much at lunch. I do this every time we get together, and then have to work out twice as hard all week to get rid of it."

"Yeah, because you're grotesquely overweight," Jayne said with a chuckle, looking at Karen's super-slim frame. Just like everything else about Karen, her weight was definitely under control. Manicured nails—check. Pixie cut hair perfectly in place—check. Snarky attitude delightfully intact—check.

"If I start doing lunch with you girls more often, I'll be headed in that direction." They all laughed.

"Oh, let's head in here," Claudia said, opening the door of a shop. "This place is so fun." They walked inside, and the usual Main Street smell of antiques and old wood in the historic buildings was intermingled with this shop's burning incense. Crystals hung from the ceiling, meditation stones were gathered in bowls and New Age books and CDs lined the shelves.

"So I've jabbered enough about my date with the über-hunky Gray Brandt," Jayne said. "What's new with you guys?"

"Well," Claudia said, "Sam is still working his butt off, trying to make partner. But if he gets this, it will bring so much security. The kids will easily have college paid for, and we can put more money into fixing up the house." Jayne loved their century-old house that they had meticulously rehabbed in a revitalized, energetic area in St. Louis city.

Karen put her hand on Claudia's shoulder. "I don't want to burst your bubble here, but you don't have any kids."

Claudia laughed. "True, but we will, soon. Once he gets this partner thing nailed down, we'll start trying. Not that we're not already practicing." She shared a devilish grin with her friends.

Jayne giggled. "Well of course we know Sam's a stud. You two can never keep your hands off each other. Not that I blame you—your hubby's so damn cute."

"He is, isn't he?" Claudia smiled. "And I picked out the most beautiful furniture for the dining room...I think he might buy it for Christmas."

"Wow, a whole set of furniture for Christmas?" Karen said. "The Knight family is high-rollin'."

"Well, we need a dining room set anyway, but it's a little out of our price range. But as a gift...hopefully he'll splurge for the extra. Oh, isn't this pretty?" She held up a beautifully woven scarf. "This could be used as a sarong, or scarf, or a bunch of different ways."

"Ooh, those are nice," Jayne said, running her fingers across the silky fabric. "So what's new with you, Ms. Karen?"

"Oh, same old, same old. Beating my head against the wall at work, trying to somehow build my client list in this shitty economy."

"How's Rick?"

"Oh…he's Rick." Karen browsed through a selection of chunky metal rings.

"What does that mean?" Jayne asked, eyeing her friend.

"You know…he's nice and not bad on the eyes, but…."

"But what?" Jayne loved Rick. He was the anti-Karen. He was sweet and tender and light-hearted. He evened her out, balanced her in a way no other man had.

"He's just rather dull, I think. No spark there, not terribly ambitious—"

"So what? He has a good job. And I think there's plenty of spark there."

"He's settled for doing graphic art work for a little small brewery. He's happy with that. Doesn't want to move onward and upward." She sighed. "He's so talented, but content with his mediocre job."

"Well, if it pays the bills and he likes it, what more is there? A lot of people hate their jobs."

"Jayne's right," Claudia popped in. "That's probably why he's such a happy, easy guy. He's not stressed about his job—he does what he enjoys."

"Everything's just so comfortable with him, though, nothing exciting there," Karen said, trying on a ring.

"You do this every time." Jayne sighed.

"Do what?"

"Just when it's time to consider actually getting vulnerable and sharing your life with someone, you call it quits."

"I don't do that." Karen's brows furrowed. "Do I?"

"Yes, you do," Claudia confirmed. "And I think Rick is a really great guy and he really loves you. I don't think you should let him go. I think you'll regret it forever."

"Me too," Jayne said, nodding her head with enthusiasm.

"Hmmm… Well if you two think he's so great, do you want him?" Karen said, rolling her eyes as she walked away.

"What are you so afraid of?" Claudia asked. "Actually needing someone? Getting too out of control with your emotions?"

"Oh Jesus, don't give me any of your psych bullshit. You watched Oprah for too many years."

"But Oprah's always right." Jayne chuckled. "Well, except for with James Frey. But besides that, she's a pretty reliable source of information."

"Well, you two can just chill out and calm down because I'm certainly not going to get rid of him at the moment. We're safe, at least 'til St. Patrick's Day."

"What are you talking about?" Claudia asked.

"Do you mean that John Mayer song, St. Patrick's Day?" Jayne asked, deciding on a blue-green scarf.

"Yeah, you know, it talks about how if you're in a relationship when the weather starts turning cold, you're safe until St. Patrick's Day. Nobody wants to be alone over the holidays, then the New Year seems so optimistic, even I'm not jaded enough to dump someone then. The next thing you know, it's Valentine's Day, and I don't need to tell either of you how fucked up that can be when you're alone." They all nodded. "But who cares if you're alone on St. Patty's Day? It's a holiday that practically celebrates public drunkenness. Perfect for a raw break up."

Claudia chuckled. "I never heard that. It's a pretty interesting concept, though. And actually pretty dead-on."

"Yep, so relax and know that you'll be seeing Mister Happy Rick throughout the holiday season."

Hmmm, Jane thought. Then maybe I'll get at least a few months with Gray…and that should be enough time to convince him that I'm the absolute perfect woman for him. Yep, I can make this happen.

"Hey, we need to plan a date for our annual holiday night get together with our men," Claudia said. Claudia and Sam hosted the couples every holiday season, and Jayne always looked forward to the festive gathering.

"Maybe I'll get to bring Gray," Jayne said, giddy with joy.

"Yes, maybe," Karen said, putting her arm around her friend. "But let's not look too far ahead. Tonight is only your second date."

"True. But a girl can dream, can't she?"

"I would expect nothing less from you."

****

Dinner with Gray went well, but Jayne began to feel a bit nervous as his BMW pulled into the tony subdivision where they were attending a house-warming party. The owners of these elaborate, palatial homes were not exactly her peeps. Being with Gray was intimidating enough; she wished she was the kind of person that carried Xanax in her purse to calm the panic that was setting in.

"Wow, this is a nice neighborhood," she said quietly.

"No, it's a fucking amazing neighborhood," he said, looking over at Jayne. "I plan to buy a house here someday."

"Really?"

"Well, I'm already making well into the six figures…another ten years and this will be home." He brought the car to a stop in front of a ridiculously large home with a six-car side-entry garage. Huge white columns flanked either side of the massive front door.

"Where do you live now?"

"I've got a condo in Clayton. It's small but in a great building." Expensive, Jayne thought. "Maybe I could show you later," he said, his dimples on full display.

Oh, God, I hope so. "Sure." She smiled, lost in the blue summer sky of his eyes.

They climbed out, and Gray walked around to her side, taking her hand. "We'll just stay for an hour or so. Rob Schmidt is kind of a prick, but he's right under my boss, which means I have to play the game and kiss his ass, too."

"I'm sure you do a good job of playing the game," she said, smiling at him.

"Oh, Jayne, I'm the best." He seemed to stand even taller, and she noticed his chest puff out as they reached the door. He rang the bell.

"Gray!" a man said, opening the door. "Glad you could stop by. Come in, come in." They shook hands. "And who's this?"

"This is Jayne Asher."

Jayne shook hands with him. "Nice to meet you, Mr. Schmidt."

"Oh, please, call me Rob." Jayne noticed the expensive watch on his wrist and what looked like a cashmere sweater on his fit frame. He was a handsome man, probably late forties. The extravagant surroundings suited him. "Well, make yourselves at home. Most of the guests are in the great room."

"Fantastic place, Rob," Gray said, surveying everything in sight. "Really amazing."

"Thank you, Gray. You'll be buying something like this before you know it."

"That's my plan." Gray grinned.

"You're on track for it, no doubt. Jayne, your friend Gray is quite the up and comer. We have big things in mind for him."

She smiled admiringly at Gray. "That doesn't surprise me at all." Gray winked at her.

As they walked toward the back of the house, Jayne whispered, "Gray?"

"Yeah?" he whispered, bending closer to her.

"I'm a little intimidated by all of this. This isn't really my usual scene...please stick close, okay?"

"Oh, you'll be fine," he said, and his smile made her think she would be.

Forty-five minutes later, Jayne realized his "you'll be fine" meant "you're on your own." He was off in another room, playing poker with a group of men, none of whom Jayne knew. They were smoking cigars, drinking hard liquor, and it was clearly a no-women-allowed event. That meant Jayne was left to her own devices, mingling with a group of women that she had never met before. Most of them were much older and as she made small talk, she realized she didn't have much in common with them. They all had children and only a couple of them worked. Most of them seemed to know each other, so she felt like the odd man out.

As she hovered around the table of hors d'oeuvres as if it was a life raft, a woman approached her. Jayne looked up, offering a timid smile.

"So you're with Gray, huh?" the woman asked.

"Uh…yeah," Jayne said, nodding her head. I am with Gray. Wow. The woman was smartly dressed, trendy and classy. Jayne figured she was in her late thirties but looked good for her age. Great body, with ample breasts peeking out of her low-cut blouse. I'm jealous.

"I'm Katherine, by the way," she said, offering her hand. They shook, and Katherine smiled. "How long have you been seeing each other?"

"Oh, this is only our second date."

Katherine raised her eyebrows. "And you're by yourself at the food table? Fun date."

Jayne was uncomfortable in Katherine's direct stare. "Well, we're just stopping by for a bit. We're going to catch a band later. So, how do you know Gray?"

"Oh, honey," Katherine said with a chuckle. "How don't I know Gray?" She took a seat at a bar stool and Jayne did the same. "Well, we work together. Our offices are across the hall from each other."

"Oh," Jayne said, smiling. "Neighbors."

"You could say that. And sometimes being neighbors leads to other things." Jayne's eyes must have bugged out of her head, because Katherine quickly said, "But that was a couple of years ago. Ancient history, really."

"So…you two were an item?" Jayne felt like someone had punched her in the stomach.

"Well, yes. It was mainly just a sex thing, I guess. He's good, am I right?" She gave Jayne a knowing smile.

"Oh, I wouldn't know…not yet, anyway." Jayne looked down at her drink. Suddenly her Coca Cola seemed incredibly inadequate. A shot of something, anything sounded good at the moment.

"I'm sorry," Katherine said, touching Jayne's arm. "Really. That was wrong of me." She smiled warmly at Jayne.

"No, that's okay. So he's good, huh?" Jayne felt the heat rise on her cheeks as she asked.

"Yeah, it almost makes putting up with him worth it. But good luck with the rest of him."

"How do you mean?"

"Don't get me wrong, Gray's a lot of fun, but...well, look at tonight. Second date and he's already off doing his own thing. Trust me, it doesn't get better."

"Oh, it's fine...."

"Jayne, my advice is to enjoy him until it's not fun anymore. He's just a man that knows what he wants and does what he wants. He wants to be with you right now, so go with it. Have some fun. Just be careful."

"Be careful?"

"Don't ever think you mean more to him than his ambitions. Everything is a distraction to him...if you're in his way, you're gone."

Jayne thought she actually saw compassion in Katherine's eyes. "I'll keep that in mind."

"I'm sorry to be so harsh, but you're young...I just want to save you some heartache. You seem like a sweet girl."

"Thanks," she said quietly.

"Katherine, what are you doing?" Gray asked, approaching them. Jayne's heart started beating faster at the sight of him. She wasn't sure if it was because of his breathtakingly attractive appearance or what Katherine had just warned her about.

"Scared?" Katherine smirked at him. "Because you should be."

"Jaynie, don't believe a word she says," he said with a smile, putting his hands on her shoulders. She could smell the strong odor of cigar smoke that lingered on him. "She's just upset because she can't have me."

"Oh, I could have you. Just don't want you. Been there, done that." Their eyes held for a moment.

"What makes you think I would want you again?" He bent over and kissed Jayne on the cheek. He looked up at Katherine. "You better watch yourself. I have to put up with you at work, but we're not at the office now."

"Charming as always," she said, standing up. "It was nice to meet you, Jayne. Good luck."

"Why don't you go hang with someone your own age?" Gray said, his voice steely. Jayne's eyes grew large as she gave Katherine a desperate smile.

"Fuck off, Gray," Katherine said, walking away.

"What a bitch," Gray said quietly, grabbing Jayne's hand. "Are you ready to take off?"

"Sure," she said, still a bit disoriented about what had just transpired.

"Let's go thank our hosts and hit the road."

****

After hearing the band play and watching from a distance as Gray cavorted with more of his friends for a couple of hours, Jayne found herself walking with him into his condo. She was tired, but somehow wide awake at the same time. He held her hand as they entered.

"Home sweet home," he said, flicking on a light. It illuminated an immaculate open floor plan, filled with contemporary furnishings and devoid of most color. It looked expensive, yes, but lacked character. Typical for an upscale bachelor pad.

"Cool place," she said as he let go of her hand and walked to the wet bar in the corner of the great room.

"Thanks. It's my crib. Do you want a drink?"

"No, I'm good."

He poured himself a scotch, and as he took a drink, he turned on some music. Chris Isaacs' voice played from speakers in the ceiling overhead. "Let me take your coat," he said, removing it. He bent down and kissed her neck as he tossed the coat onto his cream-colored leather sectional. Jayne closed her eyes, feeling tingly all over as his hot kisses moved from her neck to her lips. He knew how to kiss, that's for sure. He ended with a tender nibble on her bottom lip.

When Jayne opened her eyes, he was looking at her with desire.

"You're beautiful, Jaynie," he whispered, kissing her again. His hands ran through her hair and she couldn't help but plant hers on his perfectly sculpted rear end. He could have been an ass double for less endowed actors. Seriously. "Would you like to see my bedroom?"

"Yes," she said with a grin. "Are you seducing me?"

"Well, I'm not showing you my penchant for interior decorating, that's for damn sure." Dimples creased his cheeks and made her fire for him turn into an enormous bonfire blaze. He took her hand, leading her down a hallway and onto his king size mattress.

The lights were dim in the room, but she could make out his rippling abs and firm pecs. She'd never seen anything like it. As they climbed naked under the covers, Jayne was a bundle of nerves and desire.

Katherine was right.

Gray was known for excelling at most everything he did, and sex was definitely no exception. He knew exactly what he was doing, and easily brought Jayne to climax. Twice. He knew some positions she'd never experienced but found exhilarating. He was skilled and tenacious.

As they lay back, exhausted, an hour or so later, Jayne felt physically satisfied. But somehow, emotionally, she felt like his performance was less about passion and more like playing in a sport competition. Like he was mastering her, going for the gold.

No doubt about it, it felt fantastic. Probably better than she'd ever had. Technically perfect.

But technique wasn't everything. It was missing something. Not that I'm complaining, she thought to herself.

"That was pretty fucking great," Gray said, clearly proud of himself. He lay on his back, hands behind his head. They had just finished and were still out of breath.

"Yeah, it was," she said, throwing her leg over his and resting her head on his chest.

"For a sweet little thing, you're pretty untamed under the sheets," he said with a chuckle.

Giggling, she said, "Well, you never know what someone's really like."

"We'll have to do this again—make sure we get to know each other better."

"I certainly hope so." She loved staring into his eyes.

"But I better get you home."

What? We just made love. "I'm in no hurry…."

"I'm starting to get tired, though, and it's a good twenty minute drive to your place and then back. I'd have you stay, but I've got hockey with my guys early tomorrow morning."

"Oh, okay," she said, forcing the smile onto her face. What about cuddling? Intimacy?

He was already putting his clothes on.

Chapter Two

Karen woke up Sunday morning to the welcoming, although unnerving, sight of Rick staring at her.

"What are you doing?" she asked, offering the smallest of smiles.

"Oh, just looking at you, so at peace, so tender." He kissed her. "When you're asleep is the only time you let your guard down." He put his arm around her and pulled her closer.

He was absolutely right. He knew her so well it was almost irritating. Looking into his large, deep-brown eyes, she saw nothing but love and acceptance. Something she'd never felt from any man before. She adored the way his beard seemed to nearly grow overnight, dark brown with hints of red peeking out now and then. The stubbly growth matched his casual, unkempt appearance and his laid-back personality. His wavy brown hair fell forward, the curls framing his face in such a way that made him impossibly irresistible. God, she hated that she wanted him so much.

"You need a haircut," she proclaimed, rolling away on her back and stretching.

"No I don't," he said with a lopsided grin. "The ladies like my shaggy locks." He ran his fingers through his shoulder-length hair for emphasis.

"Oh, do they?" She landed a playful slap on his stomach before she climbed out of bed. Of course they loved his hair. It was his signature—his artsy, sexy, sultry look. Damn him for being so cute.

"They do. And I know you do, too. You're just too cynical to pay me the compliment. But I see the way you catch glimpses when you think I don't see it. And you never fail to run your fingers through it when we're having sex."

"Okay, detective Rick. You caught me." She smiled at him as she closed the bathroom door.

After relieving herself, she stared at her reflection in the mirror. For the most part, she liked what she saw. Dark blonde hair with lighter highlights, cropped short—eclectic and fun when she wanted, or businesslike when she needed it. She liked her full lips and her eyes were okay. Sure, her nose was larger than she'd like and no one would ever call her cute like Jayne. But someone once told Karen she had sophisticated looks. She could live with that.

She knew she wasn't unattractive, but anyone would pale in comparison to her friends. So she worked with what she had and told herself that her saucy personality made up for whatever small failings she had in the beauty department. And her breasts were nice, always had been. Men seemed to appreciate them; she figured they'd been responsible for some of her sales over the years. Of course someday they'll just sag.

Karen climbed on the scale: still 126. Not bad for being five feet seven inches tall. Looking closer, she noticed the mere hint of wrinkles in the corners of her hazel eyes. She dabbed on some supposed miracle elixir eye cream. Shit, Karen, you're going to be thirty soon.

"Am I starting to look old?" she asked as she walked out of the bathroom.

Rick laughed. "What are you talking about?"

"I mean it. Am I starting to age?"

"Well, I'm sure we all age, all the time, but no—you look gorgeous. Not a day over twenty-five." He reached out to her, and she sat on the bed next to him.

"Well that's just because you're old, everyone looks young to you."

"Hey, thirty-five is not old!" He nudged her. "Besides, I look like I'm thirty."

"True." She grinned at him. "I'm going to make some pancakes...do you want some?"

"Of course I want some of your special pancakes. That's the only reason I'm with you." He kissed her arm and she stood up, sticking her tongue out at him. She knew he loved her pancakes, but she didn't want him to think she was making them just for him.

Even if she was.

****

Over the next couple of weeks, Jayne and Gray settled into a casual dating routine that seemed to suit Gray but left Jayne wanting a little more of him. They usually spent one night a week together and one night on the weekend. They would talk every day—sometimes just a quick, perfunctory "How's your day?" but other times, they would chat on the phone at night for an hour or so. Jayne would be curled up on her couch, under a massive down blanket with socks and flannel pajamas to keep her warm. Sometimes he would be on the treadmill when they talked; other times, she could hear him eating his dinner.

She was learning that he was a very driven employee. It was rare that he left the office before six-thirty, and sometimes it was closer to eight. Other times, he would end their phone call by saying, "I just got an email I need to follow up on. I'll catch you tomorrow. Good night, sweet Jaynie."

That's how he ended all of their phone calls. Sweet Jaynie. Every time he said it, her heart did a little flip. Normally she would have hated someone calling her Jaynie, but the way he said it, there was no comparison. It was his way of being intimate, making her special.

Their sex life together continued to be fantastic, but Jayne was always dismayed with the speed at which he managed to hop out of bed afterward. He seemed reasonably affectionate otherwise—holding hands, kisses, arm around her. But when it came to real intimacy…that didn't seem to be his strong suit. So Jayne took what she could get from him, just delighted to have what she did.

He was extremely charming and complimentary toward her. As he loosened up around her, she found him to be really funny. It didn't take much for him to make her laugh, and she could tell he ate it up when he got her giggling.

Usually they went out on their date nights, but one night they stayed in at her place and watched a movie, scarfing down Chinese takeout. That was Jayne's favorite date. He seemed less "on" and more just Gray. For Jayne, just having him next to her, on the couch in her living room, was good enough. He generated a magnetism that she'd never experienced before…she felt giddy to just be around it.

It was the Monday before Thanksgiving, and Gray had told Jayne that afternoon on the phone that he would be working really late. She knew he often waited until he got home to eat, so she decided to surprise him with some of the Chinese carryout they'd gotten the week before.

When the elevator opened on the fifth floor, Jayne wasn't exactly sure which way to go. She'd never been on the fifth floor, where most of the executives had their digs. She could almost feel the power emanating from the large offices and dark cherry wood furniture. It was after seven o'clock, the place was bare, and she was about to just start wandering around to find him when she heard his voice to her right, down the hall.

"That doesn't get the message across enough. Doesn't drive it home the way we need it to." Hearing him in his element made her smile, and she headed his way.

"Gray," she heard a woman's voice say, "I've worked my ass off on this."

"Well, I'm sorry, but I think it needs to be stronger."

"It's fine."

"Fine? I don't want fine. I want to knock it out of the ballpark. See, that's the difference between us—I'm heading for a corner office and you'll still be across the hall in ten years. Just fine means it sucks."

Jayne reached his doorway and peeked in to see Katherine standing in front of his desk, wearing an expression of absolute irritation on her face.

"Knock knock," Jayne said, smiling. They both looked at her. A smile spread across Gray's face, dimples and all.

"Jaynie!" He stood up and greeted her at the door with a gentle kiss. She wanted him already.

"Hi, Katherine," she said, smiling.

"Hello, Jayne. Nice to see you again." Katherine headed toward the door. "Gray, let me see what I can do with this, okay?"

"No, Katherine, I'm going to take over. Email me all the files you've got on it."

"Dammit, Gray, I've got this—"

"No, you don't. I appreciate all the time you've spent on it, but I think we need some perspective from a fresh pair of eyes."

Jayne thought she could nearly see fire shooting from Katherine's eyes as she glared at him before walking out of the room.

"So," Gray said, his arms around Jayne, "what are you doing here? I told you it's gonna be a late night."

"Yeah, I know. But I thought you might get hungry, so I brought you some dinner." She held up the brown bag of Chinese.

His eyes seemed to sparkle with surprise and pleasure. "That was really sweet," he said, a small smile playing on his lips. "Very thoughtful of you."

"I just know you don't always take the time to eat until you get home."

"You're right." He took her hand and led her back to his desk, where he lifted her up and sat her on the edge, making her chuckle. "I could always just eat you."

"But then you would still be hungry."

"True." He grinned. "Well, did you bring enough for both of us? I could take a quick break and eat with you."

"Yes, I did." He kissed her again, and there was no denying the electricity in the air. She put her arms around his neck, pressing her body against his.

"I can see you two," Katherine hollered from across the hall. "At least close the door before you start."

Gray rolled his eyes. "She is such a bitch."

Jayne chuckled. "Well apparently not too much of a bitch if you slept with her."

"That was before I got to know her."

"Oh, I see," she said, dropping her arms and grabbing the food. "Can you clear a spot on your desk so we can eat?"

"Of course."

Soon they were laughing and talking in between bites of fried rice and crab Rangoon. Jayne was impressed at the size of his office; she only had a cubicle, and here he had his own office with a window, an elegant desk, and even a fern.

At a lull in the conversation, Jayne caught him staring at her as she looked up from her bite of crab Rangoon. "What?" she asked, smiling. "Do I have sour cream on my chin or something?"

"No, no, you're fine." He looked down. "You know, Jayne...I think you're great. You're beautiful and sweet...so don't take it personally that I do my own thing so much, okay? It's just who I am. I have to stay focused—I have goals set for myself."

"I understand," she said, smiling at him as their eyes met. He looked almost vulnerable...she'd never seen that in him before.

"I mean, this is fun, I love spending time with you. You're a great stress reliever, and you laugh at my jokes." He winked at her. "But I can't give you much more than what I am right now. I've got too much on my plate."

"That's fine," Jayne said, suddenly worried about what exactly he meant. She wanted to ask but didn't dare.

"Well, okay then," he said, caressing her cheek. "Hey, I keep meaning to ask if you'd like to join me on Thanksgiving to go to my parents' place."

"Sure, I'd love to." She felt her body relax after his earlier words. Meeting the family. Wow.

"Great." He patted her thigh.

"What time? We could get together with my family before or after."

"Oh, well, my parents live about an hour and a half out, in the middle of nowhere. It's a great place—several acres, a nice clearing and gorgeous lake, then lots of wooded area. But it's an all-day thing…big lunch, touch football game for all the guys, pie by the fire afterward. We probably wouldn't make it back to town until after seven or later."

"That sounds great, but I would really like to see my family for part of the day." She couldn't imagine not seeing her brother and parents and nephew.

"Well, you don't have to come," he said, polishing off his dinner and tossing the cartons in the trash can under his desk. "It's no big deal."

"No—I want to come," she said quickly. "It's just one Thanksgiving, right?"

"Right," he said, flashing a smile. "And you'll like my family and all my cousins and everyone. It's a good time."

"I bet it will be." She was so thrilled that he wanted her to spend the holiday with him. But for someone who cherished her family, being without them would be difficult. And how was she going to tell her mom?

"Well, my sweet Jaynie, I have to get back to work. Thanks so much for bringing up dinner for me—that'll give me my second wind. I have to get this project done before the holiday." He gave her a quick kiss before he turned his attention back to his computer.

"You're welcome."

"I'll be here really late, so I won't call you until tomorrow. Have a good night, okay?"

"I will," she said, waving as she stepped into the hallway.

"Good night, Jayne," Katherine's voice popped up.

"Good night, Katherine," Jayne said, smiling at her as she headed down the hall to the elevator.

****

"Hi, Mom," Jayne said, walking into her childhood home. There was nowhere else on the planet that felt more comfortable to her. Stepping inside felt like instant belonging.

"Hello, my girl," her mom exclaimed. Carol Asher was like an older version of her daughter. Jayne was always relieved to see her mom still looking good at her age; her mom gave her hope that she might hold up well, too. Since a part of Jayne still expected her mom to look like she had fifteen years earlier, she was always a little surprised to see her mom's grey hair and the wrinkles that had crept onto her face. Everything else in the house seemed to stand still in time, so it seemed out of place that her parents would be aging. "So are you ready to get to work on our Thanksgiving meal?"

It was a tradition that Jayne and her sister-in-law Melissa always came over on the Wednesday evening before Thanksgiving to prepare as much food ahead of time that they could. Pies, rolls, casseroles…just about any Thanksgiving meal staple you could imagine was being prepared in their kitchen.

"You bet, Mom," Jayne said, giving her a hug.

"So, are you going to be bringing this new handsome man tomorrow?"

Jayne took a deep breath as she grabbed an apron out of the pantry and tied it on. "Mom, I'm not going to be able to make it over tomorrow."

"What?"

Jayne hated the disappointment on her mom's face. "I'm going to spend Thanksgiving with Gray, and his parents live out of town. We won't be able to do both places this year."

Carol shook her head. "Jayne, we're your family. You've never spent a holiday without us your whole life."

"I know, Mom, and I'm so sorry. But I'll be here for Christmas."

"Are you sure about that?"

Jayne actually wasn't. But she'd have to put her foot down with Gray at Christmastime. She didn't want to miss out on the whole holiday season with her family. "Yes, I'll be here. And Gray will probably be with me."

"Well, can't you at least stop by for pie? How far away do they live?"

Jayne knew her mom wouldn't give up. She was relentless. That's where Jayne got her drive...but somehow when it came to Gray, she was much more passive. "He said it's an hour and a half away. Apparently it's an all-day thing, and it will be really late before we're heading home."

"I know it might be their tradition, but your tradition is to be with your family. There needs to be a little give and take, don't you think? Maybe he loses a couple of hours with his family so you can spend some time with yours." Carol put her hand on Jayne's shoulder. "When you care about someone, you're willing to compromise to make them happy."

Mom, just stop it. Of course you're right. I know, I know. But she wasn't going to give up on this romance; she knew she could make it work. It wasn't perfect, and Gray could be selfish, but she knew that in time, he would grow to care for her the way that she did for him. She just had to keep working at it...she didn't want another wasted relationship.

"It's not like that, Mom," she said, trying to convince herself. "If we can make it for dessert, we will, okay? And you're just going to love him."

"I'd love him more if he wasn't stealing my daughter away on a major holiday," Carol said with a huff as she greased a casserole dish.

Just then, Jayne's phone chimed with a new text message. She pulled it out of her pocket and looked; it was from Gray. Working late, won't have time to chat tonight. Look forward to spending the day w/u tomorrow.

"Is that from him?" Carol asked.

"Yeah," Jayne smiled. "Here's a picture of him." She held out her phone to her mom.

"Well...I can see how he could tempt you away from family." Carol gave her daughter a small smile. "But he shouldn't expect you to do that."

Jayne ignored her mother's comment, because what was she supposed to say to that? She was right.

But Gray was looking forward to spending the day with her. That was enough to plant a smile on her face as she started rolling out dough.

****

Gray had undersold the beauty of his parents' property. It was breathtaking, like something that would cause an artist to crack open the bag of brushes. Especially in the fall, with the trees still clinging to the last remnants of their brilliant copper, red, and golden leaves. The lake shimmered with diamond-like ripples from the brisk autumn wind. The large two-story log cabin boasted a wrap-around porch, complete with a stone chimney piping out white plumes of smoke. Altogether, it created an idyllic Thanksgiving scene.

"This place is absolutely beautiful," Jayne said as they walked up the stairs onto the wooden porch.

"Yeah, it's pretty nice. They moved out here once my brother and I were done with school. It's a fun place to hang out." He opened the door, and they were greeted with the aroma of cinnamon, turkey and pumpkin along with the loud sounds of a football game on the TV and people laughing.

"Gray!" a plump, middle-aged woman said, heading toward the door. Jayne realized right away that she was his mother; she shared the same stunning blue eyes of her son.

"Mom," he grinned, holding out his arms and giving her a big hug. "Happy Thanksgiving."

"Happy Thanksgiving to you, too." His mom smiled at Jayne. "And who do we have here?"

"Oh, Mom, this is Jayne. Jayne, this is my mom."

"Please, call me Sara," she said, shaking Jayne's hand. Jayne thought she seemed warm and welcoming. She was a pretty woman, and Jayne imagined that twenty years earlier she was probably quite stunning.

"So nice to meet you," Jayne said, feeling nervous yet somehow calmed by her. "Thank you for having me."

"Well you're welcome. I have to run back to the kitchen—cooking for twenty-one people is relentless." Her smile exuded warmth.

"I'd be happy to help. What can I do?"

"Oh, you picked a nice one, Gray," Sara said, winking at him. "Jayne, don't worry about a thing. It's just a lot of little last minute stuff. I've got it under control. But thanks so much for offering. You kids just have fun. We eat in about forty-five minutes."

"Okay, Mom," he said, pulling off his coat. He took Jayne's coat, too, and when he stepped out of the room to hang them up, a man approached her.

"Hi," he said, offering a broad smile, not unlike Gray's. "I'm Josh, Gray's big brother. Big in terms of birth order, not actual size. It's ironic when your little brother ends up two inches taller than you."

Jayne laughed as they shook hands, and she enjoyed dissecting his looks to find comparisons with Gray. There was a similarity, no doubt, but although Josh was a really good looking guy, he didn't quite have the Calvin Klein underwear model good looks that Gray had.

"I'm Jayne, so nice to meet you."

"The pleasure's all mine. So, have you been dating Gray for a while?"

"Just about three weeks. It's new."

"Oh," Josh said, raising his eyebrows. "He must like you if he's bringing you to Thanksgiving dinner." His smile put her at ease.

"I hope so." She smiled back.

"Can I get you a drink?"

"Sure, that would be great."

"Coffee, soda, water…something stiffer?"

"No," she said, "water's fine."

"Follow me." He led the way to the great room filled with people and a large stainless steel tub filled with ice and drinks. He grabbed a bottled water. "It drives Mom nuts when we get in and out of the fridge while she's working in the kitchen. So we always put the drinks out here."

"Thanks, Josh," she said, taking the bottle. As she unscrewed the top and took a gulp, she looked around the room. Some older people—uncles and aunts? Dozen or so men and women around her age she figured were probably cousins.

"Big crowd, I know…I imagine it's a little intimidating for an outsider. But trust me, the Brandts are a pretty harmless bunch." He gently elbowed her. "Except for maybe Gray."

"So I've been told," she said.

"Oh, there you are," Gray said, approaching them. "So I see you've met Josh. Has he been boring you with his tales of underperforming high school students?" Gray put his arm around her.

"Uh, no…are you a teacher?" Jayne asked.

"Yes, I teach high school English. And despite what Gray thinks about my job, I actually love what I do."

"Oh, I think teachers are amazing." Jayne offered a big smile.

"Well, I don't knock the profession," Gray said, "just the pay. Poor Josh will forever be driving the old Toyota parked out front."

"Nothing wrong with my Toyota," Josh said, clearly annoyed. "Well, it was nice to meet you, Jayne. Gray now has about twenty other people to introduce you to."

"Yeah, nice to meet you, too."

****

Jayne was enjoying herself. His family's antics kept her laughing throughout dinner, as they all seemed to be funny, down-to-earth people. She couldn't begin to keep the names of all his relatives straight—she was okay with just remembering his parents and brother. The food was good, too, but she couldn't help but miss her own family. She wondered what they were doing as she finished her meal. Were they getting ready to eat? Was her nephew doing something adorable that she was missing?

After dinner, it was apparently tradition that all of the men and older boys in the Brandt family would head outside to play their annual Thanksgiving football game. They would split into teams and play for the year's bragging rights. Jayne wasn't surprised that Gray seemed pretty competitive about it. She didn't think there was a laid-back bone in his body.

As they started their scrimmage, Jayne offered to help with dishes. She stared out the window as she dried plates, looking at Gray and his handsome figure outside. With the lake in the background and changing leaves in the surrounding trees, it looked like a Kodak moment. Although she missed her family, she was glad to see him with his. He seemed more relaxed around them, less guarded. It was nice. And she was pleased that his family seemed to like her.

She waved at him, smiling, and he nodded in acknowledgment. He was talking to his brother, who Jayne thought was a really nice guy. They'd chatted a bit throughout the day and he was easy to talk to.

Maybe if they got out early enough, they could still make it to her parents' house. She wanted to give Gray the chance to experience what she had today—home.

****

Josh noticed Jayne watching Gray through the kitchen window where she was doing dishes. The guys were taking a break from their touch football match-up, chugging bottles of water and catching their breath.

"So, little brother," Josh said, wiping sweat from his forehead, "Jayne seems really great."

"Yeah, she's a cute girl," Gray said nonchalantly, taking a drink.

"Well, yeah, she's cute, but she seems warm, and fun, and sweet, too."

"Yeah, she is." He shrugged. "It's just a fling, no big deal."

"Really?" Josh said, not at all impressed with Gray's carefree attitude. "You brought a fling to Thanksgiving dinner with your family?"

"Sure. If you don't bring a date, you look like a loser." Gray grinned. "No offense."

"Oh, no, none taken," Josh said, shaking his head. What an ass. "Don't you think you could be sending her the wrong message? I mean, most normal people only bring serious partners to family holiday gatherings."

"Most normal people don't mope around for three years after their fiancée dumps them."

"Why are you always such a prick?"

"Just being truthful." They stared at each other, Josh wanting nothing more than to punch the smirk off Gray's face. Josh loved his brother, but he sometimes wondered why. He could be such an arrogant bastard. Gray looked over at the window and nodded at Jayne's desperately happy wave.

"We were talking about you, Gray. You can tell Jayne's crazy about you—you can see it in the way she looks at you. You need to make sure you're not leading her on. Most women see meeting the family as a big step."

Gray ran his fingers through his hair and took another drink. "Well, it's not a big step. It's just the holiday season, and it's nice to have someone to take to all of these fucking events. Work parties, dinners at my bosses' place...a date makes those things easier."

"But have you told her that?"

"What, do you think I'm a complete asshole?"

Josh knew he wasn't. But Gray certainly was more opportunistic than he was.

Gray continued. "I haven't exactly told her that, but I also haven't acted like it's some big romance. I've told her I'm really focused on work now. So it's just fun and she's good in bed. Wish her tits were bigger, though."

"You're a pig," Josh said, shaking his head. "Just don't break her heart. She seems like a great girl." There was a long line of discarded women that Gray left in his path.

"Oh, okay, thanks for the lecture, Dad." Gray flashed a smile, and even Josh wasn't completely immune to his younger brother's charm. Little shit.

"You're welcome, smart ass," Josh said, smiling back. "But just because you can get any girl you want, doesn't mean you should sample them all. Women have feelings, you know."

"Yeah, I'm well aware of that. That's why I can't deal with being with any of them for more than a couple of months. Too needy, too much of a hassle."

"Not with the right one." Josh's voice was quiet.

Gray slapped Josh on the back. "And how's that going for you?"

Josh rolled his eyes. "Just because I don't screw every girl that bats her eyes at me, doesn't mean I'm failing in that area. I'm just waiting for someone special."

"Well, you keep looking for that and slaving away to educate our nation's youth on a meager salary while I climb the corporate ladder. When the dust settles, I'll have a couple of homes, a fat portfolio and the company of any woman I choose."

"Just random women to sleep with at night? That's what life is all about, huh?"

"Well, my life," Gray said, shrugging. "I'm never lonely. I can always find someone."

Only because they don't really know you. "You enjoy your fancy homes and I'll find real meaning with a wife and family. On my meager salary."

"Absolutely. Now that that's settled, let's huddle up. Hey guys!" he yelled. "Let's get back to the game. Time for the Brandt boys to finish this up with a slaughter."

Josh couldn't help but laugh at Gray's bravado. He was a lot of fun, despite his esteemed opinion of himself. Would he ever grow up? Josh glanced back at the kitchen window, not surprised to find Jayne's gaze fixed solely on Gray.

Poor girl.

****

"I can't believe we're eating this white sauce pasta," Karen said, taking a drink of wine. "I mean, Thanksgiving was just two days ago. I ate enough food then to last me a week. I think we should have limited ourselves to salad today."

"Oh, but it's sooo yummy," Jayne said, twirling creamy fettuccini noodles around her fork.

"Sorry, Karen," Claudia said as she dunked her bread in the sauce. "This was my idea. But it just sounded so good. You can never go wrong with pasta on The Hill. Best Italian food this side of the Atlantic."

"True," Karen said. "And if it wasn't this damn good I would have gone with a red sauce to be a little healthier. I'm gonna be so fat."

Jayne rolled her eyes. "Puhlease."

Karen shrugged with a grin. "So, how did everyone's holiday go?"

"Mine was really nice," Claudia said. "We did the two meal thing, first Sam's family and then mine. I was stuffed, but it was so much fun. I just love his sisters and parents. And his new baby niece is absolutely scrumptious. I couldn't get enough of her. She's six months old now, and I could stare at her forever."

"I can't wait until you get to be a mom, Claud," Jayne said, touching her hand.

"Me too, me too." Her smile was grateful. "So what did you guys do on Thanksgiving?"

"I went to Gray's."

"Oh, that's right," Karen said. "The big family meet and greet. How was it?"

"His family is great. Really warm, nice people. There were so many people there, though—cousins, aunts, uncles. I couldn't keep them straight."

"So then did you go to your folks after that?" Claudia asked.

"Well, no, his parents live out of town, and it was a long drive."

"Wow, I bet Mama Asher wasn't happy about that," Karen said, her eyes intense as she stared at Jayne.

"No, and I was really bummed to miss out on the day with my family. But it's just one day." She looked down at her plate.

"If you say so."

"So, Karen, what about you?" Claudia asked. "How was your holiday?"

"It was okay. We decided not to squeeze in Rick's family since it's a good two-hour drive to Columbia. We're going to spend a whole day there over Christmas. And I didn't really want to deal with my dad and his whole large stepfamily bullshit. So we just went to Mom's."

"Was your brother in town?"

"No, but we'll see him over Christmas. It was nice at Mom's, though…my grandma was there and my aunt and uncle. He and Rick get along great."

"Well it sounds like we all survived the first holiday of the season." Jayne added with enthusiasm, "Don't you just love this time of year?"

"You know I do," Claudia said, grinning.

"That's because your true calling should be holiday decorator extraordinaire," Karen said with a chuckle.

"What can I say? I just love the whole festive thing."

"Me too," Jayne chimed in, smiling. "And the whole season…there's just something so romantic and hopeful about it. I love chunky sweaters, chilly nights perfect for snuggling, hot chocolate around the fire, sledding…all of it."

"And you missed your calling—Hallmark card writer," Karen said with a smirk. "And I don't mean that in a bad way. I would be a dark, cynical bitch if I didn't have you to instill a little warmth in me from time to time."

"Would be?" Jayne laughed. "I think I'm too late. I think you're already dark and cynical. But you're not a bitch."

"Think how much worse I would be, though, without you guys."

"True!" They all laughed.

"So, Jayne, when are we going to meet Gray, God of Loins?"

"I guess at Claudia's Christmas party. Just two weeks away."

"Well I, for one, can't wait to see what all the hype is about."

"I'll second that," Claudia said, squeezing Jayne's hand.

Karen pushed her chair away from the table. "I ate so much, I can hardly move."

"Well, we have to move, because we have to make the 8:10 show," Claudia reminded.

"I'm warning you, I might fall asleep. Especially since you picked a romantic comedy."

"Oh, you secretly love rom-coms," Jayne said, nudging Karen. "Admit it."

"No I don't. I just enjoy the eye candy—they always cast delicious men in the lead roles. That's why I agree to your chick flicks."

"I know your pitiful little heart enjoys them. But I'll go along with your story."

"Shut it," Karen said, smiling.

December

Chapter Three

When Jayne and Gray pulled up in front, Claudia and Sam's house looked like something out of a Better Homes and Gardens magazine spread. Their nineteenth-century home was the very picture of an old-fashioned Christmas. Real pine garlands were draped grandly on the front porch, accented with pine wreaths and bright red velvet bows on each post. The front bay window displayed their perfect Christmas tree, decorated to a tee. Jayne considered Claudia her domestic idol—she was the closest thing Jayne knew to a real, live Martha Stewart.

"Isn't this just like a postcard?" Jayne said as they stepped out of the car. She noticed Rick's Jeep parked in front of Gray's BMW. "If I didn't know better, I'd think Claudia had e-mailed Mother Nature and requested the two inches of snow that fell last night. Not too much to get in the way, but just enough to make the landscape picturesque."

"Yeah, it's definitely impressive," Gray said, taking hold of her hand as he fell in step with her. Jayne couldn't help but stare at him with adoration. "What do they do for a living?"

"Sam's a lawyer, working on becoming partner. And Claudia is an office manager for a small business."

"A lawyer. Makes sense. This place isn't cheap." Gray surveyed everything as they made their way up the walk.

"Jayne!" Claudia shouted when she opened the door. The girls hugged, always happy to see each other. "And you must be Gray."

"That I am," he said, displaying the dimples that drove Jayne wild.

"Well, come in, both of you." She shut the door behind them and took their coats. "Sam? Jayne and Gray are here."

Sam darted from the living room, where he was talking with Rick. As always, Sam wore a warm, inviting smile along with his Polo sweater and flat front black slacks. His eyes lit up when he caught Jayne's eye.

"Jayne, my very favorite of all Claud's friends," he said, kissing her cheek and embracing her in a brotherly hug.

"I heard that, you asshole," piped up Karen from across the room.

They all laughed. "How could you be my favorite, Karen? You're always busting my chops about something." There was a twinkle in his eye that Jayne had always loved. "And the famous Gray we've all heard so much about," Sam said, holding his hand out. They shook firmly.

"Nice place you've got here," Gray commented, looking around at the large crown moldings and decorative woodwork.

"Oh, thanks. It's a work in progress."

Jayne tugged at Gray's hand, nudging him to follow her into the living room. She waved at Karen and Rick, a huge smile planted on her face. This was so exciting—they were all finally getting to meet Gray. It was a huge step in their relationship. Besides her family, there was no one more important to her in the world than the people in this room. They were like the family she handpicked.

Karen smiled as Jayne and Gray approached, coolly inspecting Gray. My God, Karen thought, he's like something out of a movie. Some sappy romantic chick flick. Almost too good-looking, a Greek god—no wonder Jayne is so flipped out over him. She looks absolutely love-struck.

"Hi, guys!" Jayne said, her excitement bubbling over. She wore a beautiful festive dress, fitting her demure curves to perfection. The burgundy fabric made her fair skin look nearly porcelain, and with her wavy auburn locks framing her cheeks, she looked radiant. Even Karen couldn't deny the happiness on Jayne's face. She was positively giddy.

"Hello, sweetie," Rick said, jumping up to give her a hug. "You look beautiful tonight." He reached over to

Gray, hand extended. "I'm Rick Gordon. Nice to meet you."

"Gray Brandt, pleasure is all mine," he said, flashing what Karen considered a perfect smile of ridiculous proportion.

Holy shit, he's even got dimples. In that moment, she decided he was too much. No way that a glorious male specimen like him could not be fully in love with himself. He must be a narcissistic ass. No doubt about it. Shit, Jayne was so clueless when it came to men. She was forever throwing her whole heart and soul at any man that paid attention to her. And this guy was going to stomp all over it.

"And you must be Karen. I've heard a lot about you."

Don't look into his eyes. He'll probably cast some sort of spell. Their eyes locked. Oh Jesus, he is all that, on the outside anyway. T-r-o-u-b-l-e. "Hello, Gray," she said, shaking hands and smiling ever so slightly. "I've heard a lot about you, too. Glad to finally put a face to all the hype."

"All good, I hope."

Magnetic charm, that grin was powerful. She looked over at Jayne, her desperation for approval obvious. "Oh, nothing but the best."

She squeezed Jayne's hand, giving up a big smile for her. She wanted to tell her to run, run for your life. But it was clear that Jayne wasn't going anywhere. And who could blame her?

"I'm so glad you all could come," Claudia said as she approached.

"What can we help with?" Jayne asked.

"There are just a few last minute things, if you ladies want to join me in the kitchen. We should be eating in a few minutes."

"Gray, can I get you something to drink?" Sam asked as the girls left the room.

"Scotch on the rocks would be great."

"Got it. Rick—you still working on that beer?"

"Yeah, I'm good, thanks." He sat back down in the wingback chair as Gray took a seat on the sofa across from him.

"Thanks for bringing that beer, by the way. You know I love the pumpkin beer they put out this time of year."

"Yeah, it's a huge seller for us. I like it too."

"You're in the brewery business?" Gray asked, leaning forward, resting his elbows on his knees.

"I do graphic design for Midwest Breweries. A small, local brewer."

"Yeah, I've heard of them. I've got some contacts at Anheuser-Busch if you'd like to try to get in there."

"Oh, thanks, but I'm good where I'm at. Great people, quality beer. And I like working for a smaller company."

"You do?" Gray sounded surprised. "Well, whatever works for you."

"One Scotch on the rocks," Sam said, handing Gray a drink. Sam sat down in the other wingback chair next to Rick.

"So what do you do?" Rick asked Gray.

"I'm VP of Marketing for Nixon Pharmaceutical."

"Nothing small about them," Rick chuckled.

"Definitely not," Sam agreed. "How long have you been there?"

"Started there straight out of college after a summer internship…guess it's been seven years now. Been climbing up the ladder ever since. And I hear you're a lawyer, Sam?"

"Yep, toiling away, trying to make partner." He took a drink. "I think I should be able to seal the deal next year. I've been there almost eight years now, and I've worked my ass off every one of those…I'm due."

"And then I hear it will be baby-making time in the Knight household," Rick said, grinning. Sam laughed.

"You heard right. I mean, it's not like we're not practicing all the time…" Sam pointed to the kitchen. "Look at Claud…she's gorgeous. I'm a lucky guy." They all turned to look, and there was no denying that. Her dark hair was swept up in a loose knot at the back of her head, tendrils cascading down in front. The dress she wore accentuated her thin but voluptuous frame, and her face would have seemed appropriate gracing the cover of any magazine.

"Yes you are," Gray said, obviously admiring what he saw.

"So, you met Jayne at work?" Sam asked, as Gray turned to face him.

"Uh, yeah. At lunch. We've got this huge cafeteria with a salad bar, and like three days in a row we ended up in the salad bar line together. So I asked her out."

"Love across the lettuce," Rick said, finishing off his beer.

"Oh, we're just having fun," Gray corrected. "She's a sweet girl."

Rick and Sam glanced at each other. Just then, Claudia announced, "Time to eat. Everyone take a seat...I've got place cards on the table."

"Of course you do," Karen said, shaking her head while she smiled at her friend.

"And they're so cute," Jayne commented, holding up a Christmas ornament with card attached.

"Thank you," Claudia said, taking her place at one end of the table. Sam sat at the head, while the other couples found their spots on each side. The table was beautiful: decked out with a festive holiday centerpiece, fine china, and even matching salad plates with a Christmas motif. Each wine goblet was adorned with a holly leaf pattern.

"Claudia, you've outdone yourself," Karen said, surveying the spread. "Gorgeous table as always."

"Thanks," she beamed. "Sweetheart, can you please start passing the food around from your end?"

"Of course," Sam said, smiling at her. Their eyes caught, and they shared a knowing look full of love that anyone at the table could see.

Jayne saw the way Sam and Claudia were looking at each other and was struck with a pang of longing. That's what she wanted—what they had. A mutual love and friendship. They had a great life together and were creating their lovely home together, piece by piece. Soon they'd be starting a family...all things that Jayne hoped for herself. She didn't feel jealous. She was just anxious to find what they had.

Jayne patted Gray's thigh under the table, and he took her hand in response. She loved the feel of his strong, powerful fingers entwined in hers. She stared at him and he turned to look at her, catching her gaze upon him.

"What?" he asked, his dimples peeking out as he grinned.

"Nothing, just thinking how handsome you look tonight," she said quietly.

"You mean I normally don't?"

"No, of course you're always hot," she said, smiling. "But tonight especially so."

"Well, thank you then. Just wanted to make sure you weren't dissing me." He took the steaming hot plate of juicy sliced pork roast from Claudia, and filled his plate. "Do you want some?"

"Yes, please, just a couple of pieces." As Gray dished it up for her, she was thrilled that he was finally here, with her best friends. She knew she was kind of jumping the gun, but she wondered if he could be the one. The one to settle down with, create a life with like Sam and Claudia had. Gray seemed to fit in, and she adored him. Things weren't perfect, but in time...maybe things would get better. And what beautiful babies they would have.

"That enough?" he asked, bringing her back to reality.

"Yeah, thanks," she said, her cheeks burning, hoping he was not a mind reader.

Once they'd all dished up and starting eating, the conversation started to pick back up.

"So, do any of you ski?" Gray asked after swallowing a bite of creamy mashed potatoes.

"I like skiing," Sam said, "but it's been a couple of years since I've been."

"I'm allergic to outdoor activities," Claudia said with a chuckle.

"So I take it you're a skier, Gray?" Sam asked.

"Yeah, I really enjoy it. I try to make it to Vail or Telluride at least once a year. And of course I hit the slopes here at Hidden Valley quite a bit to practice and keep in the game."

"I haven't been on a ski trip in about three years," Sam commented.

"I took Jaynie here with me last weekend to Hidden Valley."

"You went skiing?" Karen asked Jayne, her eyebrows arched in surprise. Jayne wasn't exactly known for her athleticism.

"Well, I gave it a shot," Jayne said, looking down.

"Poor thing only lasted about twenty minutes before she headed to the lodge," Gray said, taking another bite. "She missed a nice day. I stayed out for another two or three hours."

"So, Jayne, what were you doing all that time?" Karen asked.

"Oh, I was just keeping warm at the lodge, reading a book."

"Sounds like a romantic day together," Karen said, her disapproval thinly disguised in sarcasm. "Did you at least help her out, Gray, when she was on the slopes?"

"I tried," he said, shrugging, "but the bunny slopes are just so boring. I couldn't take them for long. But Jayne didn't mind, did you?"

"No, it was fine," she said, looking up at him with a smile.

"Rick, do you golf?"

"Uh, no, I'm not really into golfing. Sam's your man for golf."

"We should play then sometime," Gray said to Sam. "I've got a couple of club memberships."

"I'd love to. There's no such thing as too much golf."

"So, Rick, you're in great shape—what do you play?"

"Well, I guess I don't play too many sports. I'm more into hiking, biking, swimming, that sort of thing."

"So the whole outdoors-y chunky granola thing. I can see that about you."

Jayne swallowed a piece of pork as she looked at Rick. He looked annoyed. She wasn't sure if Gray meant to be condescending, but it sure came across that way.

"Chunky granola?" Rick asked, putting his elbows on the table. "Not sure where you're going with this."

"Oh, just that you look artsy with your hair and everything."

Jayne shifted in her seat. The tension was palpable. She had to intervene. "Actually," she piped up, "Rick is an amazing artist. He paints...you've got to see his work sometime."

"Thanks, Jayne," Rick smiled at her. She noticed how nice he looked in his casual blazer and button-down shirt opened a couple of buttons. He was normally a worn Henley, jeans and hiking boots kind of guy. So when he dressed up a bit, Jayne was always impressed with how classy and hip he looked.

"Are you putting together pieces for a showing?" Gray asked, seemingly oblivious to the friction he'd caused.

"No, not in particular. I don't really sell my work."

"Then why do you paint?"

The question hung uncomfortably in the air as no one spoke for a moment. Jayne thought Gray's question didn't come across as rude, but rather as if he couldn't fathom why someone would paint if they weren't doing it for profit.

"Why?" Rick sat back in his seat and crossed his arms. Jayne thought she could actually see Karen biting her tongue. Oh, no. "Because it's who I am. I have to—it's how I express myself."

Karen shot Gray a steely, menacing smile as she said, "I imagine it's like how you probably feel the urge to collect expensive watches or buy fancy cars."

"Or how Claud expresses herself by redecorating a room every month," Sam said with a chuckle, attempting to lighten the mood.

Gray glanced around the table. "I didn't mean anything by that, I was just wondering. Sorry if I offended you." No one spoke. He smiled, dimples appearing. "And the artsy comment—that's just the marketing side of me. Always trying to figure out the demographic, what kind of category everybody fits in."

"No offense taken," Rick said, putting his arms down and resuming his meal. Jayne loosened the grip on her fork; she hadn't realized how tense she'd become.

"So, is everybody staying in town for the holidays?" Claudia asked, looking a bit flustered. She wasn't used to friction at her dinner parties.

"We'll take the two-hour trek to Columbia to see my folks," Rick said. "Not sure what day yet, though."

"Oh, gee, I can't wait," Karen sighed, but she smiled at Rick.

"Oh, like your family gatherings are so much more appealing," he teased. "Visiting two different homes since your parents are divorced—every man's dream." Everybody laughed.

"Touché my dear." Rick kissed her hand, but she quickly pulled it away, looking uncomfortable. PDA was not something she participated in, if she could help it.

"Are you guys off the last two weeks of the year again?" Claudia asked Jayne and Gray.

"Yeah," Jayne said, nodding. Their company shut down that same time every year.

"You lucky dogs, must be nice."

"Well, I'll be going in at least a couple of days," Gray said. "Ambition can't always take a day off."

"I know what you mean," Karen agreed. "I'm in sales, so I make my own hours. And although I want to blow off work sometimes, it's almost impossible to do it. Every minute I'm not trying to sell is a minute someone else is selling."

"Yeah, if you don't do it, someone else will." Gray nodded with enthusiasm.

"Well, I'm not that driven," Jayne said, giggling. "I won't be setting foot in that place."

"I can't say I'll be working that hard, either," Sam added.

"So I might actually get to see my handsome husband?" Claudia asked with a smile.

"For a day or two, anyway," he said with a grin.

The rest of dinner went well and afterward, the men headed to the living room for another cocktail while the women cleaned up in the kitchen.

"I still think it's bullshit that we're expected to do all this work," Karen muttered, carrying dishes to the sink. "What is this—1950?"

"No, dear, then you'd be wearing pearls," Claudia said as Jayne laughed. Karen chuckled, too.

"I don't mind," Jayne said. "I mean, I don't like doing the dishes all the time, but for the holidays it seems like kind of a tradition."

"Drinking eggnog and opening gifts are traditions," Karen corrected. "Cleaning up dinner because I have a vagina is just sexist."

"Lighten up—it's the holidays," Jayne said, sighing.

Karen grinned. "Turn on some fucking Christmas carols, and then maybe it will feel like some glorious holiday tradition."

"You got it," Claudia said, touching the control panel on the wall. Soon Johnny Mathis was crooning It's Beginning to Look a Lot Like Christmas.

Jayne took Karen by the hands and started dancing around the kitchen with her. Claudia watched as her two friends twirled about, especially enjoying seeing Karen dance with abandon. It was rare to see her loosen up that way, but when she did, there was a spark in her eyes that was unmatched. And Jayne had seemed joyous all evening.

Laughing, the two stopped dancing before they resumed cleaning up.

"Everything was so delicious, Claudia," Jayne said.

"Oh, thanks, sweetie," she said, smiling. "I love having you guys over. And we finally got to meet Gray."

"So…what do you think of him?"

Looking at Jayne with her big eyes full of a mixture of worry and hope, Claudia felt conflicted. Gray was handsome, charming…but seemed quite full of himself. Yet there was something almost magnetic about him. And it was clear Jayne adored him.

"I think he's one of the best looking men I've ever laid my eyes on," Claudia reassured. "It's obvious he's a pretty cocky guy, but show me a successful guy that's not."

"Yeah, he's certainly not insecure." Jayne chuckled. "But I think he's a good guy." Karen was noticeably silent as she scraped food off plates. "Karen? What about you? What do you think?"

Claudia's heart nearly stopped as she looked at Karen. They caught each other's eyes, and Claudia tried to tell Karen with a look, Don't crush her. Be kind.

"Well," Karen said, looking back at the dish she was cleaning, "he ought to stop working so hard at his job and just hop a flight to L.A. He'd be the next big thing in no time."

"I know, sometimes when I look at him, he's too perfect," Jayne said, smiling. "But do you like him?"

Karen looked at Jayne, tilting her head. "Jayne, just be careful with him, okay?"

"What do you mean?"

She sighed. "I know he's charming and going places, but…" Karen swallowed. "He's a lot, Jayne. And I can see how hard you've fallen for him, but I'm worried maybe he's a bit of a player. So just be cautious."

"But do you like him?"

"He needs a little more tact, but yeah, what's not to like?"

"You just said someone needs tact?" Claudia laughed.

"Yeah, imagine that," Karen said as they all laughed.

****

They played poker for a couple of hours with Christmas carols playing in the background and spiked eggnog in their glasses. Everyone laughed and had a good time while Rick cleaned up, pocketing sixty dollars. It wasn't a high stakes game, but they all contributed a bit to make it interesting.

After poker, they sat down in the den on cozy leather couches, with a blazing fire to keep them toasty. Jayne cuddled up next to Gray, who didn't seem to mind, but Jayne also noticed that he didn't lean into her. He was busy telling some stories about his college days. Jayne watched Rick put his arm around Karen, who stiffened up. Why does she do that? Jayne wondered. Unfazed, Rick kissed the top of her head. Glancing over at Sam and Claudia, Jayne smiled. They were snuggled up together in an oversized chair, with Claudia on his lap. Sam stroked her hair as they laughed at something Gray said. Rick chimed in with a comment, making them all laugh harder.

Jayne felt so sleepy in front of the warm fire, and so content, her head lying on Gray's rock hard chest, surrounded by her friends.

"Hey, sleepyhead," Gray said, nudging Jayne awake. "It's time to go."

"Oh," she said, disoriented, sitting up. "Was I asleep long?"

"Maybe twenty or thirty minutes," Karen said, patting Jayne on the leg. "We're going to go. Loved seeing you— call me this week. Nice to meet you, Gray."

"Yes, nice to meet you too," he said, standing up as Karen allowed him to give her a perfunctory hug. He shook Rick's hand.

"Good bye, Miss Jayne," Rick said, bending down and kissing her on the cheek.

"Bye guys," Jayne said, standing up, still a bit foggy. Gray handed over her coat, and she slid her arms inside. "Sam, Claudia—thanks so much for having us. This was so much fun. And so festive."

They all hugged, and Jayne yawned as they made their way out the front door. The instant they hit the cold air she began to shiver. As they walked to the car, it was quiet outside, almost serene, with snow blanketing the lawns. It really was beginning to look a lot like Christmas.

"Too tired for a nightcap at your place?" Gray asked with a twinkle in his eye.

"No, not too tired for you," she smiled. But she actually was too tired. She just wanted to crawl into bed, but she couldn't imagine ever telling him no. Not about sex, or anything else, for that matter.

As she climbed into the car, she realized how dangerous that was. She'd never let a man have that kind of power over her. So why was she letting him?

****

Claudia and Sam stood at the front door, watching their friends drive away. She let out a long, contented sigh. Sam put his arms around her and they kissed.

"That was fun, wasn't it?" she asked.

"The kiss, or our evening?" he asked with a grin.

"Your kisses are always fun," she said, smiling, "but I meant having them over."

"Yeah, that was a good time. You throw a great dinner party, my dear." He closed and locked the door and turned out the living room lights. "Let's go to bed."

Claudia was tired but also in a great mood. She gave him her best come hither look. "Do you want to sleep just yet?"

"Well, well, Mrs. Knight. If you have something better in mind, sleep can wait."

"Oh, I have something in mind." She grinned at Sam, still completely in love and turned on by her husband after being together for ten years, eight of them married.

"Well, let's turn out the rest of the lights and you can show me what you're talking about."

"Yes sir." She flicked out the kitchen lights.

"You look so beautiful tonight, Claud," he said with a quiet voice. "I love you so much."

"I love you too, Sam," she said as he put his arm around her. As they headed up the stairs together, arm in arm, Claudia asked, "What did you think of Gray?"

"Oh...he's arrogant and cocky, that's for damn sure. But I think he's an okay guy. Not so sure he's as into Jayne as she is into him."

"Really? Why do you say that?"

"He made a comment about how they're just having fun. I think Jayne's heart is in much deeper than that."

"Yeah, me too," she said, sighing. "He looks like a model or something though, doesn't he?"

"You got that right. Made me feel like the ugly duckling." They walked into the bedroom.

"Oh, Mr. Knight, there's absolutely nothing ugly about you." She unzipped her dress, pulled off her bra and panties, and climbed into bed. "Come here and I'll show you just how hot I think you are."

"Yes ma'am." There was a huge grin on his face as he climbed in beside her.

****

Jayne was thrilled when more snow fell on Tuesday, so much so that the campus of Nixon Pharmaceutical closed for the day. No work! She felt like a schoolgirl who just saw on TV that her district had called a snow day. An unexpected day off was divine.

She drew a bath, filled it with some decadent sweet-smelling potion she'd gotten from Karen and Claudia on her last birthday, and climbed in. Soaking in the soothing hot bath was way better than anything she'd be doing at the office. She had some laid-back music from The Civil Wars quietly playing from her iPod. Perfection. The only distraction was the damn dripping faucet in the nearby sink that felt like a woodpecker poking at her brain. She managed to wipe off her hands and lean far enough to reach her iPod and turn up the music to drown out the drip of doom. Ah, much better.

When the water cooled to room temperature and her fingers and toes looked like the raisins she used to eat out of the red box when she was a kid, she climbed out and called Gray. It was around ten o'clock, and, true to form, he was working. Albeit at home, since the campus was closed.

"So you don't think you'll have time to play today?" she asked him in a seductive tone.

"Oh, well, you make a play date sound pretty appealing." He chuckled. "Let me see how much work I can get done, okay? Please don't bet on it, but I'll call you later and let you know if I can get away for a bit."

"That's fine. I've got stuff I can do around here."

"Okay, sweet Jaynie. I'll talk to you later."

"Bye." She hung up the phone, grinning as always with him.

She started her Christmas music play list on her MP3 player, got busy cleaning up around her condo, and baked some chocolate chip cookies. Then she plopped down in front of the television, put in her Bridges of Madison County DVD, and cried while wrapping presents. She put extra time and thought into wrapping Gray's gift, which she was excited to give him. It was a Movado watch she'd bought him—a bit extravagant, she knew, but he seemed worth every penny of the five hundred dollars she'd spent. She just knew he'd love it.

Jayne was packing up her wrapping supplies when her phone rang. Gray.

"Hi," she answered with her usual cheer.

"Hello. Can you come out and play?"

She laughed. "I'd love to. I didn't really think you'd get your work done."

"Well, I didn't, but watching the snow fall outside and thinking about you all alone at home...I couldn't concentrate. So let's go sledding."

"Sledding?"

"Yeah, I've got a great sled we can both fit on, and I thought it would be a blast to head up to Art Hill."

"Sure! I haven't gone since I was a kid, though."

"It'll be great. Tell you what. I'll be over to get you in about forty-five minutes. Is that good?"

"That's fine."

"Dress warm."

"I will. See you in a bit."

"See you soon, sweet Jaynie."

****

A sea of moving people scattered all over Art Hill when Jayne and Gray arrived. The popular St. Louis sledding destination grew crowded on snowy days like this, filled with families, teenagers and others young at heart. The snow had stopped falling, leaving about a three to four inch deep cold, white blanket on the ground. Gray had to park his car far away, and they trudged through the snow for about ten minutes before arriving at the top of the hill. Jayne was tired already.

Standing there, the view was impressive. Behind them stood the massive, elegant St. Louis Art Museum, and at the bottom of the huge hill, was a lake that spouted fountains in the warmer months. This was the site of the 1904 World's Fair and ever since had become a winter gathering spot. Jayne spent many days of her youth bundled up in the cold, sliding down and climbing back up this hill.

"I'm glad you wore a snowsuit," Gray said. "It is damn cold out here."

"You could say that," Jayne said with a smile, looking at him. She thought he looked adorable in his Ralph Lauren Polo stocking cap, ski jacket and matching pants. He looked like a professional—like he was a member of the U.S. luge team on his way to compete in the Olympic trials.

"You look cute, Jaynie." He grinned at her, giving a quick kiss. She'd had that snowsuit for a few years and had only worn it a handful of times. It was powder blue and always made her feel like a snow angel. "Your cheeks are getting all rosy."

"That was quite a workout, walking up here."

"Yeah, now I'm ready to have some fun."

Jayne couldn't remember the last time she'd laughed so hard or felt so exhilarated. It was wonderful. They had a blast, acting like a couple of twelve-year-olds, riding down the hill, screaming with abandon and tearing back up the hill for another go 'round. She was getting tired, but didn't want to stop. It was like riding a roller coaster over and over again.

They tried going down backwards, they tried Jayne sitting on his lap, Jayne in front, Jayne in back, on their knees, on their butts...experimenting was half the fun. When they decided to go down facing each other, with Jayne riding backward and Gray facing forward—it ended with a crash landing at the bottom of the hill. They were both hysterical with laughter as Gray landed on top of her.

Jayne looked up at his face, snow clinging to his hat, cheeks red, vibrant blue eyes twinkling. His dimples seemed even deeper as he laughed with abandon. Her heart overflowed.

"I love you, Gray," she said, staring into his eyes.

As soon as she'd said it, she wished she could take it back—it was too soon. But she felt it, and as her eyes searched his, she waited, breathless, to see what he would say. Maybe...just maybe, he loved her, too.

"Well...that's nice," he said, kissing her. Then he stood up and held out his hand to her.

As he pulled her to standing, her mind was screaming, That's nice? That's nice? What the hell kind of response is that? Then, internally, she beat herself up for going too far, for making herself even more vulnerable than she already felt.

She could barely manage to make eye contact with him after that, and they left about twenty minutes later. She tried to play it off like she'd never said the "L" word and he'd never responded with something as ridiculous and evasive as, "That's nice."

But they both knew what happened. He drove her home, declining an offer for dinner, saying he'd better catch up on the work he'd left waiting for him. As always, he kissed her with tenderness before leaving—but she rushed out of the car before he could tell her good night.

****

"That's nice?" Claudia repeated on the other end of the phone.

"Yes." Jayne sighed. "It was mortifying." It was the next morning, and she busied herself at work with deleting all the spam in her inbox as she chatted with Claudia. The previous night she'd been entirely too embarrassed and upset to call anyone.

"Well...I guess it could have been worse."

"What could have possibly been worse?"

"I don't know...if he'd said, 'Oh shit' or something like that. Or if he'd said, 'Well I don't love you.'"

"Yeah, I suppose." Jayne took a sip of her latte. "He did say it was nice. Not horrifying or awful. Nice. So maybe he's glad I love him, but he's just not ready to say it himself yet."

"That could be." Claudia didn't sound convinced.

"But probably not." As Jayne stared off into space, her mind wandering, she was brought back to reality with the sight of Gray strolling toward her cubicle. She whispered, "Oh shit! Here he comes. Gray never comes down here. I'll call you back."

"Hello, my sweet Jaynie," he said, smiling as he approached her. He walked into her cube and leaned against her desk. "Will you get busted if I kiss you here?"

"No, I don't think I'll get in trouble, but I've seen my boss' husband, and I'm sure she'll wish you were kissing her instead," she said with a giggle.

Gray shrugged his shoulders and winked when he said, "Let's make her jealous." He leaned over and kissed her gently, once, twice. He was smiling as he pulled away.

"So what are you doing, slumming down here with the common folk?"

"We had a meeting and all of the meeting rooms upstairs were already booked. A lot of end of year strategizing and finishing stuff, I guess."

"And in the process, you get to see how the other half lives, huh? No walls, just partitions. Not nearly as nice as your floor."

"Oh, but you're among the partitions. Looks pretty damn good to me."

Jayne felt her face grow warm. "Well, thank you."

"You're welcome." He grinned. "I know how you can repay me."

"How?"

"I was so busy yesterday after you tempted me to play outdoors—"

"I didn't tempt you. You called me."

"True, but it was the thought of you and that gorgeous ass of yours that kept distracting me from my work."

"Okay, keep talking." She laughed. "How can I repay you?"

"You can come over to my place tonight and let me see you without all the layers of your snowsuit. I was actually thinking a different kind of suit—your birthday suit."

"You want to see me naked?" she whispered with a broad smile. "Mr. Brandt, that is naughty."

"I know. That's why I want to." He bent over, whispering, "And wear something hot."

"I never said I was coming." She chuckled as their eyes met.

"Ooh, hard to get. I've never seen this side of you. Now I want you even more." He stood up. "I should be home by seven-thirty. Be there."

"Yes sir," she said with a grin. He walked away, and Jayne noticed that instead of walking, he always seemed to strut. Female heads turned to watch him all the way down the long aisle of cubicles.

Well, I must not have scared him too badly. She picked up the phone and called Claudia back.

"Well?" Claudia's eager voice answered.

"He acted fine, actually. Maybe more than fine. He wants me to come over tonight for a little...you know..."

"Yes," she said, chuckling. "I know. So he's obviously not running for the hills. That's good. You might be right—maybe he's just not there yet, but he's okay that you are."

"I hope so. I feel a little relieved now."

"So are you going to say anything to him about it?"

"God, no. I'm perfectly happy to just let it lie and pretend it never happened. I think that's what he's doing, anyway."

"But do you think bringing it out in the open would help?"

"Who would it help? Certainly not me…it would give me a nervous breakdown."

Claudia laughed. "Okay then. Just thought I'd mention it. Well, I hope everything will seem normal tonight."

"I sure hope so."

****

When Jayne arrived at Gray's condo, she was wearing nothing but a white silk teddy with a matching thong underneath her black wool coat. She also wore sky-high red patent leather Isaac Mizrahi pumps. She felt sexy, yes, but also a little out of character. Sex kitten was not exactly how she saw herself.

But for Gray, she found herself doing whatever it took.

He opened the door, with an impossibly thick, fuzzy towel tied around his hips. Drops of water glistened on his chest like something out of a Hot Midwestern Males calendar spread. His wet hair was slicked back, giving him an almost debonair appearance. Jayne thought he'd never looked more attractive or more desirable. Sex personified.

"Come in, come in," he said, a wide smile spreading across his face as she walked inside. "I didn't have time to get dressed, but I don't suppose that really matters, do you?"

"And here I got all dressed up for you," she said with a grin, unbuttoning her coat and giving him a good preview.

"Wow. I mean, wow." She'd never seen his eyes get so big.

She chuckled. "So you like?"

"Me like very much." He put his arms around her and pulled her close. As they kissed, the towel came loose and dropped to the floor. "Oops." They both laughed. "I guess

I need to take this slinky little negligee off of you so we can be even."

"Sounds fair to me," she said, breathless, more aroused than she'd ever been in her life. His powerful chest, clean scent, and unbelievable smile were nearly too much for her. Their attraction was magnetic.

Soon they were in bed, and Jayne was sure all was right with the world.

"You could become addicting, you know that?" Gray said, lying down next to her when they were done, his breathing still heavy.

"Nothing wrong with that," she said, kissing his sweaty chest.

"Oh, there's a lot wrong with that." He chuckled.

"Like what?"

"Let's not do this, Jaynie, okay?" His tone had turned to one of irritation, and he sat up.

"Do what? What are we doing?" She didn't know what he meant but was hurt by the annoyance in his voice.

He turned to look at her, and said gently, "I told you, I've got goals, I have plans. I can't get too involved."

"I know. I didn't mean anything—" Her eyes pleaded with him.

"Okay." He bent over, kissing her. "Forget it, okay? I'm just a little tense right now. There's a lot of pressure on me at work."

"Is there anything I can do to help?"

He climbed out of bed, heading to the bathroom. "You just did."

Jayne lay there, wondering if, by some chance, he would climb back into bed with her to cuddle. Maybe. Their passion had been intense, although she still had the nagging sense that sex was more like a workout regimen to him than making love. She was still naked, on her side, her head propped up on her hand when he walked back in the room.

His eyes lit up at the sight of her. "You have a phenomenal body, did you know that?"

"Thank you," she said coyly. In that moment, with the most handsome man she'd ever seen telling her she had a great body, she felt truly beautiful.

"Have you ever thought of getting a boob job?"

What? Did he really just say that? She felt like she was going to throw up.

"I mean, if you had larger breasts, your body would be unbeatable."

Jayne wasn't even aware that she'd pulled the sheets over her body. She just knew she had to get out of there. He was putting on clothes anyway. Of course he wasn't going to cuddle.

She pulled the teddy over her head, wishing with desperation now that she'd brought a sweatshirt to cover her apparently pitifully small breasts. Her mom had big breasts; why had she gotten screwed in the mammary department?

"Jaynie?" Gray stood in front of her, and touched her cheek. "I'm sorry. Did I hurt your feelings? I didn't mean to—"

"No, no, you're right, they're small." She stepped into her shoes and headed out of the bedroom.

"I just meant, you're a solid eight-point-five and with larger breasts you'd easily be a ten—"

"Please stop," she said, surprising herself when it came out incredibly harsh. She pulled on her coat, all the while never making eye contact with Gray.

"Hey," he said, pulling her toward him. She was staring at the floor. He pushed her chin up and she was forced to look at him. His deep blue eyes looked right into hers. "You're hot, you're incredible. I'm sorry." He gave her a tender kiss. "Okay?"

"Okay," she said, unable to resist those eyes. Then he smiled, and his dimples made an appearance. She couldn't possibly stay mad at him.

"And there's your smile," he said, chuckling. "So we're still on for Friday night, right? Christmas party for my department."

"Yes. I've got the perfect outfit picked out."

"I don't know…I kind of like what you wore tonight."

She giggled. "I have something more appropriate in mind."

"Not too appropriate, I hope." He winked at her.

"All eight-point-five of me will be on sultry display, don't worry." She kissed him. "Good night."

"Good night, sweet Jaynie," he said, opening the door for her. "I'll call you tomorrow."

When she got into her car, she wanted to cry. She felt humiliated and embarrassed. But even worse, she felt empty.

Chapter Four

Karen was relieved that since Rick worked for a brewery, there was an endless supply of beer at his holiday party. Because the whole being festive with co-workers bit was definitely not her scene. But the Pumpkin Spice beer helped. So did being there with Rick.

It was obvious to her that everyone at Midwest Breweries adored Rick. And she knew why. He was a great guy. Easy going, always quick with a joke or kind smile, hardworking, creative. The guys were all his buddies, and the women all flirted with him. She couldn't blame them.

It was a casual event at a local tavern. They had rented the back room for the thirty or so employees and their dates. People were chatting, mingling, and enjoying the music from the live band in the main room. Karen was tapping her foot to the surprisingly good music, sitting with a couple of Rick's colleagues going on and on about some distributor they were at war with. It was hard enough for Karen to make small, banal talk with customers for her job, but it was torture doing it in her free time.

"You're the most beautiful woman in the room," Rick whispered from behind. He sat a martini in front of her. "Your non-hops alcoholic beverage, miss."

"I had no idea they had such smart, hot waiters here," Karen said, grinning as Rick sat down next to her.

"You should get out more."

"I don't exactly call this getting out," she whispered in his ear.

"What do you mean?"

One of the guys across the table said with vehemence, "That's why distribution is the key to everything!"

Karen rolled her eyes, saying, "Case in point."

"Touché," Rick said, his grin sheepish. "Wanna go hit the buffet again?"

"Oh, Christ, I might as well get fat. Beats getting bored."

As they made their way through the buffet line of appetizers, Karen was pretty certain she could feel her thighs expanding just from smelling all the grease. Loaded potato skins, toasted ravioli—a St. Louis staple, crab Rangoon, meatballs…the usual suspects. So yummy.

"So is Jayne still dating that ass, what's his name?" Rick asked, piling meatballs onto his plate.

"Gray. Yes," she said, shaking her head in disgust. "And Claudia told me Jayne actually told him that she loved him."

"She does?"

Karen sighed. "Poor thing thinks she does. I personally think she has better taste than that, but his glistening white teeth and impossible dimples have put her under some kind of spell."

Rick laughed. "Could be. So what was his reaction to her blurting those three little words?"

"Oh, it was good, that's for sure. If you like someone to respond with, 'That's nice.'"

"Are you serious?" Rick couldn't help but chuckle as he shook his head. "What a tool."

"Uh, yeah, you could say that. But I don't know what poor Jayne was thinking. He is going to crush her."

"Have you talked to Jayne about it yet?"

"No…I'm worried I won't be able to hold back and I'll tell her what I really think of him." As they left the buffet, Karen added, "I hate him."

"Oh, I don't think he was that bad," Rick said, pulling out Karen's chair.

"He was worse."

"So he wasn't an all-around fantastic guy like me?" Rick smiled at her.

"No, he wasn't," Karen said, offering a small grin. *Damn, he is too sexy,* she thought to herself as she looked at the sparkle in Rick's dark eyes. "But don't get too big of a head."

"Why not? I need a big head to hold all this gorgeous hair," he chuckled, swishing his hair.

Karen laughed out loud. "Stop. Really."

****

As she surveyed the room, Jayne figured she hadn't seen this many people dressed up since her senior prom. And that had been a decade earlier. They were in a fancy ballroom at a fancy hotel, but unlike prom, there was an open bar and drinks were free.

She was used to playing her part when she went out with Gray—smiling on his arm, dolled up, making a witty comment when she knew it would score, and otherwise keeping quiet. And of course there was the obligatory time spent alone, watching Gray yuck it up with his cronies. Kissing ass, making strategic political moves, always playing an angle. Sometimes she enjoyed watching him, like now, as she sat at a table by herself, a dozen feet away from him.

He was standing with a group of guys, wearing a suit that must have been custom tailored for him. It was a slim cut, very fitted—showing off every curl, push up and lunge he'd been doing for the past few years. He looked fantastic in it. Not that he looked bad in anything, but he looked even better in a suit. Jayne took a sip of her fuzzy navel and watched him tilt his head back, laughing. Dimples on full display. He said something that made all the other men laugh, and one of the guys slapped him on the back.

Gray turned in her direction, caught her staring at him, causing Jayne's face to grow hot. She figured it was glowing bright red, surely enough to match the lipstick she was wearing. He grinned, nodding at her. They'd been there for almost three hours…Jayne was tired and bored and her feet were killing her. Although the shoes were worth the pain— they were sublime. While she still had his eye, she pointed to her watch. He just shrugged and turned his attention back to the boys club.

As Jayne contemplated whether it would be rude to lay her head down on the table and take a nap, she heard: "Jayne? Jayne Asher, is that you?"

She turned to see a familiar smiling face. "Scott," she said, jumping out of her seat and giving him a hug. He was an old friend from high school; they'd done theater together and yearbook. A lot of good memories.

"Oh my God, do you work here?" he asked.

"Yes, on the second floor. You must be on the fifth floor."

"Well, yeah."

"Impressive," she grinned. She was somehow comforted to see that Scott looked pretty much the same. Maybe ever so slightly heavier but not a trace of wrinkles. He looked good, just as she'd remembered.

"But I'm actually fifth floor ghetto. No office for me, though my cube is pretty sweet. I'm second assistant to the head of marketing."

Jayne laughed. "Nothing wrong with a cubicle. I've got one myself. So, are you married, kids, what?"

"Sadly, already married and divorced. No kids."

"Oh, I'm sorry," she said, thinking to herself that she couldn't believe he'd already burned through one marriage before she'd even started one.

"It's been a couple of years, I'm over it. So are you here with someone, since this is the marketing department's shindig and you work in customer relations?"

"Actually, yes." She looked with pride at Gray. "My boyfriend, Gray Brandt."

"Gray Brandt? Gray Brandt is your boyfriend?"

The surprise on his face made her laugh.

"Yes. Why are you so surprised?"

"Oh, well...he's the wonder boy of the department. Aggressive, driven, smart guy."

"And you didn't think someone like him would want to be with me?" Jayne couldn't help but be hurt.

"No, no," Scott said, taking her hand. "I just didn't think you'd go for a guy like him."

"Oh," she said, relieved. "Why?"

"I don't know…" He let go of her hand and glanced over at Gray. "I mean, I get it, he's a great looking guy and all. I just figured you would be with someone a little more laid back. And a little more…monogamous."

"So he gets around, does he?" she asked, nudging Scott. "We've only been dating for about seven weeks."

"Not that you're counting." He chuckled.

"Oh, hush. He can be a lot of fun when you get him away from the office."

"And when is that? He's always there when I arrive and there when I leave."

"We squeeze some time in here and there. But, yeah, he's a busy guy." Jayne caught Gray's eye as he glanced over at her. For a moment she thought he might be jealous that she was talking to another guy. But no reaction—he just looked away. "So what about you? Are you dating anyone?"

"Yeah, her name's Julie. But I didn't want to bore her with my work party, so I told her I'll crawl into her bed afterwards."

"Boring? No, this is just great," Jayne said, laughing. "It's much better now that you're here. Let's refill our drinks and dish on everyone from school."

"Works for me."

****

Nearly an hour later, Jayne had indulged in far too many cocktails. She was a lightweight when it came to drinking anyway, but after four fuzzy navels and two shots, it was amazing she was still functioning. Somewhat.

Gray had largely ignored her as she and Scott got hammered together, reminiscing about the good ol' days and catching up on their lives post high school. Gray was unconcerned, that is, until Jayne and Scott convinced the DJ to play You're the One That I Want from Grease. It held a soft spot in both of their hearts since it was their senior musical. The DJ gave them each a mic, and they belted it out with abandon. What they lacked in technical expertise they made up in enthusiasm. At least they thought so.

Gray apparently didn't.

Jayne was facing Scott, dancing around and doing her best Olivia Newton-John sex kitten impression from the movie when Gray came up behind her and snatched the mic away.

"Concert's over, Jaynie," he said, setting the mic down and grabbing her hand rather brusquely. He looked at Scott with disdain. "Aren't you one of Mac's assistants?"

"Uh, yes...I went to high school with Jayne." John Travolta's voice piped in with the chorus.

"Well, this isn't high school—it's the Ritz Carlton, and my boss is over there." He put his arm around Jayne and started steering her out of the room.

"I'll call you," she said to Scott, looking back as Gray dragged her away. She thought Scott looked sad as he nodded his head.

"Looks like you've got a wild one there," one of the men from Gray's clique shouted, and all the others laughed.

Gray looked sheepish as he grinned. "Nothing a little coffee won't cure."

"Or maybe she'll do a different kind of performance for you when you get her home," another guy chuckled.

By then he'd successfully ushered her out of the ballroom and was quick to grab their coats from the coat check girl. All the while he said nothing to her, and Jayne was afraid to talk. She felt like the teacher had caught her smoking in the bathroom or something. Which had never really happened to her, of course, because she always did what people expected of her.

When they stepped out of the hotel, the cold air seemed to snap her out of her drunken haze in an instant. Gray gave the valet his ticket and as they stood there shivering, she looked over at him.

He let out a loud sigh, his breath visible as plumes of white in the chilled night air. "What the fuck, Jayne?"

Her voice was quiet when she said, "We were just singing—"

"You were drunk and making a spectacle of yourself. You embarrassed me in front of my colleagues." He wouldn't even turn to look at her.

"I didn't mean to embarrass you...I was just trying to have fun. I'm sorry, Gray." She put her hand on his arm but he jerked it away as his car pulled up. He tersely opened the door for her and after she climbed in, he slammed it shut with great force.

Tears started forming in her eyes. She didn't want them to, but she couldn't stop it. Maybe it was the booze, the late hour, the fact that she'd disappointed him...or she wondered if it was just because she was so terrified to make him mad. To give him a reason to leave.

"Gray, I really am sorry. Please don't be mad." She figured it was the tremble in her voice that made him look at her. He looked angry, but his jaw softened a bit.

He focused straight ahead as he pulled the car into the busy Clayton suburban traffic. All the lights looked fuzzy to Jayne and through her tears, she could barely make out the Christmas decorations scattered along the streets.

"I need to know you're not going to do something like that again," he said, his voice subdued and quiet. "I mean, I depend on you to be an asset when I take you places, not a liability."

Assets? Liabilities? Was that all she was to him? A business arrangement? "An asset?" Her voice was just a whisper.

"Jayne, don't take it like that."

"Like I'm just a tool you use?"

"Oh, come on, you know it's not like that. I was just using that as a symbol." Neither of them spoke for a moment. "Please don't cry, okay?"

She wiped her eyes on the back of her hand. "I won't embarrass you again."

"Thank you."

Jayne was surprised that he pulled the car into his parking garage. She had figured he was angry and would take her straight home. After he'd parked and come around to her side of the car, he opened the door and said gently, "I guess you need some help getting in."

"I'm fine." Truth was she felt a little thickheaded. But not too wobbly. Her painful shoes were more of an impediment to her mobility than her drunkenness. He kept his arm around her as they made their way up the elevator, down the hall, and into his condo.

"I had a fair amount to drink, so I didn't really think I should drive any more than the three miles home. I figured you could just crash here tonight if that's okay."

She'd never stayed overnight before. Unfortunately, now she would be, but only because they'd had too much to drink. Nonetheless, it would feel good to sleep in his arms.

"Thank you," she said, unsure if he was still upset with her. She pulled off her coat and draped it over the edge of his leather couch. It felt cold to the touch. As she stepped out of her shoes, feeling short, he touched her bare back where her dress scooped down low.

"You look stunning tonight." He kissed her neck. "I'm sorry for getting so upset with you. It probably wasn't all that bad."

"I really didn't think it was a big deal. I was just bored, and Scott is so much fun—"

"Yeah, who is that guy?"

"An old friend from school. He's a great guy." She grinned. "Are you jealous?"

"Of a chubby little assistant?" He laughed. "Uh, no. He's hardly a threat. But it was a little embarrassing that my date was hanging out with him."

"That's kind of elitist, don't you think?" she asked quietly.

"No, it's realistic. I'm in marketing. My whole job is all about creating an image. For my company, for our products. So my image is just as important if I'm going to get ahead."

"So I can't hang out with people beneath you?"

"Why are you trying to make it sound like I'm an asshole? I'm not. But I have to think of how things look. I'm sorry, but I've set my sights pretty high, and I have to do everything right." He kissed her. "You're right."

"Until I start singing show tunes?"

"Exactly." He grinned at her. "So now that we've had our first fight, are you sober enough to have some make-up sex?"

"As long as you're on top," she said with a giggle.

"Oh, I think I can handle that." He unzipped her dress, kissed her shoulder and Jayne suddenly didn't care about his earlier words. Her mind gave in, her body took over, and when they finished she fell asleep in his arms.

****

As Jayne opened her eyes, it took a minute to remember where she was. Gray's place. She rolled over, expecting to see his sculpture-like body next to her, but instead his side of the bed was empty. And cold. He'd been up for a while.

"Gray?" she called out, hearing her voice echo in the sparse surroundings. Then she saw a note on the nightstand with some money: I'm sure you're wiped out, so I let you sleep. I'm going to work out & then to the office. Help yourself to food, coffee, whatever. I left some money for a cab so you can get home. I'll call you later about what we want to do tonight.—Gray

She was disappointed but not surprised. As she drifted off to sleep last night, she had visions of making breakfast for Gray and spending the morning together. What was she thinking? And she was not going to call a cab.

Should she call Karen or Claudia? Karen would judge. Rightfully so, but Jayne really didn't want to get a dose of reality at the moment. Cab fare on a nightstand was enough reality. Claudia would be perfect.

The phone only rang a couple of times when Claudia picked up. "Hello?"

"It's me, Jayne," she said, always happy to hear her friend's pleasant voice on the other end of the line.

"Hi. What's new?"

"Well, I was wondering if you could do me a favor."

"For you, anything. What do you need?"

"A ride."

"Oh, sure. Is your car in the shop or something?"

"No, I went out with Gray last night, and we had a little too much to drink so I crashed at his place. When I woke up, he was already gone and left me money for a cab, but I really don't want to call a cab."

After a pause: "Yeah, that's fine, I can pick you up from Gray's. He's in Clayton, right?"

"Yes. And thank you so much. I'm sure you have better things to do—"

"No, I'm just hanging around the house, so it's no problem. Text me the address and I'll be there in about thirty minutes, okay?"

"You're a lifesaver, Claud."

"You'd do the same for me."

"Without a doubt." Jayne smiled to herself, feeling so lucky to have wonderful friends in her life. "See you in a little while."

She hung up and wandered into the kitchen, wearing nothing but a blanket around her. She checked the fridge…not much in there. The coffee was still warm, so she poured a cup and after a few sips, some of the fog that was clouding her seemed to dispel. Looking around, it was obvious that Gray didn't really live here. It was just a place to sleep and take a shower. A very expensive place to sleep and take a shower.

The thought of walking out of his building in the morning light wearing what, obviously, was last night's dress, was just too embarrassing. So she rifled through his closet and drawers, finding a pair of sweatpants and a T-shirt. Yes, she would still be wearing satin sling-back pumps, but it was the best she could do.

Jayne sat down on his seldom-used couch, in his sterile room, and sighed. She shook her head, angry at herself for wanting to spend the night with him so much. She'd finally gotten that wish and was drunk enough that she immediately fell asleep in his arms and didn't even remember cuddling or the feeling of lying against him. And how could she have ever thought the next morning would be cozy and intimate, when it was clear those were two things he was incapable of?

She was beginning to realize, slowly, that although he was perfect on paper...that wasn't real. But he was the ideal image of the man she wanted to share her life with.

Image. Isn't that what he said his life was all about, creating an image? And here she was starting to see that maybe that's all he was for her...the perfect image of a man that was anything but perfect for her.

But as hopeless as it seemed, she wasn't ready to give up on the dream yet that he could be something more. She had been down this road so many times with other men...trying to force something that just wasn't meant to be. But I'm almost thirty. I have to make this work. I can't fail again.

Maybe Gray would come around. Maybe he would grow to need her as much as she wanted him to. He seemed to like her enough...Jayne could only hope that in time, that would turn to love.

****

After taking Jayne home, Claudia stopped at the mall and did some shopping. As she browsed through stores, she couldn't help thinking about her friend. Jayne had looked ashamed, defeated. Not her usual bubbly self. Claudia had tried to reassure her that Gray was just a guy, and guys in general are insensitive and clueless. He'd at least left her cab fare.

But she could see that Jayne was so disappointed. And Claudia was fairly sure that Gray was not the guy that Jayne so desperately wanted and needed him to be. But how could she tell her that?

How do you stop your friend from hurting herself without hurting your friendship?

When Claudia got home, she walked into the house, glad to be out of the cold, and dropped her bags on the table in the hallway.

"Hello, sweetheart," Sam said, walking into the room.

"You're home early," she said with a smile. "For a Saturday. Normally you're stuck at the office until at least two or three."

"I just decided I was done working for the weekend." He kissed her. "What did you buy?"

"Oh, nothing, really…" She didn't want him to see what she'd bought. He'd get irritated, and she didn't want to have this conversation again.

"Let me see," he said, opening one up. She saw his face harden. "Claud? Again?"

"They were on clearance, and so cute…I couldn't resist."

"But they're baby clothes. And we don't have a baby, we don't have one on the way, and we're not even trying." He was shaking his head.

"Will you just let me dream a little bit? Please?" Her tone was pleading. "I wanted to start a family three years ago, but you wanted to wait, so I'm waiting…but it's not easy. And buying baby things makes me feel just a little closer to having one someday."

Sam put his arms around her. "But you've bought a lot of stuff. Don't you think it's a little crazy—"

"I am not crazy." She pushed him away. Tears threatened to spill from her eyes, but she used all her strength to keep them at bay. "But you're asking your wife to deny her instinct, her urges, her desire to start a family. This has been going on for three years. It's hard, Sam, okay? I can't wait much longer."

"I'm sorry, sweetheart," he said, his voice quiet as he pulled her back in his arms. "Tell you what. Why don't we start trying in the summer? Whether I've made partner or not, let's put it on the calendar."

"Really?" Her heart started beating faster; she couldn't believe what he was saying.

"Really." He smiled at her, and she was reminded how much she truly loved him. And she could only imagine how wonderful it would be to start a family with the man she loved so much.

His cell phone rang from his pocket; he made no move to get it.

"Aren't you going to answer that?" Claudia asked.

"No, I'm done working today. I'm here with my beautiful wife. Phone calls can wait."

She kissed him. "Why don't I make some lunch then?"

"And she cooks, too," he said, planting a playful smack on her bottom as she headed to the kitchen. She was practically skipping, so overjoyed that he had finally committed to a time to start their family.

The best Christmas present she could ever get.

****

Jayne always thought there was something absolutely magical about a lit Christmas tree at night. Especially when the lights in the house were out, and the tree seemed to glow. It evoked such feelings of warmth and hope and joy.

Maybe it had less to do with the tree itself and more to do with the memories it was associated with. When she was growing up, the Christmas season was Jayne's favorite time of year. The Ashers weren't exactly the Cleavers, but they were about the closest real family she knew to that ideal. Her parents had now been married for thirty-three years, and although she was aware that their marriage wasn't perfect, it was strong and filled with love. They created a wonderful environment to grow up in, and Jayne knew that she had never once felt unloved or less than special.

Christmas was the celebration of the closeness their family shared. Her mom seemed always to be baking cookies, letting her kids work alongside her and design their own sugar cookies. They would make homemade ornaments and play Christmas music while they decorated the tree, mugs of steaming hot chocolate on standby.

The tree. The symbol of the season. The one tradition Jayne couldn't imagine celebrating the holiday without. She had a small one at her place and had also tacked up garlands around her living room to make it seem more festive. But as she and Gray walked up to her childhood home, she could see the familiar sight of the Asher family Christmas tree twinkling and welcoming them from the front picture window. That was the tree she waited to see, every year. The tree that meant home.

Although she was so excited to have Gray with her on Christmas Eve, to meet her family, he seemed less than enthusiastic.

"Now you know we can't stay very late," he reminded as they reached the front porch.

"I know, Gray, but we can stay for at least a couple of hours. My mom's still upset that I didn't come home for Thanksgiving. You need to work your charms on her."

"Well that's no problem," he said with confidence. He looked at his watch. "It's four o'clock. We need to be hitting the road by six. That will get us to my parents' by seven thirty."

"Okay," Jayne said, irritated that he was putting her family on a strict time schedule when they'd spent the entire day on Thanksgiving with his. Oh well. She was starting to realize that Gray was used to getting his way. And although it made her feel ashamed of herself, she didn't want to push it.

They walked in the house, undetected amid the sounds of her family in the back of the house. Christmas music was playing and Jayne could hear her three year old nephew saying, "Santa! Santa!"

Jayne looked over at Gray. "So this is where I grew up."

"Looks like a great place to grow up," he said, looking around the room. "Little Jayne Asher...is this the room where the boys would come calling?" He winked at her.

"Something like that," she said, grinning. "Give me your coat, and I'll hang it up." As she was putting them in the closet, her mom came in the room.

"Jayne—you're here!" she exclaimed.

"It's so nice to meet you, Mrs. Asher," Gray said with a big smile, showing off his dimples. He held his hand out and Jayne could see her mother melting under his gaze. They shook hands.

"So you're Gray, the man that stole my daughter on Thanksgiving," she said with a chuckle. She was smiling and practically batting her eyes at him.

"I am so sorry about that. I promise not to steal her like that again. It's just apparent you've raised a young lady who's in high demand."

"Oh, I forgive you," Carol said, still smiling at him. Jayne couldn't believe it. Her mom was almost swooning, which was really something for a no-nonsense woman like her. The powers of Gray's charms were in full effect in the Asher household.

"Do I get a Merry Christmas hug?" Jayne said, and her mom tore her eyes from Gray. They embraced, and Jayne whispered in her ear, "No flirting with him. He's mine."

Carol pulled away, chuckling. "Oh, please."

"Let me take you to meet everyone else," Jayne said, proudly dragging Gray into the family room. Soon he'd been introduced to everyone—her dad, brother, sister-in-law, nephew. It felt good to have him there, in the one place in the world that felt more like home than anywhere else. As she watched him pick up her little nephew in his big, strong arms, she decided she could get very used to having him around.

****

It was five minutes before six when Gray leaned over and whispered in Jayne's ear, "We need to go now."

Jayne looked at him, at his beautiful blue eyes that were so easy to lose herself in, and saw by the expression on his face that he was not kidding around. She glanced back at her family—her nephew banging on a new drum that

Grandma and Grandpa had gotten for him, her brother's arm around his wife, Mom and Dad looking so happy sitting on the love seat together. It looked exactly like Christmas should.

She didn't want to leave.

"Just a little bit longer?" Jayne whispered, pleading with him. "We just opened presents—"

"I told my family we'd be there by 7:30. It's a long drive. Say your goodbyes, and quickly."

Jayne didn't like taking orders from anyone she wasn't getting a paycheck from. But now was certainly not the time to assert herself with Gray, on Christmas Eve.

"Hey Mom, Dad," she said, approaching them. "We have to get going. It's an hour and a half drive out to Gray's family."

"But you just got here," her father protested, looking over at Gray. "We just barely met Gray."

"Well, we've got a long weekend coming up, sir," Gray said, sure to present one of his biggest smiles. "We can come visit on Sunday...maybe watch some football?"

"Sure, that would be great," Harry Asher said with enthusiasm.

"Really, you have to leave?" her brother Ryan asked. People always told Jayne he looked like a male version of her.

"Yes, I'm sorry," Jayne said, thinking, You have no idea how sorry I am. This is the only place I want to be today. She swooped up her nephew, tickling him and slathering him with kisses.

Soon they were in the car, waving goodbye to her mom, who was standing in the doorway watching them leave. Jayne felt like crying.

Gray looked over at her. "You know, I can go to my parents' without you. I can tell you're upset, so why don't you just stay with your family?"

"Because I want to spend Christmas Eve with you."

He smiled at her, and put his hand on her chin. "Then chin up, Jaynie. Stop moping and let's enjoy the rest of the evening, okay?"

"Okay," she said quietly, unable to prevent the smile from creeping onto her lips. When he looked right at someone, it was impossible to resist his charms. "Can we please listen to Christmas music?"

"Oh, jeez," he said with a sigh. Looking at her, he chuckled. "Just for the first thirty minutes."

"Forty-five?"

"Fine," he said, laughing.

****

Jayne was relieved to learn that it was just going to be the immediate Brandt family for this holiday. Although Thanksgiving had been fun, it was a little overwhelming with all of the unfamiliar faces.

When they walked in the house, they were greeted by a large brown Labrador retriever jumping on them and attacking with furious licks. Jayne laughed as the dog gave her face a bath.

"Damn it," Gray said, shoving the dog away as his brother Josh came running up.

"Atticus, off!" Josh commanded, and the dog retreated, tail still wagging. "Sorry, guys. He just gets so excited. He's harmless."

"Josh, your dog just jumped all over my Tommy Hilfiger cashmere sweater," Gray said with disgust.

"Well then, good dog, Atticus. I trained him specifically to attack cashmere or overpriced high-end labels." Jayne and Josh laughed as Gray looked at them with disapproval. "Lighten up, little brother. Your sweater's fine."

"Lucky for you. Why'd you bring your dog, anyway?"

"Why not? And why are you so crabby? It's Christmas," Josh said with false enthusiasm. "Good to see you, Jayne." He gave her a hug.

"Good to see you, too," she said, petting Atticus. "Beautiful dog. Is he a chocolate lab?"

"Thanks. He's actually a mutt, but it's obvious he's got a lot of lab in there with some other stuff, too. Got him from the rescue shelter where I volunteer. He's my baby."

"Gotta have something to keep you warm at night, huh?" Gray said.

Josh glared at him. "We aren't all lucky enough to have a Jayne."

"That's right," Gray said, putting his arm around her and leading her into the family room.

Jayne participated in the Brandt Christmas Eve tradition of having chili before opening gifts. When they exchanged presents, Jayne was surprised that his parents had included her, giving her a lovely scarf. The boys made out with quite a bit of loot, and they'd gone in together to get their parents a brand new, state-of-the art computer. Theirs was several years old and their mother complained incessantly about how slow pages loaded on the internet.

After presents, they sat at the big farmhouse-style kitchen table and played games. First Outburst, then Life. Plenty of laughter and fun. Jayne was struck by how laid back and fun his family was, when Gray was the epitome of work hard, play hard. Or maybe it was work hard, work hard some more, and eventually play hard—but not for long.

Jayne yawned and Gray said, "It's almost ten-thirty…we've got a long drive…I better get you home."

"Aren't you going to stay here?" his mom, Sara, asked. "Josh is staying, and I put clean sheets in the other guest room for you two."

"No, Mom, we've got stuff planned for tomorrow, so we might as well head back tonight."

"But it's such a long drive."

Jayne thought staying sounded nice, and said, "Yeah, if we stay, we can just crawl into bed right now."

"Maybe next time," Gray insisted. "Jaynie, I'll go get our coats."

Jayne figured he didn't want her to stay the night at his parents' because he wouldn't be able to take off and leave her again in the morning. He'd be trapped, with her. Which sounded like heaven to Jayne but obviously not to him.

On the drive home, Jayne dozed off and on, having dreams of Gray needing her, begging her to stay. The dreams seemed so real. Or maybe she just wanted them to be.

When they pulled in front of her condo, he said, "I had fun with you today. Merry Christmas—I'll see you tomorrow." He kissed her with tenderness, and she always felt that, unlike sex together, the kisses meant something. His kisses seemed sincere.

"You can stay tonight, if you want." Please want to, please, her eyes begged.

He hesitated for a moment, looking right at her, his face wearing a conflicted expression. Then he said, "No, I need to get home. But I'm coming over tomorrow, right?"

"Yeah," she said, looking down, trying not to let her disappointment show.

"What time do you want me over?"

"Well, we're making dinner together so...I don't know...maybe four?"

"Four it is then. Good night, sweet Jaynie." He kissed her again before she climbed out of the car.

So much for dreams.

Chapter Five

Across town, Karen was in a dream of her own, this one being a real-life nightmare. Christmas Eve at her dad's house.

Her parents had divorced when she was fifteen, and her father had promptly gotten remarried to a woman he'd most likely been having an affair with. Karen found out over the years that there had been many dalliances, so she wouldn't have been surprised if his second wife, Kim, had been one of them. Secretly, Karen hoped that Kim was being screwed around on like her mother had been.

So now Christmas with her dad didn't just mean Christmas with her dad—it meant Christmas with him and a whole slew of pseudo-relatives that she would have never associated with otherwise. Lazy, sloppy, ridiculous people. If they were co-workers of hers, they would have been the ones that when they approached her desk to chat, she would have pretended to be on the phone. Or if they wanted to go to lunch, she would have lied and said she had a lunch appointment, while she sat alone in her car in the parking lot of Taco Bell instead.

They were nice enough, sure, but they weren't her kind of people. And all they did was prevent her from even the remotest possibility of enjoying the holiday with her dad.

Thank God her brother Jon was there, or she most likely would have stuck her finger down her throat to make herself vomit, just to feign illness and leave. And of course Rick came, too. What would she do without him?

It was the afternoon of Christmas Eve, and as she looked over at Rick talking to her dad, she decided that was her Christmas gift. Watching the two of them talking about football, Rick making her dad laugh...that was good stuff.

She realized while watching them that she'd fallen for Rick because he was all the good things about her dad. Easygoing, fun, everybody's friend. Gentle, caring. But as far as Karen could tell, Rick didn't possess the flaws of her father—self-absorption, lying, cheating, and selfishness. No, Rick was pretty much the opposite of those things.

As a kid, Karen remembered worshipping her father. She loved both of her parents, but her dad was pretty much her hero. Until that day. The day he not only broke her mother's heart, but hers as well.

Watching him leave, suitcases in hand, was the single most miserable day of her life. She'd never forget as long as she lived, how it felt to have her heart shatter. She thought she would not physically survive. She was weak, lonely, and afraid.

Over time, the feeling began to dull, and she knew she never ever wanted to feel that way again. She wouldn't allow herself to love someone like that again. With her dad, she had given her whole entire heart to him. She had been vulnerable. He held all the power—she was putty in his hands.

No more.

She still loved her dad, but from behind a huge wall of pain that had grown between them. Over the years, she expected the wall to slowly break down, but it hadn't. Maybe she hadn't let it; maybe she was the one holding it up.

Either way, she was doing the best she could. His crazy family wasn't helping.

Rick caught her eye from across the room. "What are you looking at?" he asked, grinning at her.

A practically perfect guy. "Nothing," she said instead. She walked over to him and her dad. "So what's new, Dad?"

"Oh, you know, same old, same old." She really didn't know though.

Looking at her father, with his white hair and handsome face—just starting to wrinkle around the hazel eyes he'd passed onto her—she realized she didn't really know him anymore. Certainly not like she once had. Hal Taggart used to camp out with Karen and Jon on the family room floor in sleeping bags and stay up late, laughing and telling stories. She used to go to work with him sometimes in the summer and sit in his office, coloring, reading and listening to him wheel and deal with customers on the phone. Those were her first lessons in sales, learned from her dad as she worshiped him from her chair in the corner of his office.

"So how's work?" she asked, knowing that was something they always shared. They were both in sales. He was the first one she always called when she landed a big client or sold a big order. He understood; in that way they were the same. They connected.

"Oh, it's been better. This economy is a bitch, isn't it?"

"It's killing me, Dad. I'm supposed to be growing my sales, and I can't even keep them stagnant. I'm down about twelve percent."

"Well I imagine it's like that for all your sales people, isn't it?"

"For the most part, yeah. There's one bastard who grew his numbers eight percent in the last quarter, making the rest of us look bad. But he's the only one." She sighed, sitting down next to her dad. "I mean, I'm not worried about losing my job or anything, but I sure would like to be making more money, not less."

"You'll get there, once this economy picks up. You're a damn good sales person, Karen." He put his hand on her leg, which she was quick to jerk away.

"All I can tell you," Rick said, sitting down in a chair across from them, "is that beer sales are up. When the economy's down the drain, people want to drink away their sorrows and use beer to cheer them up. You're just selling the wrong stuff. Come work for us, Karen."

"Work with my boyfriend, all day? I don't think so." She shook her head, though she smiled.

"Actually, you're right. I probably wouldn't like you very much if I had to work with you." They all laughed.

"And what makes you think I would still like you?"

"Because I'm irresistible, you know that." He kissed her on the cheek, and she shot him a look that said, Do that again and you'll regret it. She couldn't stand PDA. At least not when it involved her. "Sorry," he whispered.

"So beer sales are up, huh?" her dad asked.

"Yeah, Hal, it's apparently pretty common when the market tanks. It's up for us, and even more so for the big breweries."

Karen was distracted by somebody's child wailing in the next room and loud laughter from nearby. She could barely keep everyone straight. In sales, it was her job to remember names. But that's because clients mattered to her. It's how she made her money. These people meant nothing to her.

Three stepsisters and two stepbrothers. A myriad of step-nieces and -nephews. Too many to count or worry about remembering. They were inconsequential to her. And sometimes, it seemed like her dad shared the sentiment. He'd never wanted a big family; it was just her and her brother. So why on earth did he marry a woman with so many fucking kids?

Her brother Jon stepped into the room. "Hey, sis," he said, sitting on the arm of the couch next to her. "Hey Dad." He fist pumped Rick and they all started talking.

Karen watched her stepmother, Kim, doting over some of her grandchildren. She wasn't so bad. Kim seemed to really love Karen's dad, Hal. Why, she couldn't fathom. Except that she probably only saw the good parts, the parts that Karen adored for her first fifteen years. But maybe Kim hadn't seen the darker side of him, the one that Karen had spent the last fifteen trying to reconcile and forgive.

She didn't know that she could ever forgive.

Watching all the commotion was too much for Karen. She got up and stepped out on the back deck. It was freezing cold, yes, but it was quiet. Still.

As she shivered, rubbing her arms up and down, her dad stepped out with her. He put his arm around her; and although she tried to stop it, she naturally pulled away just a bit. Instinct. Preservation.

He chuckled. "Like a fuckin' circus in there, isn't it?"

"Yeah, Dad, you could say that." She looked at him, saw the smile in his eyes, but maybe a hint of sadness too. "What the hell were you thinking when you married her? Five kids? And they've all procreated."

"Yeah, whether they could afford to or not." He smiled, but it looked bitter. "Maybe I wasn't thinking. But she's good to me, she loves me."

"Mom loved you."

"Yes, but she didn't understand me, Karen."

"No, she just wasn't content to be a doormat."

"Karen—"

"Why did you leave us?"

"I didn't leave you. I left your mother—"

"You left me, Dad. You left Jonathan. All of us." She looked away. "You fucked me up forever, did you know that?"

"I didn't mean to—"

"Well of course you didn't, you're not a cruel person. But you're selfish, Dad, okay? You've always only thought about yourself. I loved you like you were some god or hero or some bullshit like that. And after you betrayed us, I can't ever love again. Not like I should." She turned and looked him right in the eyes. "That man in there, that fantastic man, loves me. I know he does. And I'm going to leave him, like I've left all the rest of them, and it's all your fault."

He looked back at her, his gaze never faltering. "Don't let what I did have that kind of power over you—"

Karen laughed, a bitter, cynical laugh. "I'm not letting it, Dad. If I had a choice, trust me, I wouldn't be this way. But I don't have a choice—this is how I am now. This is what you've done to me."

"It's not too late to learn to change. I've changed."

"How? How have you changed?" She nearly spit the words out of her mouth.

"I don't lie any more. I don't cheat."

"Well, that's a great comfort. You only lied to and cheated on the people that should have mattered to you the most."

She looked away, sickened at the sight of him, and went back inside. He didn't follow.

****

"I come bearing gifts of groceries," Gray said, standing in Jayne's doorway, with a crooked smile and a stuffed paper bag.

"Food and a hot body," Jayne said as she shut the door behind him. "Merry Christmas to me."

"Yes, Merry Christmas," he said, kissing her. "So what can I do to help?"

He followed her in the kitchen and she soon had him mashing potatoes and carving the turkey. Gray didn't know how to cook, but he was good at following directions and eager to help. It was just going to be the two of them, laid back but with the traditional meal.

Jayne turned on her Christmas music playlist as Gray carried the turkey to the dining room. Looking at the festive table, the decorated tree in the background and the gorgeous man standing beside it—she decided this was a wonderful Christmas. She knew things with Gray weren't ideal, but they were still pretty good. She just knew that in time, she could make things work.

They chatted with ease during dinner; they always had lively conversation. He had great stories, and she loved hearing them. He seemed to think she was funny, and they shared a lot of laughs. Jayne was just anxious to get through the meal and finally give him his present.

"That was all so delicious," he said, brushing his fingers over her hair as she stood up to clear the plates.

"Thanks," she said, taking his hand and kissing it.

"We could leave the dishes and celebrate the rest of the night in your bed—"

"No, we still have presents to exchange and spiked eggnog to drink." She grinned at him as she left the room carrying plates to the sink.

"Then we can finish Christmas off with a bang? Pun intended."

"We'll see, Mr. Brandt," she teased.

Within a few minutes, she was nestled in his arms, next to her small but expertly decorated Christmas tree. She handed him his gift, wrapped with a satin bow and paper that she'd picked out just for him.

"Wow, Jaynie, this looks almost too pretty to open."

"I wanted it to be perfect for you."

"Well yours isn't wrapped quite as fancy, but it's the thought the counts." He handed her the small package, very lightweight. Maybe jewelry? She wondered. "Go ahead, open it."

"Okay, I will," she said, tearing into the paper. When she opened the small box, she was shocked...absolutely stunned. She had no idea what to say and couldn't say what was really on her mind.

"I know you're big into music," he said, "but I wasn't sure exactly what you have, so I figured with a Best Buy gift card you could get whatever you want."

"It's great," she said, sick to her stomach at the thought that he would soon be opening her gift worth ten times what the fifty dollar gift card was. A gift card? Could he have come up with anything more impersonal? And it wasn't even to a spa or department store or someplace like that. It felt like he'd been at Best Buy to get the latest edition of Mortal Kombat for his PlayStation and picked up her gift card at the register on his way out the door.

"I'm sorry, I'm not that great at buying gifts," he said, putting his hand on hers.

"No, it's perfect. I do love music. Thank you." Her performance was worthy of an Academy Award nomination, at the very least.

"Now it's my turn," he said with glee, ripping his open.

Oh God, oh God, oh God. I so messed up. I went way overboard.

He opened the box, his mouth dropped open, and neither of them spoke. Jayne thought Brenda Lee's voice belting out Rockin' Around the Christmas Tree suddenly sounded incredibly loud. Her eyes were glued to Gray, and she wanted to look away and run from the room, but much like a train wreck—she couldn't.

Finally, after what felt like forever, he cleared his throat. He turned and looked at her, his eyes full of apology. "Jayne, this is a beautiful watch, a fabulous gift...but it's just too much. I can't accept this."

"I want you to have it," she said, nodding her head.

"I can't keep it. And I'm sorry for the small gift card. It's only been a couple of months...I didn't think we were there yet, you know? With big gifts."

"I understand," she said, using every bit of her will power to keep from crying. It was just a gift exchange, but it told so much more. Of where they were...and how far apart.

"Please, take this back." He pushed the box toward her. "But thank you so much for picking it out—you know my tastes. It's exquisite."

Without looking at him, she snatched the box and quickly stood up. She rushed into the kitchen and put the box in a drawer. Closing her eyes, she took a deep breath before heading back in the living room. Gray was standing up.

"Hey, this is a great Christmas tune...may I have this dance?" He was smiling at her, his dimples peeking out, his hand outstretched.

"Sure," she said quietly, falling easily into his arms. He slowly twirled her around to the velvety voice of Harry Connick, Jr. crooning What Are You Doing New Year's Eve? Jayne closed her eyes, both comforted and frightened to feel and smell and hold him so close. She was getting so attached to him, so used to how he cradled her in his arms.

But she didn't really know if she could count on that for much longer.

She opened her eyes as Gray sang the chorus, slightly off-key. He stopped dancing and kissed her. Slow, gentle, then with more intensity. "So? Even though I completely botched your Christmas gift, will you be my New Year's date?"

"Yes, of course." As she smiled at him, she felt the slightest bit of hope.

As usual, they enjoyed themselves in the bedroom, and he seemed even more attentive than normal. Probably trying to make up for the gift card. This time, Jayne wasn't at all expecting him to stay the night. She knew he wouldn't.

He put his clothes back on approximately three minutes and two seconds after he'd reached orgasm, and although entirely expected, it still broke her heart.

Once completely dressed, he leaned over and kissed her…why did his kisses always have to feel so good?

"You can just stay in bed—I'll let myself out. Merry Christmas, sweet Jaynie."

It was nine-thirty on Christmas night, and Jayne was alone. Thoughts drifted to her parents, her nephew, Claudia and Karen. She wondered if they were all happy, filled with the joy of the season. She thought about calling one of them, but couldn't bring herself to.

She pulled the covers over her head, and even with Christmas music still playing softly in the background, she could hear the bathroom faucet dripping. Mocking her.

"Damn it!" she yelled, climbing out of bed. She'd long since given up on fixing it herself, so she turned up the music in an effort to drown out the drip. It worked.

But for the first time, as she waited for sleep to take her and put her out of her misery, she noticed that a lot of Christmas songs sound melancholy and sad. Despite the magic of the season, so many of the melodies were less than joyful.

She understood why.

Chapter Six

Karen and Rick spent Christmas day in Columbia, Missouri, with his family. Just like Rick, his family was easy to get along with. Karen enjoyed spending time with them but was glad to get back home. They got back into town around six-thirty, put on some comfy clothes and ate leftovers while watching a movie they'd rented.

As they sat on the couch, Rick said, "Hey, let's go do something fun. Throw on some shoes and your coat." He got up, sliding on his loafers.

"Where are we going? I'm wearing sweats."

"Doesn't matter, just grab your coat." She stared at him, looking doubtful. "Come on, Karen, be spontaneous for once. Trust me. It'll be fun." He was smiling with glee, and his dark eyes sparkled; he looked like a little kid on Christmas morning.

Well, it is Christmas, Karen reasoned. I'll indulge him.

"Fine," she said, slipping her arms into her pea coat.

They got in his Jeep, and he turned on the radio to an all-Christmas music station. Normally Karen would have objected, but it was Christmas day, after all. And the songs reminded her of being a kid and her mom playing them all through the house.

"So where are we going?"

"Just chill, Ms. Taggart," he said, patting her leg. He smiled at her, and Karen loved how he looked at her. Like he adored her.

So she chilled, and about fifteen minutes later, he pulled into an unfamiliar subdivision.

"So, this is it," he said, slowing the car down. "I just thought it would be fun on Christmas night to drive through some neighborhoods and enjoy the Christmas lights. I've always thought that was neat."

"Really?" Karen grunted.

"Well, yeah," he said, sounding hurt. "It's festive, the lights look cool—"

"I just don't get the point of wandering around, staring at Christmas lights."

Rick abruptly stopped the car and put it in neutral. Glaring at Karen he said, "Not everything has to have a point, Karen. Some things in life are just about enjoying the moment, about sharing something with someone."

The hostility in his voice and contempt in his eyes caught Karen off guard. She'd never seen him that way before.

"But then again," he continued with a sad chuckle as he looked away, "you don't really share anything with anyone, do you? Not your innermost thoughts, your emotions...certainly not your life." He turned to stare at her, his dark eyes piercing into her very soul. "Why are you even with me, Karen?"

"What...what do you mean?" Her heart was pounding wildly. The night had turned from what she viewed as an annoying waste of her time into a scary, threatening condemnation. His tone scared her; it reeked of disgust, of disappointment.

"Why are you with me? You won't let go of...of...whatever the hell it is that's keeping you from me. If you're never going to give me all of you, then what's the point? Isn't that what you want—-to know the purpose, the point of something before you waste your time on it?" He had raised his voice, something she'd never heard before. "So what's the fucking point?"

"Because..." her voice trailed off, she was trembling. Scared. An emotion she didn't allow herself to feel very often. After all her thoughts of bailing on their relationship, when confronted, she realized the thought of losing Rick scared her. "Because I love you."

"Oh, you do?" he asked, his voice still dripping with anger. "Honey, I don't think you understand the point of love." He put the car into gear and started driving.

Neither of them spoke for at least a couple of minutes. To Karen, it felt longer. Finally she said, her voice soft, "I do love you. Maybe not in the way you want me to, but I do."

The car came to a stop at a light. He looked over at her, his face softening a bit. "I know."

They drove the last few minutes back home in complete silence. When they got to the loft, Rick strode quickly ahead of her, tossed his keys on the kitchen counter, and headed to the bedroom. Karen sat on one of the barstools at the counter, nervously biting the dry skin on her bottom lip. He came back out of the bedroom, wearing a ratty old shirt and sweatpants, heading toward the door.

"Where are you going?"

"I'm going up to the attic to paint." He had a small studio set up in the cramped, dark attic. Floodlights did their best to illuminate the space for him.

"I thought we were going to watch the movie—"

"You watch the movie." His eyes were pleading with her, somehow, but Karen didn't know how to respond. Without another word, he headed out the door.

She fell asleep on the couch within a couple of hours and woke up much later, disoriented. She looked around, glanced in the bedroom. No Rick. The clock on the microwave said it was three-seventeen in the morning. She threw on a jacket and headed up to the attic.

When she peeked in, she could see him asleep on the floor, underneath a tarp serving as a blanket. Even in slumber, Karen thought he looked perfect. She looked at the canvas on the easel. There was a blackened silhouette of a man and woman at opposite sides of the painting, both reaching their hands out to each other, but not quite touching. Trying to touch. The woman had light illuminating from deep within her, shooting out in delicate rays like sunshine. But surrounding her were chains, connected with a padlock across her chest.

Tears sprang to Karen's eyes, and she wanted to lie down in Rick's arms and hold him tight and beg him to help her. And to never leave.

Instead, she wiped her eyes and went back downstairs, embarrassed to be so emotional. I'm probably going to start my period soon. Damn hormones. She climbed into bed, begging slumber to take her. To relieve her of these emotions that she couldn't seem to control.

****

Claudia couldn't stop drinking champagne, although she knew she'd probably regret it in the morning. Everyone was in such a great mood, music was playing, trays of food were everywhere—it was the perfect New Year's Eve party. She knew a fair amount of the people there, primarily Sam's colleagues. They were at the large, beautiful home of one of the law firm's partners.

Some of his colleagues were much older, in their fifties or beyond, so Claudia struggled to connect with their wives. But a couple of the younger guys' wives she knew well, and they got along great. So she spent most of the evening with Cindy, Sherry, Nina, and Sam's assistant, Rachel. Sam mingled with the crowd but never too far or too long from Claudia. She thought he looked great in his fitted T-shirt, blazer, and dark jeans. He was the best-looking guy in the room.

"That's it," she said after polishing off her glass of champagne, "I'm taking these shoes off. My feet are killing me, and I'm done with them." The women around her laughed as she unzipped the sky-high black ankle boots. They were her favorite and most stylish boots; Sam affectionately called them her hooker boots. But he liked them, which was partly why she wore them.

"Those boots are fantastic," said Rachel.

"Thanks, Rachel," Claudia said, smiling at her. She seemed like a sweet girl, and Claudia knew she did a good job for Sam. This was the first time they'd met, although they'd talked on the phone many times. "I need to thank you, by the way, for taking such good care of my Sam at work. It's nice to know he's got you to depend on."

"Oh, no problem, that's my job." The young girl smiled up at Claudia. Even though she'd taken off her tall boots, Claudia still had three or four inches on Rachel. I remember being her age. I know I'm getting older when I think of someone in her early twenties as a young girl. That was me, seven or eight years ago.

"So I can't believe you don't have a boyfriend," Claudia said and one of the other women agreed. "You're so cute." Whereas Claudia had a classic, sophisticated look with her dark hair, lean lines and striking features, Rachel was blonde, short, and curvy. Her upturned nose was undeniably cute, lending her a childish, innocent look.

"Well, I split up with my boyfriend a few months ago. I've been too busy to really look for a new one."

"We should find her one," Nina said, putting her arm around Rachel. Nina herself was a beautiful woman, with exotic looks and gorgeous caramel colored skin. "So who do we know?"

Sam joined the group at that time. "You ladies look like you're conspiring," he said, chuckling. "Should the men you came with be worried?"

"We're just trying to find a man for Rachel," Nina said, as they all murmured in agreement.

"Oh really?" Sam said, glancing at Rachel. "I imagine she's capable of finding her own man."

"I just thought of someone!" Claudia squealed. "My friend Karen's boyfriend, Rick, has the cutest younger brother. Do you remember him, sweetheart? We met him at the Cardinals game this summer."

"Yeah, I do." Sam looked irritated. "I don't like setting people up. It can backfire."

"Oh, don't be such a Debbie Downer." Claudia put her arm around Rachel. "You would love him. He's got a gorgeous body—he's a fireman."

"A fireman?" Cindy said. "Oh, wow, isn't that like every woman's fantasy?"

"I thought every woman's fantasy is a lawyer," Sam said.

"To marry, yes," said Sherry. "But to have sex with—a hot fireman."

"Okay, I'm out of here with that comment," he said, shaking his head. "And Sherry, I'm going to tell your husband you said that."

"Who says he doesn't have a fireman's uniform stashed in the closet?" Everyone laughed hysterically as Sam blushed.

"Sherry, you're a mess. And just for the record, I think you should all leave Rachel alone. Don't let these women corrupt you."

"Wait, Sam, don't go too far," Claudia said, grabbing his arm. "It's almost midnight. We have to kiss at midnight."

"You're right," Sherry said, "just five minutes left."

"I'm going to get going," Rachel said.

"Why?" asked Nina.

"Well, it's such a romantic moment, but if you're not kissing someone you love at midnight…well, it's kind of depressing." She looked down, and Claudia felt bad for her.

"But it's not just about kissing somebody," Claudia said. "It's about cheering on the New Year, and welcoming all the good things to come."

"Maybe," she said, giving up a small smile. "But I'm gonna take off anyway. Happy New Year's, everyone!"

They all wished her well and told her good night.

"See you in a couple of days, Sam," she said as she walked away.

"See ya."

"Let's refill our glasses with champagne," Cindy said, pouring more bubbly into hers.

"Just two minutes left," Nina cheered. Soon all of their glasses were filled, and Sam put his arms around Claudia.

"Poor Rachel," she said. "She looked so sad. We definitely have to set her up with Rick's younger brother."

"Enough about Rachel." Sam put his finger on her lips. Suddenly the whole room started chanting: "Ten, nine, eight, seven, six, five, four…."

Claudia looked into Sam's eyes, realizing this was their eleventh New Year spent together. She couldn't imagine any better way to start the year than in his arms, looking in his eyes.

"Three!"

This would be the year they would start their family. The year she'd been awaiting for so long. Children. What she'd dreamt of since she was a child herself—having a baby of her own.

"Two!"

Sam pulled her closer, smiling as he shouted with her, "One!" They kissed, full of passion, full of joy.

"I love you, Samuel Knight."

"I love you, Claudia Knight." They kissed again. Then her phone buzzed with a new text message. It was from Karen: Happy New Year to the 2 best friends a girl could ask for! I'm just glad I don't have to hear any more fucking Xmas songs. Much love.

Claudia laughed out loud.

"What?" Sam asked. She showed it to him, and he couldn't help but laugh, too. Her phone beeped again. This time it was from Jayne: Wish I was w/my BFFs instead of at this boring black-tie thing. Drink a shot for me; I'm not allowed to get drunk in front of Gray's boss. Luv u— Happy New Year!

Sipping her champagne with the obligatory Auld Lang Syne playing in the background, Claudia couldn't help but think about her friends. She hoped the new year would be as kind to them as she knew it would be to her. That Jayne would find the man to share the rest of her life with, whether that was Gray or someone else, and that Karen would finally let Rick in, instead of letting him go.

She held up her glass, a silent toast to the fates, and whispered, "To my friends, to the new year."

January

Chapter Seven

"Claudia? It's me, it's Jayne." She was sitting on her couch, eating a sleeve of chocolate chip cookie dough batter with a spoon. Pathetic, she knew, but warranted. Yet not exactly the way to honor her "eat healthier" New Year's resolution. Week two and she was already cheating.

"Hey, girl," Claudia replied in her typical soothing tone. "What's new?"

"I think Gray is doing that St. Patrick's Day thing to me."

"What?"

"You know, the John Mayer song. Where you're staying with someone just through all the holidays."

"Oh, yeah. Why on earth do you think that?"

"Well...there have been a few things. But what really has me worried is that all of a sudden, he's not wanting to make any extended plans. It's always, 'Well let's see what's going on then' or 'Hold on, let's not get ahead of ourselves.'" She'd mentioned a concert in March that tickets were going on sale for, and he gave a noncommittal response. Then she suggested they head to Chicago for a long weekend in the spring, which resulted in the "Let's not get ahead of ourselves" comment.

"Hmmm...well that might not mean anything."

Jayne wanted so badly to believe that, but her gut told her differently. They enjoyed a nice New Year's Eve together, but he seemed to be a bit more distant, if that was possible. She'd spent the past two months making excuses and explaining away his behavior, happy to do so since she was so completely enraptured with him. But the fog of idolatry was finally starting to dissipate—and she was worried with what she now saw.

"Maybe not by itself," Jayne explained, putting another gooey decadent glob of dough in her mouth, "but it's part of a bigger picture."

"Like what?"

"Well, at Christmas, he gave me a really impersonal gift."

"What?"

Jayne sighed. "A Best Buy gift card." It sounded even worse when she said it out loud.

"No!"

"Yes." Another spoonful went in.

"How much was it for?"

"Fifty dollars. He said he knew I liked music, so I could buy some CDs."

"Well, at least he put some thought in it."

"But if he'd ever paid any attention, he'd know I don't own a CD player. I have an iPod and an iPhone and just plug them into speakers at my house or in the car."

"Well, what did you get him?"

"A Movado watch."

"Oh, wow…how much did that cost you?"

"Five hundred dollars. It normally costs a lot more—I got a great deal on it."

"Oh, sweetie…I don't know what to say." The pity in her voice was obvious, and although embarrassing, Claudia had such a caring, loving way about her that Jayne felt some comfort. "What did he say when you gave him the watch?"

Tears threatened at her eyes. "He said, 'I didn't think we were there yet.'"

"Oh." Silence.

"He refused to keep it, said it was too much."

"Well, hon, maybe it was a little too soon to buy him something that expensive."

"Could be, but that doesn't explain the damn gift card." She finished off the tube of dough. Now she was upset and bloated. Great.

"Maybe he's just a terrible gift-giver—"

"Don't sugar coat it, Claudia. Be honest."

There was silence for almost a minute before Claudia said quietly, "It doesn't look good." With that, Jayne let the floodgates open and started to cry. "Oh, Jayne, don't cry. I'm so sorry. I shouldn't have said that. I didn't mean to make you cry."

"No, I'm not crying because you said it. I'm crying because it's true." Her sobbing made it difficult to talk. She contained it enough to say, "So what do I do now?"

"Well, you could confront him."

The thought terrified Jayne. She always just agreed with him and went along with him because...why? Because she was afraid of losing him. She never really felt worthy of him, and so she did whatever he wanted in order to please him. Didn't want to rock the boat. And confronting him about where their relationship was going...well that would pretty much capsize the boat.

"I...I can't do that. I know I should, but with Gray I'm just so...so damn weak. I'm afraid of losing him."

"Well, if you talk to him, at least you'll know where you stand."

"But it might also make him leave, if that's where this is headed."

"So what? You should only be with someone because they love you and see a possible future with you."

"Why am I so weak when it comes to him? I am a strong, smart woman. And I'm acting like a lovesick thirteen-year-old with no self-esteem."

"Sometimes when we're with the wrong man, it brings out the worst in us. The trick is to find a man you love that lets you be the best version of yourself. The strong, smart one."

"So you think he's the wrong man?"

"Jayne, I don't know...that's for you to figure out. But if you're feeling insecure with him and like you can't even be honest about your feelings with him...that should tell you something."

"I knew he was too good to be true," Jayne said quietly. She chuckled—a sad, mournful sound. "I think I've been blinded by his sparkling pearly whites."

Claudia laughed too. "Trust me, sweetie, if there's anyone that could cast a spell on a woman, it's him. He looks like a fairy tale Prince Charming."

"Well, unfortunately, I don't think that he is. At least not for me, anyway."

****

In addition to the worries about Gray, Jayne was equally stressed about some recent developments at work. Kelly, the supervisor she was so happy working for, had been transferred to a different position due to a company-wide reorganization at the beginning of the year.

When they'd all gotten the email with the new organizational chart, she had to admit it felt good to see her boyfriend's name near the top of the list under the Marketing division. There was Richard Mackenzie (commonly referred to as just Mac) as the head of both Customer Relations and Marketing, Robert Schmidt under him as head of the Marketing division, followed by Vice President Gray Brandt (and two other counterparts at his level), and it showed eight people directly under Gray, including Katherine.

Jayne, however, was so inconsequential that she didn't even show up on the organizational chart. But her Customer Relations department did, and instead of being under Kelly Sullivan, it was now showing Tony Green as the department head. He had been transferred from a position on the fifth floor, and when Jayne asked Gray about him, his response was, "He used to work in Marketing—an underachieving prick. Good luck with that." Sounded promising. On the first day back from the New Year break, Jayne was determined to make the best of the situation, and was hoping that Gray's judgment of Tony was off the mark.

It wasn't.

Jayne came into the office early in the morning, cleaned out all the junk that had piled up in her inbox over the holiday, grabbed some coffee and greeted her coworkers. Then she headed into Tony's office to introduce herself.

"Excuse me," she said quietly, standing in his doorway.

"Yes?" he said, his gaze looking away from his computer screen and directed at Jayne. He looked to Jayne to be in his fifties, rather overweight and nondescript. His expression relayed nothing more than annoyance.

"Hi, I'm Jayne Asher," she said in her usual chipper voice, smiling broadly. "I just wanted to introduce myself—"

"I know who you are. I saw you at the Marketing holiday party with Gray Brandt." His tone made it obvious that he was not a fan of Gray. "Don't think for a minute that screwing him is going to help any with me. You better carry your own weight."

Jayne was in shock…she couldn't speak for a moment. Her face must have shown as much because he said, "And don't look so surprised. I don't need your innocent, chipper act. I know how this works. You think you can sleep your way to the top or land a high earning husband so you don't have to work. Well that bs might have worked with Kelly, but not with me."

"Sir, I can assure you—"

"I don't need your assurances, I need you to get to work and know that I'm gonna be watching you very closely. Don't mess with me."

A million thoughts swirled through Jayne's mind, but it was obvious he wasn't going to let her talk. So, although she had started sweating and her face felt flushed, she managed to look him in the eye, conjure up her most sickeningly sweet smile, and say, "So nice to meet you."

It was his turn to look shocked as she turned on her red patent leather high heels and headed back to her desk.

Her heart was pounding, her palms clammy as she sat down. In the next cube, her friend Dawn asked, "What's wrong? You look like you're sick."

You have no idea. Instead, she said, "Just met the new boss. Don't think he's a fan of mine."

Dawn chuckled. "How could anyone not like you? Besides, he just met you."

"Yeah, maybe you're right. I might have misread him." Not a chance. And I don't have the strength to deal with this right now. As she got back to her email, she considered telling Gray about Tony's remarks. But their relationship was so precarious now…she didn't dare do anything to make it worse.

Jayne was glad she was meeting with Karen for lunch in a couple of hours. She really needed to vent. Tony doesn't know me. Once he sees my work, my attitude, my effort— he'll know Gray has nothing to do with my job.

At least she hoped he would. She was already stressed about having a talk with Gray, but maybe she could make that work and iron out things with Tony, too. I can fix this.

****

"Gray is absolutely not the right guy for you." Karen was emphatic as she sat across the café table from Jayne.

"No, tell me what you really think," Jayne said, smiling. She took a sip of her coffee.

"Well, you asked, so I'm telling you. I think he's a cad, a player, only out for himself. Sure he's fucking gorgeous, but what good does gorgeous do you? It looks nice in a photograph, but does he make you feel special? Loved? Important?"

No, no, and no. Jayne was glad the café was noisy and packed with people—it helped to distract her just enough to not lose it in the middle of a public place. "I guess I was just so wrapped up in being with a guy like him that I couldn't really see what was going on. Which was nothing…for him, anyway. I'm just a date, a romp in bed."

"Is the sex at least good?"

"Yeah, it really is. That's probably the best part of our relationship. The rest of it is just me doing whatever he wants and smiling the whole time like a dope."

"Oh, Jayne, you're not a dope. You just fell for a narcissistic ass. Do you really think you're the only woman to fall for Gray Brandt?"

"No…every single girl at work would love a chance to be with him."

"See? It's not you. It's that we're pre-wired to look for an Adonis like him. It's in our chromosomes to look for a strong, handsome man to procreate with. So you're being animalistic, that's all. But now that you're starting to use your brain, too, you see maybe he's not really the kind of man you want." Karen polished off her coffee and sat back in her seat, arms crossed.

"How do you drink your coffee black? It must be nasty to drink it straight."

Karen shrugged. "I like everything to get to the point. Even my coffee."

Jayne laughed. "God, I love you. Even when you drive me nuts."

"It's part of my charm to irritate people." Karen offered a grin. "So, what are you going to do?"

"I guess I'm going to talk to him soon, which I'm sure means I'll end up alone again."

"Well, it's better to be alone than to be played. And at least it will be you bringing it up, not him."

"True." Jayne looked around, seeing everyone chatting, working, and bustling about. She really wanted things to be okay with Gray, but she knew deep down that he didn't love her. There was no way even the ever-optimistic Jayne could fix that. She loved the idea of them together, but she'd have to get past that. He was never going to be the man she hoped he would be. She looked up at Karen. "So what's going on with you and Rick? You said a couple of months ago that you didn't know how much longer you'd be with him."

"Yeah…I don't know. He blew up at me over Christmas, which he's never, ever done. Now things seem a little forced. I should just get out."

"Well, what did he blow up about?"

Karen sighed. "My bullshit. I'm just not a sentimental, needy woman. I don't think I can be the woman he wants."

"Does that bother you? Do you want to be the one for him?"

Karen looked away from Jayne. "The thing is, I'm to the point and brutally honest with everyone, but I'm not sure if I am to myself. So I don't know, Jayne. And sometimes it's just easier to walk away than deal with all the emotional bullshit."

"Well, I think he's worth dealing with the emotional stuff. He loves you, Karen. I have no idea why," she said, chuckling, "but he does. And he's great for you. Claudia said to me last night that the trick is to find a man you love that lets you be the best version of yourself. And I think that's exactly what you have with Rick."

"Fucking Claudia," Karen said, rolling her eyes. "Why is she right about everything?" Karen and Jayne shared a smile.

"Because she's in a great place, so it's easier to help us with our problems."

"I guess." Karen leaned forward. "Rick does get me, he really does. But even knowing who I am hasn't scared him away."

"Well, then what's the problem?"

"I'm fucked up, that's what the problem is. I need a psychiatrist or something, but I'm way too cynical to believe in that."

"Don't give up on him. You've done that so many times, but Rick is a great guy. You might not admit it, but I think you need him. And that scares you, doesn't it?"

Karen stood up. "We came here to discuss your disaster of a relationship, not mine. I've got to get to an appointment, and I'm sure you need to get back to the office, too." She threw her coffee cup in a trashcan behind her.

"I didn't mean to make you mad," Jayne said, standing up. She knew Karen enough to know she should have left all the emotions out of the conversation. Emotions were like Karen's kryptonite.

"I'm not mad, just tired of talking about this crap. I have to try to sell my new concept to an idiot that won't get it and probably won't buy it because he wants to keep doing things the way he has been for the last twenty years. Doesn't matter that it's inefficient and costly, it's how he's always done it."

"I don't know how you do your job."

"Well from what you told me about your new boss, I wouldn't want your job."

"Yeah, well, it's obvious he got the wrong impression of me so I'll just have to prove him wrong. But your job is a struggle every day. I couldn't handle it."

"That's because you have a heart and all the rejection would crush you. I, however, as we all know—have a cold lump of steel where my heart should be. So I handle it just fine."

No you don't. Jayne looked at her friend with tenderness. You just pretend to. Please don't let Rick go. She silently tried to will her friend. You do need him, because you do have a heart.

And he's the one man that's gotten through to see it.

****

Karen waited in the lobby for her client, anxious to start their meeting. She crossed her legs and bounced her foot up and down, wishing he would just hurry up.

Before she got out of her car to come inside, she'd checked in her mirror to make sure everything looked okay. Cherry red lipstick was perfectly intact. Hair was sleek but messed up just a bit to soften the look. Eyebrows looked great after yesterday's waxing. She looked pretty, yet determined. And she hoped the low-cut blouse would garner some points; if his old-fashioned ways wouldn't let him see how she could benefit his company, perhaps her cleavage would open up his mind a bit. Anything was worth a shot.

She turned her phone to vibrate and slipped it in the pocket of her jacket, just as Mr. Winters approached her.

"Karen, hello," he said with a smile, his hand extended. They shook, and Karen flashed him her brightest smile.

"Mr. Winters, so nice to see you again."

"Oh, call me Al. Let's head to the conference room. My operations manager and production supervisor are both going to join us." They walked into the beautifully appointed room, covered in expensive wood paneling with high back leather chairs surrounding the dark wood table.

As she was introduced to the other men in the room, she noticed that one of them had hair like Rick's, but he wasn't near as attractive. Oh, Rick, she thought. Of course Jayne was right. I do need you. But I hate that I need you. It makes me feel weak and...vulnerable. And dammit—why am I thinking about this now? Get out of my head, you and your adorable damn smile and hot shaggy hair. I have a business meeting. I need to be on my game.

"Well, Karen, what do you have for us?"

Karen pulled out her laptop and started showing the PowerPoint presentation of how she planned to make their operations more efficient and save them money. Al seemed more receptive to her ideas as she went along. He asked some good questions and even smiled a couple of times and nodded his head. The youngest guy in the room, with Rick's haircut, seemed to really be buying into it, and he was commenting on it to Al.

Surprised at how well it was going, she was momentarily distracted when her phone started vibrating in her pocket. It stopped, and then immediately started again. And again. After the third time, Karen said, "Excuse me, I'm sorry, I never answer my phone when I'm in a meeting, but someone has called me three times in a row." She grabbed her phone out of her pocket and it started vibrating again. Her stepmother's cell phone. "This is my stepmother—she never calls me. There might be an emergency."

"Go ahead, no problem," Al said warmly.

"Thank you," she said, answering the phone as she turned her back. "Hello?"

"Karen, thank God you answered."

"What's going on? I'm in the middle of a meeting—"

"Your father had a massive heart attack, and things don't look good."

"What?" Karen's heart started beating wildly and she felt the color drain from her face. "Where is he?"

"He's at Mercy—can you come up now?"

"Yes, yes of course. I'll be right there."

"Hurry, Karen."

"I will." She turned back around to face Al and his associates, her mind vacant. Instead of a rush of emotions, she seemed to feel...nothing.

"Is everything okay?" Al asked. "You're white as a ghost."

"Um...my dad just had a heart attack and they say it doesn't look good. I...I need to go."

"Oh, my goodness, of course. I hope he's okay."

"I'm sorry about the presentation...I'll email it to you from the hospital."

"No, no, don't worry about it. You've got some great ideas. We'll just reschedule for another day."

"Good luck," said the longhaired man.

"Thanks," she said, frantically shaking as she loaded her laptop into the bag. She couldn't seem to get it to fit. Al pushed it in for her and zipped it shut. "Thank you."

"Do you need a ride to the hospital?"

"No, no, I'm fine. I'm really sorry—"

"Just go to your family," he said, practically pushing her out the door.

****

Jayne thought that maybe tonight would be the night she would confront Gray. After talking with Karen over coffee earlier in the day, she'd felt a little stronger, and she'd successfully dodged her boss, Tony, all afternoon. When Gray called and said he'd grabbed a movie and carryout and would be over in a bit, she figured she should probably have a talk with him. She hadn't seen him all week, and it was Thursday already. As usual, he didn't ask her what movie she wanted to see or what she wanted for dinner. She was certain the DVD would involve plenty of explosions and gunfire and gratuitous violence. The kind of movies she hated.

So she might as well get it over with.

But the minute she opened the door and took one look at him, she wasn't sure she was ready to say goodbye to him yet. Wasn't ready for that smile and that blue-eyed gaze to stop shining on her. She also wasn't quite ready to admit to herself that, once again, all her wishful thinking and optimism were all for naught. Jayne didn't know how she would handle another failed relationship when that's all she really wanted out of life.

Gray made her laugh during dinner as he told a funny story, and she thought to herself that she wished she could just freeze time. This is when she felt like they had a shot, like they could be something together. His tie was off; he was relaxed, barefoot, sitting on the floor around her coffee table eating Chinese. It was Gray, minus the edge that drove him to succeed at all costs. Just a guy that she loved. A very good-looking guy.

After dinner, Jayne was sitting alone on the couch, dreading what she knew she had to do, when Gray came out of the bathroom.

"Jaynie, your faucet's still dripping in there." He sat down next to her and grabbed the remote. "You need to get that fixed."

"Yeah, I know." Jayne watched him as he turned on the TV, recognizing that he managed to look handsome even when just staring at CNN. Wistful, Jayne wondered how she was going to end the charade that was their relationship, when her phone rang. Karen.

"Hey, lady," Jayne answered.

"Jayne," Karen said, her voice sounding weak and subdued, "my dad just died."

Tears sprang to Jayne's eyes. "Oh, God, Karen...I'm so sorry. Where are you?"

"Just got home from the hospital."

"Are you okay? Why don't I come over?"

"No, no, that's okay. Rick's here...I'm fine, really. Just kind of in shock."

"What happened?"

"Massive heart attack. I was in the middle of that sales call and my stepmom called me. I rushed to the hospital, but he was already gone when I got there. I didn't get to say goodbye."

"Oh, sweetie..." Gray looked at her with questions in his eyes, and she held up her finger to indicate "just a minute."

"Do you want to know the last thing I said to my dad?" Karen chuckled, but this time it sounded sad. "I told him he lied to and cheated on the people that should have mattered most to him."

"Well, you didn't know—"

"I mean, I feel awful those were my last words to him, but the fact is, it was true. I don't regret saying it. Maybe Christmas Eve wasn't exactly the best time for it, but it was true." She sighed. "But I didn't get a chance to tell him that I loved him anyway. Despite all of it."

"I'm sure he knew."

"Well, he's gone, so I guess it doesn't really matter now, does it?"

"Are you sure you don't want me to come over?"

"No, I just wanted to let you know."

"Well if you need anything, anything at all, just call me. I'm here for you."

"I know." Jayne could hear the smile in Karen's voice. "And thank you. I gotta go."

The line went dead and as she hung up the phone, Gray asked, "What happened?"

"Karen's dad died." And for so many reasons, she started to cry. Gray put his strong arms around her and held her. No, tonight was definitely not the night.

****

Karen finished pulling on her tights and slipped on her black high-heel pumps. Glancing in the mirror, she wondered if it would be okay to add a splash of color. She needed something...she looked so drab in black from head to toe. Made her look even more pale than normal.

"Are you almost ready?" Rick asked, poking his head in the room. Karen noticed how handsome he looked in a suit. She'd only seen him in a suit once, when they went to a wedding together a year before.

"Yes, just wondering if I can add something like this." She held up a bright multi-colored scarf.

"Hmmm," Rick said. "It looks great, but maybe a bit too festive for your father's funeral. How about this one?" He pulled out a dove-grey silk scarf from her opened drawer.

"Yeah, that would be better. You're right." She twisted it around her neck, and did like the life it breathed into the ensemble. As she went to close the drawer, she caught her index finger in the drawer. "Ow!"

"Oh, you slammed that hard. Are you okay?"

Looking down at her finger, she saw the jagged remnants of her acrylic nail. Red, shiny nail broken off. "Look. Now what am I gonna do?"

"Well, we can file it or put on a Band-Aid—"

"It will look terrible." She leaned against the dresser and did something she'd never done in front of Rick before. She started crying. "I can't do this—I can't go looking like this!" She sounded hysterical and felt it, too. Like she was drowning.

"Sweetheart, it's okay—"

"No it's not! I can't do this." She fell into his arms, barely able to stand on her own. Rick's grip tightened as he supported her. Her crying turned into sobbing...painful, powerful sobs. "I can't do this. I can't."

He cradled her head against his chest, stroking her back and saying quietly, "Shhh, it's okay."

"I just can't..." Her voice trailed off.

"Shhh… You can do it, but you don't have to do it alone. I'm here, Karen, I'm not going anywhere."

The impossible strength in his arms, the depth of his words, the comfort of his chest all overwhelmed her. She'd never felt so frail, so weak. Or so sheltered.

"He's gone…."

"Yeah, he is. I'm sorry. But I'm here for you."

Karen looked up at him, at the tenderness and love in his eyes. For the first time, she really saw that. And acceptance. He loved her, just the way she was. In spite of the way she was. How on earth could he love her, when she did everything she could to be unlovable?

"Why?" she whispered.

"Why?" His brows furrowed. "Why what?"

"Why are you here for me? I've been so hard on you, so distant. Why are you still here?"

"Oh, that," he said with a chuckle, still holding her tight. "Because I knew the real you was in here somewhere. I saw a glimpse every now and then. And I loved you enough to try to find that girl."

"But look at me, I'm a wreck…I'm weak and needy and—"

"Human, Karen. That's called being human." He caressed her with gentle, tender kisses. "It's okay to need me. I need you, too."

"You do?"

"Of course I do. Why else would I put up with your bullshit?" They both laughed through their tears.

"I can't get through this day without you." Or this life.

"Well, you don't have to." He pulled away, wiped the tears off her cheeks, and kissed her again. "Let's go get this over with."

"Okay," she said, sighing. She knew she might have a shot at making it through the day, if he was by her side.

****

As their car pulled up in front of the church, Rick looked over at Karen. She looked beautiful, no doubt about it. But she looked somehow delicate today, something he would have never said about her before. It bothered him to see her so upset earlier, but he was grateful that something, anything had broken through to her. To have her give in to him that way, to show vulnerability…it was something he thought would never happen.

Just when he was starting to think he would never get through to her and it was time to move on—there it was. The Karen that she didn't let anyone see. The real Karen. And she had not only shown herself, she admitted that she needed him. Too bad it had taken the loss of her father to make her finally be whole.

They stepped out of the Jeep and into the cold, blustery day. As he walked around to her side of the car, she took his hand and smiled.

"Well, that's different," he said, grinning at her. She never liked to hold hands and certainly had never initiated doing so.

"Oh, stop, or I'm going to put my hands in my pockets," she said, laughing.

"I'm not complaining, not at all." He kissed her hand.

"Don't push your luck." Her words were terse, but he saw the smile in the corners of her mouth. And he thought she may have actually moved closer to him as they made their way inside.

"I won't." His voice was almost a whisper.

"I guess I figure we're burying one emotionally immature member of my family today…maybe it's time I break the cycle and actually grow up."

"I'm good with that. I'm worried that someone or something has possessed my girlfriend, but I like it." They both chuckled. When they reached the top step of the church, they stopped and Karen took a deep breath.

Rick put his arm around her. "I'm right here." She looked up at him, teary-eyed, as he opened the door.

****

"Holy fuck, I needed this," Karen said, taking a very long drink of her martini.

"Yeah, I think you've earned that drink," Claudia said, rubbing her hand on Karen's back. "How are you holding up?" The funeral had been three days earlier, and although Claudia and Jayne had been there to support Karen, they hadn't really found a chance to talk. This was the first time they were getting together since her father died.

"I'm okay, I really am." She flashed a grateful smiled at her friends. "It just doesn't seem real yet. Maybe it hasn't really hit me, I don't know."

"Well when it does," Jayne said, "you know we're here for you. Day or night."

"Yeah, I do know that," she said, taking another gulp. "And thank you."

The waiter brought their food and as they all dug in, Karen said, "So enough about my dad. What's new with you guys? Feels like we haven't talked in ages."

"Well," Claudia said, absolutely beaming, "I have some good news."

"What's that?"

"Sam agreed that we could start trying for a baby this summer."

"What if he hasn't made partner yet?" Jayne asked.

"He said we'd start our family, regardless."

"This is so exciting," Jayne said, digging into her white chili.

"Slow down," Karen said. "She's not pregnant. They're just going to start having lots of sex in a few months." They all laughed.

"But thanks for the enthusiasm," Claudia said, grinning at Jayne. "Trust me, I'm plenty excited."

Jayne thought she'd never seen Claudia look happier. Claudia pulled some Kleenex out of her purse and said, "Sorry, guys, I know this is gross, but I've had a cold for like a week now." She turned away from the table and blew her nose.

"I thought you sounded kind of stopped up," Karen said. "So when you have the beautiful babies that you and

Sam will inevitably make, are you going to call us Aunt Karen and Aunt Jayne?"

"Well there's no one else in the world that feels more like sisters to me, so you bet."

"So, Miss Jayne," Karen said, looking directly at her, "what's the 411 on the infamous Mr. Brandt?"

"Oh, well…" Jayne stared into her bowl.

"Don't tell me you haven't talked with him."

"Okay." She grinned. "I won't tell you."

"But you haven't, have you?" Karen raised her eyebrows.

"Guilty as charged." She looked over to Claudia. "But I'm going to, really I am. Soon." Karen was shaking her head.

"Why haven't you?" Claudia asked in a gentle tone. Concern filled her eyes.

"I don't know…" Jayne sighed. "I guess it's because he's an awful lot to walk away from. And I just know that when we talk, it will be his out to bolt. And maybe I've just been wanting to enjoy being in his arms a little while longer."

"No one faults you for that," Karen said. "I wouldn't mind being in those arms, either. But at what cost to your self-esteem?"

"I know, Karen, I know." Jayne hated when people told her what she already knew but was afraid to admit to herself. And she hated even more that she'd allowed herself to be reduced to a shrinking violet that felt like she couldn't be without a man. "Maybe I'll talk to him tomorrow after work. We don't have any plans, but he might get together with me. Then I'll see what he has to say."

"It's like pulling off a Band-Aid," Karen said. "Better to do it quick."

"Yeah, you're right. But sometimes easier said than done." She saw real compassion in Karen's expression; it felt good to know her friends were there for her.

"Hey, what's going on with that new boss of yours?" Claudia asked.

"Oh, that," Jayne sighed, shaking her head. "He is horrible. He's not really nice to anyone, but it's like he's singled me out for specific torture because of Gray. Which is ironic, because Gray has never had anything to do with my job whatsoever. We work in the same building, but that's where our business together ends. But I can't tell Tony that because he won't even let me speak."

"Maybe you could send him an email or something?" Karen suggested.

"I thought about that, but I really think it would just enrage him more."

"Have you talked to Gray about it?" Claudia asked.

"No, and now I can't imagine saying, 'Hey, do you love me like I love you or are you stringing me along? And by the way, can you help me with this work problem?'"

"True. So what are you going to do?"

"I don't know. He's just riding me so hard and complaining all the time." Jayne didn't want to make Karen feel bad, but when she took off a day to attend Karen's father's funeral, Tony had read her the riot act. "It's not your family," he'd barked at her. Never mind the fact that she had plenty of vacation time accrued and she never used all of it in a year so she usually lost some of it anyway.

"So what's going on with you and Rick?" Jayne said, looking at Karen. "I know at Christmas you guys were having a rough time, but you seemed really close at the funeral."

"Actually," Karen said, smiling much broader than she normally allowed, "things are better than ever."

"Really?" Claudia asked, after blowing her nose again.

"Yeah," Karen said, practically gushing, "I think he really is the one."

"I'm impressed." Claudia smiled at Karen.

"What happened to the whole 'I might get rid of him after St. Patrick's Day' thing?" Jayne asked.

"Let's first say I was acting like a cold-hearted, stupid bitch," Karen said with a chuckle. "Why is no one disagreeing with me?" They all laughed. "And, I don't know…losing my dad kind of opened up the floodgates for me. Like maybe, I don't know…losing the man that for me, represented all men, and how they can hurt you…well, it was somehow liberating. It made me let go of some of that hurt, some of the defenses I'd built up."

"Wow," Claudia said, patting Karen's hand. "How very self-realized of you."

"Jesus, I sound like fucking Oprah or something." She laughed at herself, but her eyes were sparkling. "I officially just made myself sick. But on the plus side, I think I finally, for the first time, let a man in. Really in, to see the real me."

"Karen, that's huge," Jayne said. "And with Rick—I just love Rick. I've always thought he was perfect for you."

"Yeah, he kind of is."

"You actually look like you're in love. I don't think I've ever seen you look like this before."

"Shit, is it that obvious? This doesn't mean I have to be optimistic and hopeful now, does it?" She couldn't resist smiling.

"Sorry, Karen," Claudia said with a big smile of her own. "It kind of goes with the territory. Love will do that to you."

"I guess he's worth the self-loathing and love songs," she deadpanned. They all laughed. "Rick can't believe the difference in me. He's been so great."

"Oh, speaking of Rick," Claudia said, "is his little brother still single? The fireman…what's his name?"

"Ethan? Yeah, he's single. Why?"

"I was thinking we should set him up with Rachel, Sam's assistant. She's a cute little thing, early twenties…is he still available?"

"I think so, I can check with Rick."

"I never met Rick's brother," Jayne said. "When did you meet him?"

"At a ball game last summer," Claudia explained. "Sam got tickets from his boss, and you couldn't go, you had plans or something. So Rick and Karen brought Ethan with them."

"Oh, I kind of remember that. So he's cute?"

"Oh yeah," Claudia said. "Kind of like a younger, clean-cut version of Rick."

"Well, hey—after I talk to Gray, maybe I'll need you to set him up with me."

"I don't know if I'd like that," Karen said. "That would seem weird."

"It would? Why?"

Karen shrugged her shoulders. "I don't know, maybe not."

"If you and Rick got married, and Ethan and I got married, we'd be sisters-in-law!"

"Whoa, Nelly," Karen said as they all laughed. "No one is talking marriage here. You're about to make me break out into hives."

"I was just speculating, that's all."

"Well stop speculating and start eating, okay?"

"Yes, ma'am."

"But we'll put Ethan on hold for you, okay? Just in case."

"Like layaway?" Jayne giggled.

"Yes," Claudia said. "But if you don't pick him up in a month, he goes back out in the dating pool."

Jayne loved the sound of her friends' laughter and was overjoyed to see them both in such a good place. Karen was finally learning how to let herself love and be loved. Contentment looked good on her. And Claudia was getting so close to having the perfect life she'd always wanted.

In some ways, it was going to make it even harder for Jayne to finally have a heart to heart with Gray. Because she was pretty sure she wouldn't be sharing any great news about him the next time she saw her friends.

Chapter Eight

Gray's head was buried in the documents on his desk, his focus so intense that he didn't realize anyone was at his door until Jayne's voice rang out.

"Knock, knock."

He looked up to see her smiling face staring at him from the doorway. His first reaction was to smile, which he couldn't resist. She had one of the prettiest, friendliest faces he'd ever seen. It didn't surprise him that he felt glad to see her, but he didn't have time for frivolity. *What is she doing here? I told her I was slammed with a project all week. I can't deal with her distractions right now.*

"Hey, Jaynie!" He noticed she didn't step into his office like she usually did. "Come on in."

"No, that's okay, you're busy," she said, leaning against the doorframe. Her legs looked gorgeous in the skirt and heels she was wearing. "I'm sorry to bug you—"

"I've got a minute, and it's always good to see you in my office." *Shit, why did I say that? Don't encourage her, even if it's true.*

"Well, I was just hoping that we could get together tonight. I mean, I know you're probably working late, that's fine. Just whenever."

"Uh...sure." The look on her face wasn't one he was familiar with. A feeling of dread crept over him. "I figure I'll be here until at least seven."

"Why don't you just call me when you're leaving? I can meet you at your place, if that's okay."

"Yeah, Jaynie, sure." He didn't get the feeling this was a booty call or a social visit. He could tell something was up. *Why do women always have to complicate things?* "Is everything okay?"

"Yeah," she said quietly, looking down.

Christ. She wants to talk, that's what it is. I don't have time for this in my life. Here we go. "Okay, I'll call you when I'm leaving." Their eyes met, and it was obvious to both of them that everything was not okay. After hesitating a moment, she walked away from his door, and Gray leaned back in his chair, taking a long, deep breath.

"Fuck," he said out loud.

"I heard that, Gray," Katherine hollered from across the hall. "Time to pay the piper, huh?"

"Katherine, why don't you just do your job and then go straight to hell?" He threw his pen down on his desk. He could hear her laughing. Bitch.

"I have to say I'm impressed, Brandt. This one lasted a few months...must be some kind of record for you. You usually bail much sooner. Either you're getting soft, or she was just that good."

With that, he got up and slammed his door shut.

****

All that kept running through Jayne's head as she walked back to her desk was that he hadn't called her sweet Jaynie when she'd left his office. He always said, "Good bye, sweet Jaynie" whenever they parted, whether in person or on the phone. But not this time.

He'd smiled at her when he saw her in the doorway, and she felt like it was genuine. He actually looked glad to see her. But she apparently wasn't a good actress, because she could see it on his face as they talked—he knew something was up. And he didn't look happy about it.

She kept telling herself that maybe he really did want a relationship with her. Maybe he just wasn't good at expressing how he felt. Well, she was about to find out, and she felt sick to her stomach. A part of her just wanted to keep the charade alive, if there was one. But she remembered Karen's words: "It's better to be alone than be played."

True. She wanted to get this over with.

When she reached her desk, she hadn't even had time to sit down when Tony barked from his office, "Jayne—

130

come see me!" Oh crap, what am I going to get yelled at about now?

"Yes, sir?" she asked when she reached his door. She didn't want to cross the threshold into his office; God only knew what would happen when you entered the vortex of animosity.

"Where were you? You're supposed to be working at your desk." His look was full of contempt.

"I went to the restroom," she lied.

"Well that's funny, because you came from the direction of the elevators, not the restrooms."

I work my ass off for this company, work through lunch with a sandwich at my desk most days and you're going to monitor me like I'm a third grader? Fuming, she tried to justify by saying, "I also dropped off some papers—"

"Don't lie to me, Ms. Asher. I'm not paying you to visit that backstabbing, ladder-climbing SOB you sleep with. I've compiled a nice list of disciplinary issues with you, and I'm adding personal visits to the fifth floor on company time to that list."

"What is your problem with me? What have I done to you besides give you stellar work?" She was shaking but finally so angry she couldn't hold back anymore.

"You better watch your tone with me," he said, standing up. "I'm adding that to the report, too. My problem is people that skate by on other people's coattails."

"I've had this job for five years, and I've only known Gray for three months. My job has nothing to do with him—"

"Save it, Jayne. I don't want to hear your pathetic excuses. But you better get with the program or you're outta here."

Completely stunned, she walked back to her desk, wanting desperately to run to the restroom and cry her eyes out in a stall. But it was obvious he was watching her like a hawk, so there would be none of that. She couldn't believe this was happening. She'd worked there for five years, three of them for Kelly, and she'd always gotten the highest ratings on her performance reviews and was considered one of the best in the department. *I am one of the best in the department,* she told herself, dabbing her eyes.

Grabbing a report from her file, she could barely concentrate as her mind raced with the stress of the impending talk with Gray and dealing with Tony the Dictator. *How did it all turn to shit?*

****

When Gray called her to say he was on his way home, he sounded unlike himself. He said he was grabbing some fast food on the way and asked if she wanted anything. Of course she'd said no; she was far too nervous to think about putting something in her stomach. Again, no *sweet Jaynie* before he hung up.

Her knock on his door was timid, she knew. Maybe she was secretly hoping he wouldn't hear it, he wouldn't answer it, and she could go one more day as Gray Brandt's girlfriend.

"Hey, Jaynie," he said after opening the door. She stepped inside, he took off her coat, and gave her a kiss. A long kiss, a nice kiss. They both let it linger before they pulled away. "So why do I get the feeling you didn't just come here for that?" His eyes searched hers.

"No, I guess I didn't."

"Do you want to sit down?"

"Sure." He took her hand, and she loved the way her hand felt in his. He had very strong hands, just like the rest of him. But his hands seemed gentler somehow. They sat on the couch, facing each other.

"Do you want something to drink?"

She saw that he had already started on a drink for himself. Probably Scotch. "No, but thanks." She looked up at him, wondering how to start. What to say. *How do you ask, Do you love me? Will you ever love me? Could I grow to mean something to you?*

"So what's going on? I guess you want to talk about something." He sounded tired.

"Yeah, I do. I've been wanting to for a while, but I wasn't sure what to say." I'm still not. She took a deep breath. "Gray, I feel like we're in two different places. In this relationship."

He nodded his head. "Maybe."

"How do you see us?" Her lip trembled; fear gripped her. In her fantasy, he would say he loved her more than he'd ever loved anyone. But this wasn't a fantasy; even as she looked in his incredible transfixing blue eyes, she knew this was real. No more dreaming…she had to know.

It was his turn to sigh. To his credit, he didn't look away. His gaze was steady. "I'm not sure how you want me to answer that."

"I want you to be honest, Gray."

"Okay." He swallowed. "I guess I see you as someone that I adore, I love to spend time with, love to have sex with. You're a good friend, such a sweet person." He squeezed her hand.

"Well I love you, and I think you know that. I told you that once." He looked away. "Do you love me?"

He sat back but still held her hand. "Jaynie…"

The tears started filling in her eyes, but she didn't look away from him. "You don't love me, I get it—"

"No, you don't get it, Jaynie. It's not about whether or not I love you. It's that I can't ever love you the way you deserve to be loved, okay? I've been honest with you all along about my ambition, about what I'm trying to do with my life." His stare was intense. "You're not part of my master plan. I can't do what I need to and be preoccupied by love."

"Is that supposed to make me feel better?" She wiped the tears from her eyes.

"No, it's just supposed to explain that it has nothing to do with you. It's about me…please don't cry."

"Sure, the man I've spent the last three months falling in love with tells me I'm not part of his 'master plan,' and you don't want me to cry?" She stood up. All the tension, all the feelings of inadequacy, all the hurt she'd bottled up finally exploded. "Well for once, Gray, you don't get what you want. I am crying, okay? And you know what? I think you've just been stringing me along. I was handy to have around for the holidays—work parties, family events, all of that crap. So when were you going to dump me, huh, Gray?"

"Jayne, don't do this, please." He stood up, tried to put his arms around her, but she pulled away. "Sure, you were a great date to take with me. But don't act like you don't mean anything to me, because you do. But I never promised you some big relationship. I have to stay focused. You started to become a real distraction for me…a good one, but a distraction nonetheless. And I never led you on, I was upfront—"

"I know you were, Gray. But it's hard to remember that when we're making love." She chuckled. "Well, I was making love. You, apparently, were just having sex and then racing out the door."

His face hardened. "I didn't want to give you the wrong idea—"

"You didn't want to give anything. You just took. We did what you wanted, when you wanted, how you wanted. And I was stupid enough to think that if I gave you everything, that maybe you would give something back. You made me feel like I wasn't good enough for you."

"I'm sorry you feel that way. That's not how I see it."

She glared at him and saw resignation on his face. "So how much longer were you going to keep me hanging?"

"I could see you were getting more attached…I was trying to pull back a little. I like being with you, I would have been content to keep seeing you…"

"But not now, after I actually call you out on your bullshit, huh? Not when I actually say, out loud, eye to eye that I love you."

"You're the one that's trying to change things. We agreed that this was all I could give you—"

"No, Gray, we never agreed. You never asked. You just told me."

"Well, sweetheart, you didn't have to stick around if you didn't like it." He took a drink. "But I didn't see you in any hurry to leave."

"That's because I thought that in time…"

"What? That I would suddenly give up everything I've been working for, all these years…for a woman?"

Jayne wiped the tears that had started again and grabbed her coat. "I thought maybe I was worth it. I was wrong."

"Jaynie…" Their eyes locked, and held for a long time. She wasn't sure exactly what she saw, but there was conflict there. "You know, it doesn't have to be like this."

"Then how can it be, Gray?" Her voice was almost a whisper.

"You could just be okay with what I'm willing to give. We could still spend time together, still share something."

"I can't stop loving you if we're together. I can't stop wanting more. Is that okay with you?"

He looked away. Swallowed. He turned back to her, his eyes bluer than she'd ever seen. "No, it's not okay. I'm sorry, but I can't do that."

She nodded her head, tears still flowing. "I didn't think so." He walked up and embraced her, and this time, she didn't pull away. She wanted to sear into her memory forever the way it felt for those strong, solid arms to hold her. To remember the way he smelled, and oh, how she wished she would have gotten a chance to see those dimples one last time. "Gray?"

"Yeah?" He didn't let go, although her tears and mascara were dampening his designer label shirt.

"Can I ask you something?"

"Sure. What?"

She looked up at him, wiping her eyes. "When we kissed…it didn't feel like just any kiss. It felt like…like it meant something. Did it mean something?"

"Yeah," he said, a sad smile showing a hint of his dimples, "it always meant something with you." At that moment, she didn't care if he was lying or not. She believed him. She had to.

Jayne pulled away, her body quivering. He followed her to the door, but she didn't look back. She hoped he would still change his mind, that seeing her leave would make him ask her to stay.

But as she stepped out into the hallway, he only said, very quietly, "Goodbye, sweet Jaynie."

****

Through her tear-soaked eyes, Jayne could barely make out the roads. She kept wiping them, trying to clear her vision. The blurry image of the clock on her dashboard said it was ten after eight. Claudia's house was just ten minutes away...she couldn't go home to her lonely place just yet. *I should get a pet. Something to hold while I cry.* She needed someone to comfort her, and Claudia was perfect for that.

As she pulled up in front of Claudia's house, it looked so warm and welcoming. Gone were the signs of Christmas, but the oversized chair filling the large bay window and warm lighting inside was like an architectural hug. She felt a little better just seeing it.

She knew she looked horrible, but Claudia wouldn't care. And she would listen, she would soothe...she was a natural mom if ever there was one. Jayne wiped her eyes for the umpteenth time as she rang the doorbell. Sam opened the door.

"Hi, Jayne—what's wrong?" he asked, ushering her inside. "What's the matter?"

The kindness in his voice and look of worry on his face was enough to start the waterworks again.

"Bad night," she said, trying to smile. "Can you tell Claudia I'm here?"

"Oh, sorry Jayne, she's not here."

"She's not?"

"No, but she should be back any minute. It turns out that nasty cold she had was actually a sinus infection, and she went to the drug store to pick up her antibiotics."

"Well, I'm sorry, I should have called first—"

"No, no, you're fine. Stay. She'll be here before you know it." His handsome face was a safe, familiar one. Taking a deep breath, she decided she would stay.

"Okay. I'm sorry to barge in like this."

"Come on in the living room," he urged, leading the way. "Why don't I get you some coffee? I've got a lot of work tonight, and I just made a pot to help keep me awake."

"Actually, that sounds great."

Just then, his phone rang, and he looked at it, irritation evident on his face. "I'm sorry, I need to grab this—"

"That's okay, I can get my own cup of coffee."

"Sorry," he said, stepping out of the room with his phone. As Jayne headed into their warm, cheery kitchen, she heard him say quietly on the phone, "I can't talk now. I told you I'm done for the night, okay?"

His talking got more muffled as she grabbed a mug that said, "World's Best Wife" on it. She snorted. Yeah, that's me all right. If I could find anyone to marry. She poured the coffee in and just smelling it seemed to soothe her.

"Sorry about that," Sam said, walking into the room. "Work never ends."

"I can't imagine all the pressure you must be under, trying to make partner."

"You have no idea." He sounded rather frazzled. "So what's going on? I mean, I know I'm no Claudia, but I have a good set of ears."

Jayne smiled. "Oh...men troubles."

"Gray Brandt?"

"Yeah." She stared down into her cup of coffee, noticing the way the cream swirled around, as if in a whirlpool, as the steam rose above. "I just left his place. It's over."

"Jayne, I'm sorry." He put his arm around her. "Why don't we go sit down?" He motioned to the living room, and she followed him in and sat on the couch next to him. "So, what happened?"

"Well...I never felt like he was really in the relationship one hundred percent. And honestly, he was upfront about what he was up for. He told me early on that he was very ambitious, had goals in mind, and couldn't give me any more than he was." She sighed. "But I'm a woman. So I guess I heard that but didn't believe it. He sent some mixed signals, so I figured that over time, he would grow to love me, as I love him." Tears threatened again, but she held them at bay. "Turns out I was wrong. He said I'm not part of his master plan, but he still wanted to see me if I was okay with what little he's willing to give. But the thing is, I'm not. I want more."

Sam nodded, offering a pat on the leg. "I know it hurts now, Jayne, but be glad that he knows what he wants and that he's honest about it. Some guys aren't honest about what they're looking for, and the next thing you know, it's years down the road and you're left with a lot more heartache."

Jayne sighed. "Yeah, I guess so. I've only wasted three months of my life."

"But you had some fun, didn't you?"

"I suppose." And plenty of embarrassment, loneliness, and shame, too. "But who says, 'You're not part of my master plan'?"

"Well, romantic and sensitive it's not. But he's a guy that knows what he wants. And he wanted to be with you, in a small capacity, but he did. Try to look at what you did have with him."

"The problem with that is, when it was good, it just made me want all of him. But he never gave all of himself to me."

"Sounds like he's not capable of that."

"I feel like he used me, though. I was the girl on his arm at all of his holiday events, but that's all I was."

"Well I'm sorry if that's what he was doing. But you're a beautiful girl, Jayne. There are plenty of men that would die to be with you."

But I just want to be with Gray. As ridiculous as it is, as pointless as it was, as insignificant as he made me feel...I still wanted him to be with me.

Just then, the door opened, and Claudia walked in. One look at Claudia's puffy eyes and pale face, and Jayne could tell she felt awful.

"Jayne, what's wrong?" Claudia asked, rushing to her friend.

The tears began. "It's Gray..." Claudia hugged her, and Jayne began sobbing like a baby. "But you're so sick, I'm sorry for coming over—"

"No, don't you worry about me. Let me just take these pills and then I'll get a fire going and you can tell me what happened."

"I've got work to do," Sam said, standing up. "I'll leave you two alone."

"Thanks, Sam," Jayne said, still crying. "Claudia, you've got a great guy."

Sam hurried out of the room as Claudia said, "I know, we need to find you a Sam."

****

When Sam came home from work early the next day, Claudia was lying on the couch in the hearth room. A mountain of used Kleenex surrounded her, and only her head poked out from beneath the down comforter. She was so glad to see his smiling face.

"Hi, sweetheart," she said, coughing.

"You look like you feel awful," he said, setting down his briefcase and finding a spot on the couch next to her.

"I do," she nodded, blowing her nose. "But it's good to see you home so early."

"Well, I had to take care of my girl," he said with a broad smile. "Are you hungry? Why don't I heat up some soup?"

"That sounds great, actually. Thank you."

"No problem. I'll get it going."

A few minutes later, he brought out a tray with soup, crackers, and a slice of cheddar cheese. He helped Claudia

139

sit up and get settled. They chatted while she ate; she hadn't eaten all day and was ravenous.

"It feels like your fever may have broken," he said, feeling her forehead. "You were burning up when I left for work this morning."

"Yeah, I do feel a little better. I'm just achy all over."

"Tell you what…why don't I draw you a nice warm bath?"

"That would be magical," she said, her smile grateful.

"Okay, I'll come back down and get you in a few minutes."

Sure enough, soon she was climbing into a soothing warm bubble-filled bath.

"Wow, even sick, you look amazing," Sam said, pouring warm water down her back. Their eyes met and Claudia felt such a familiar comfort and longing. Sam kissed her neck once, then gently again. "I'm sorry, you don't feel good…this is no time for foreplay."

Claudia smiled. "Well I've certainly felt a lot better, but if I can just lay there while you do the work, I wouldn't mind a little something…."

"Really?" he asked, grinning.

"Sam, I'm always turned on by you."

"Are you sure…?"

"Just be gentle and I'm all for it."

When her bath was done, Sam helped dry her off and then they climbed naked into bed together. Claudia always felt like she won the lottery with Sam; he was a wonderful, considerate, caring lover. He knew all her right spots and what to do with them.

Afterward, she fell asleep and when she awoke a while later, Sam was tucking the blankets around her. He was dressed.

"That was nice," she said, her voice dripping with drowsiness.

"Yeah, it was, wasn't it?" A mischievous grin filled his face.

"Are you going somewhere?"

"Yeah, I have to head back to the office. I came home early to get you some dinner, but I left a lot of work waiting for me."

"Okay, well thank you. It was lovely."

"Do you need anything else before I leave?"

"No, I think I'll just go back to sleep."

As he caressed her cheek, he said quietly, "I love you, Claud."

"I love you, too." She was asleep before he even left the room.

February

Chapter Nine

Damn Valentine's Day, thought Jayne. What's so great about it, anyway? Oh sure, roses and chocolates and romantic evenings spent with the one you love. If you have a special someone, it's a pretty great day. If you don't...well, then, call in sick and pretend it doesn't exist.

At least that's what she'd done. Emailed Tony, saying she had the stomach flu, and since she virtually never called in sick, she figured even he wouldn't be able to complain about it. Then she shut off her laptop and spent all of Valentine's Friday in bed, in her pajamas, staring at the TV. Just fine with her. Her relationship with Gray had ended just two weeks earlier, the pain was still raw...she was due for a little self-pity.

Claudia and Karen hadn't forgotten about her. They'd even sent flowers and then called to cheer her up, too. It was sweet, and it really did mean a lot to her. But at the end of the day, there was no one to cuddle with, or kiss, or make dreams with. Just a down comforter, DirecTV, a box of tissues and of course her roommate—the dripping faucet from hell.

The next morning she woke up feeling a little better, until she pulled up her email to see a Nastygram from Tony about how she didn't take her job seriously and was frivolous with taking time off and bla bla bla. The letter ended with Expect serious disciplinary action when you return from "the stomach flu."

Although heartbroken about Gray, she wasn't too lovelorn to get pissed off. That email made her angry—it was the final straw. She decided to talk to HR about him on Monday. He was not following company guidelines, spoke to her inappropriately, and was basically harassing her. You won't be bullying me much longer.

She wandered into the bathroom and noticed in the mirror that her eyelids were white and puffy from all the Valentine's Day tears. She wanted to get out of the house, even though it was cold. Spending two days cooped up inside would be too much.

So she threw on a pair of yoga pants, a T-shirt, her coat, and a dark pair of sunglasses. No makeup, no frills. She was lucky to get herself out the door; vanity had no place for her today.

Instead of hitting her local Starbucks, she felt like going someplace different. With sudden inspiration, she headed to Old St. Charles and a fun little café she'd gone to with the girls. Maybe she'd even feel like browsing through some stores.

When she arrived on Main Street, she remembered with irritation that she had to parallel park. Not one of her strong suits. She found a spot and was mortified when it took four tries to get her car parked. *I should have just stayed in bed.* Her face burning with embarrassment, she climbed out of the car. *Hopefully no one noticed.*

"Jayne?" A man standing on the cobblestone sidewalk called her name. With the way the sun was hitting, she couldn't see his face, but his voice sounded vaguely familiar. "Yeah, I thought that was you."

Just then, she reached the curb and could see him. It was Josh Brandt, Gray's brother. *Like she wanted to see any man with the last name of Brandt.*

"Josh?" she asked, in shock.

"So good to see you," he said, surprising Jayne as he embraced her in an exuberant hug. "What are you doing down here? Are you meeting Gray?"

"Uh…no," she said quietly. *Oh my God. He doesn't even know. I was so inconsequential to Gray that he didn't even tell his brother we broke up.*

"Is something wrong?" Josh cocked his head to the side, his brows furrowed in concern. "Are you okay?"

Don't cry, don't cry, don't cry, she pleaded with herself. Then the tears came. "Yes, I'm fine," she said, breaking into a sob.

"Oh, Jayne," Josh said, putting his arm around her and guiding her from the center of the sidewalk, out of the way of pedestrians staring at the hysterical crying woman. "What's wrong?" She realized the tenderness in his voice showed more compassion in thirty seconds than Gray had shown their entire relationship.

"He didn't even tell you, did he?" she managed to spit out between sobs.

"What? Who—Gray?"

"Yes, your arrogant brother. It's over between us. Said I wasn't part of his 'master plan.'" She wiped her eyes, getting her tears under control as the sadness turned to anger.

Josh let go of her, shaking his head and sighed. "No, he didn't tell me. I'm so sorry, Jayne."

"I shouldn't have called him a name just now…he's your brother, and that was rude of me."

"Oh, trust me. I'm thinking of some much more appropriate names for him right now, and most of them you can't say on network TV."

Jayne giggled, relieved he wasn't angry with her. "I bet I could add to your list."

"Yeah, I imagine you could." He smiled at her, and Jayne noticed for the first time that although he didn't have his brother's dimples, he did have a great smile. It was contagious, for sure. He put his hand on her shoulder. "Hey, it's pretty cold out here. I was going to grab a coffee—do you want to join me?"

"Sure, I was here for the same thing anyway."

"Well, good. I brought some papers to grade, but enjoying a cup of java with you sounds much better than reading freshman papers analyzing To Kill a Mockingbird."

"Oh, I love that book."

"It used to be my favorite. But after teaching it for nine years and reading approximately seven hundred papers about it written by fourteen-year-olds, it's kind of lost its allure." They both laughed as they walked into the café.

After ordering drinks, they took a seat by the window. It was a funky little coffee house, with mismatching wood tables, great artwork, wood floors, and free Wi-Fi. Folk music, piped through the speakers above, suited the decor. Glancing around, Jayne noticed young college students frantically typing on laptops, an older couple sharing a laugh, and a group of girls gossiping—reminding her of Claudia and Karen.

"You know, Jayne, the drink you ordered can't technically be called coffee," Josh said, smiling at her from across the table. "It's more like sugar and chocolate, with a dash of coffee."

Their eyes met as Jayne chuckled. "Is there something wrong with that?"

"No, not at all. But you shouldn't say you're getting coffee. You're getting hot chocolate with a shot of caffeine."

"Guilty as charged. I like things sweet." Karen always joked that Jayne liked life to be as sweet as the treats she craved.

"Nothing wrong with that." He took a sip of his coffee, and then his face turned somber. "So, knowing my brother's track record, I will apologize on behalf of the Brandt family. I'm sure he was not a gentleman."

"No kidding," she said, anger rising in her again. "I mean, just the fact that he didn't tell you we'd broken up shows me how little I meant to him. Here I've been, crying my eyes out and moping around, and I'm sure he hasn't given it a second thought."

"I don't necessarily think that's true. It's just that we don't talk very often, actually." Josh took a big gulp of coffee. "I mean, he's my brother and I love him—"

"Of course you do."

"But…let's just say I don't exactly see eye to eye with Gray on a lot of issues."

Jayne sat back in her chair and sighed. "That makes two of us."

Josh's look was direct. "If you want to tell me what happened, I'm a good listener."

The thing was, she did want to talk about it. She was so angry and hurt and embarrassed. It was almost difficult to tell her friends, after gushing about him for so long. But here was Josh, with an earnest look on his face and the most caring eyes she had ever seen.

Without giving it a second thought, she began unloading.

He was a great listener and seemed appropriately upset with his brother's behavior. He gave her smiles from time to time and patted her hand when she got upset. And for Jayne, it felt so good to let it all out, to maybe start to let it go.

"Why don't I go grab us two more coffees?" Josh asked when she stopped to take a breath some thirty minutes later.

"That would be great. Don't forget, mine's hot chocolate with a shot of caffeine." She grinned at him.

"Of course."

"Here," Jayne said, pulling a five-dollar bill out of her wallet.

"No, put that away. You endured my brother the prick—the very least I can do is buy you a coffee."

When he returned with their drinks, Jayne was suddenly embarrassed at the way she had dumped on him.

"Josh, I'm sorry, I shouldn't have unloaded on you like that."

"No, it's fine. Really."

"Then do you want to know the most disturbing thing he said to me?" She was smiling...it was painful at the time, but actually funny now. What an asshole.

"I can't even begin to imagine."

"One time, after we'd just had sex, and we were lying there...you know, how afterward you kind of just bask in the glow?"

147

"Yeah, I know what you mean." He looked a little uncomfortable.

"Well, he told me I had an incredible body. So I'm feeling all happy about myself and feeling sexy. And then he asked if I'd ever thought of getting a boob job."

Josh's eyes nearly bulged out of his head. "Please tell me you're joking."

"I wish I was, trust me."

"Wow!" He looked down before he took a drink. "I'm so sorry he said something so insensitive and sexist to you."

"Thank you. It's actually kind of funny to me now. I mean, who does that? The sheets were still warm."

"Just for the record, he was right about you having an incredible body. But your breasts are just fine the way they are."

Jayne offered a shy smile as she felt a flush hit her cheeks. "Thanks, Josh."

"You're welcome," he said, winking at her.

She let out a huge sigh. "Enough about Gray. But thank you so much...it felt good to get some of that off my chest."

"Glad I could help. And I am really sorry he treated you that way."

"I think I'm more disappointed in myself than him."

"What do you mean?"

"Well, I let him do all those things to me. I could have objected. I could have left. But I didn't. And it's so frustrating to me, because I am a strong woman. At work, I'm strong, assertive, on the ball. With my friends, I'm confident and outgoing." Jayne stared at the worn, scuffed wood planks of the floor. "Why did I put up with that?"

"Hey," Josh said quietly, touching her arm. "Don't be so hard on yourself. You're not exactly the first person to use poor judgment when it comes to love."

She looked up, offering a grateful smile. "Yeah, I guess you're right. It's just embarrassing, you know?"

"Actually, I know more than you can imagine." He sat back and crossed his arms. "I've had my share of looking the other way for love."

"You? You seem so together."

"It's an illusion," he said with a grin, and Jayne noticed a sadness she hadn't seen before in his eyes.

"Yeah, what's your story? I'm surprised someone hasn't snatched you up yet."

"I was engaged once. It didn't end well."

"I'm sorry." It was her turn to offer a comforting touch. "What happened? If you don't mind me asking."

"No, I don't mind. After all, you did just bare your disastrous history with Gray." He tried to smile, but this time, it looked forced. "It was two months before the wedding. Everything was booked, invitations were filled out...and there were signs. Many signs. But I chose to ignore them—I buried my head in the sand. Then she was gone."

"Oh, Josh, that must have been terrible. Why did she leave?"

"Apparently she found her sister's husband to be a better catch than me."

"No!" Jayne couldn't believe what she'd heard.

"Oh, yes." He chuckled. "But they deserve each other. That was three years ago, and I hear he left her high and dry a couple of years after that. Gotta say that brought me some laughs." They laughed together, sharing in the joy that lives perilously close to pain. Just as their laughter died down, they started up again. By the time they quieted down, tears of happiness streaked down her face.

"That felt good," she said, wiping her cheeks. "I needed that. I haven't had any laughter in me the last couple of weeks."

"Well, here's to more laughter," Josh said, holding up his coffee cup. Jayne tapped his cup with her own, and they both took a drink.

"Thank you so much for cheering me up and listening to my horrible whining."

"The pleasure was all mine. Beats the hell out of grading papers."

Jayne finished off her coffee and grabbed her purse off the back of the chair. "I better get going. Thanks again. Oh, and if you see your brother, you can tell him I said to fuck off." There was a grin on her face, but her words were firm.

"Will do," he said with a chuckle, nodding his head. "Do you... Would you want to do this again sometime? I'm fairly certain you haven't shared all of Gray's bullshit with me. We could meet for coffee, or maybe grab some lunch."

What the hell? Might as well. He's fun, and I could use a distraction from Gray. "Yeah, that sounds nice."

"Got plans next Saturday?"

"Uh...no."

"Where would you like to meet?"

"Wherever you want is fine with me."

"Well, Jayne, what do you like?"

"Really, whatever you want."

"Then how about lunch at Winery of the Little Hills?"

"Sure. Noon?"

"Noon it is. It was really nice to see you today, Jayne." He stood up and gave her a quick kiss on the cheek. "Oh, and by the way—nice parking job."

She giggled, rolling her eyes. "Gee, thanks. Nice to see you too, Josh. Goodbye." She turned to look at him before stepping outside, and he waved.

A bit of a smile played at her lips as she made her way back to her car. When she climbed inside and glanced at herself in the rear-view mirror, she said out loud, "Oh, shit." She'd forgotten that she went out without makeup. Oh God. No wonder he took pity on her. She looked pathetic.

As she started her Honda, she realized she was in a much better mood than when she'd arrived. Despite being sans makeup when seeing her ex's brother.

****

Gray looked away from his computer monitor when he heard a knock on his open door. It was one of Mac's assistants, the one that Jayne had embarrassed herself with at the holiday party. That still pissed him off.

"Yes?" he asked, glancing at the guy.

"Mr. Brandt, I need to talk to you about something…" His voice trailed off, and Gray wondered why people thought it necessary to waste his time.

"What?" He was doing his best not to sound annoyed, but even he could hear it in his voice.

"It's about Jayne—"

"Jayne and I aren't together anymore," he said, turning back to his computer.

"Well, I know, I heard that—"

"Then what do you want? I'm really busy here." Gray saw the guy flinch.

"Never mind. I thought if you cared about her at all, maybe you could help—"

Gray sighed. "Help with what?"

"This came across my desk this morning," he said, walking into Gray's office and laying a paper on his desk. "I'm supposed to forward this to Mac to sign off on, but I'm hoping maybe you can do something about it."

Gray picked up the paper and quickly saw the words: "Termination and Exit Paperwork. Employee: Jayne Asher."

"What the hell?" he muttered under his breath, scanning the document. Why on earth would she be getting fired? He knew she was a good employee—he'd asked around himself before they went on their first date. He wouldn't compromise his reputation by dating someone at Nixon Pharmaceutical that was a problem employee.

"She's been having a lot of trouble with Tony. Apparently he has some issues with you, and since you two were dating…well, he's kind of been out to get her."

Gray wasn't surprised to hear that Tony had a problem with him. Gray expected nothing short of excellence out of his workers, and he viewed Tony Green as an untalented, middle-management hack. Gray had personally seen to it that Tony was passed over for two promotions because he thought he was incompetent and uninspired. Word had probably gotten back to Tony.

Looking over the paperwork, Tony was claiming that she'd had two unexcused absences in the last thirty days, her work had a lot of errors, she lacked initiative, was defiant of his authority, and took "frequent unauthorized personal visits to the fifth floor on company time." Gray searched his memory...he knew Jayne was at work every day in January, except for the day she went to Karen's father's funeral. They were only two weeks into February and he was no longer in contact with her, so he wasn't sure about that, but he'd never known her to take a day off. As far as frequent unauthorized visits to the fifth floor on company time...she'd only stopped by his office once this year during business hours.

"Has she been coming up here to see you?" Gray asked.

"No, never. We talk on the phone, had lunch a couple of times."

"Do you know of anyone else she might be coming up here to see?"

"No, not at all."

"Yeah, well I think most of these accusations are probably bullshit." Gray looked up. "So what do you want me to do?"

"Well...I don't know...I know you carry a lot of weight around here. I thought maybe you could help."

Gray sighed, glancing down again at the paper in front of him. Shit. I've never used my authority to help anyone but myself. I don't want to jeopardize my position that I've worked so hard for.

But it's Jayne. Damn it. If I do this, I have to make sure it doesn't look like I'm just covering for some woman I slept with. It has to be justified.

"How long can we stall this before Tony will expect to see the paperwork signed off?" Gray asked.

"Mac usually signs off in a day or two."

"What's his schedule look like today?"

"Meetings most of the day…he's got some free time in the late afternoon, around three-thirty or four."

"Okay. I'll see what I can do."

"Thank you so much—"

"Do not say a word to Jayne about this, okay?"

"Uh, sure." He had a perplexed look on his face as he stared at Gray.

"You can leave now," Gray said with a dismissive tone. After the assistant left his office, Gray looked back down at the termination paperwork. Shaking his head, he sighed as he stood up. *I hope I don't regret this.*

****

Walking into the Human Resources department on the first floor, Gray noticed many women look his way. *Who can I massage to get what I need?* Then, he saw a blonde who was always flirting with him peek out from her cubicle. He headed toward her. *Yep, she'll do. I've heard she's slept with half the guys here. What's her name? Chris? Carrie?* He smiled at her and noticed the nameplate on her cubicle: Christy.

"Christy," he said, producing the biggest grin he could for her. "So good to see you."

"Good to see you too," she smiled, practically fawning over him. "What brings your handsome self to HR?"

"Oh, just need to get some info on an employee. I was hoping you could help me out." He leaned against the edge of her desk, making sure he was as close to her as propriety would allow. She swallowed.

"Well, sure. What do you need?"

"I need the last five years' performance appraisals for Jayne Asher."

"I'm not supposed to release those to anyone but a department head…"

"Mac asked me check into it for him." Gray's demeanor and tone displayed a confidence he wasn't feeling.

"I didn't get an email or anything—"

"His assistant knows all about it, give him a call."

"Scott Hickman?"

"Yeah, Scott." So that's his name.

She picked up the phone and dialed. "Hi, Scott, this is Christy from HR. I'm just trying to get authorization for Mr. Brandt to pull some performance appraisals he said Mac wants for Jayne Asher... Oh, okay then. Thanks so much." She hung up. "Sorry, Gray, I just had to make sure...cover my butt, ya know."

"Oh, I know all about that," he said suggestively, winking at her.

"I'm just surprised he sent you down here instead of Scott or Leslie. I would think someone important like you has better things to do."

Yeah, no shit. "You know, when your boss asks you to do something, you just do it, right?" He smiled.

"That must be how you keep climbing the ladder, huh?"

"Something like that." Just get me the damn files.

"Okay...do you want me to print them off?"

"Please."

He had to endure her mundane chatter about God knows what until she finally put the printouts in his hand. "Thank you so much, Christy," he said, flashing a grin as he stood up.

"We should go out for drinks sometime," she said, batting her eyes.

"Yeah, we'll have to plan something," he said as he walked away. I don't need to have drinks with the office slut when I can have anyone in here I want.

As soon as he got back to his desk, he sat down and started pouring over her reviews. Words like hard-working, team player, great initiative, superior accuracy, self-starter, bright and dependable were frequently repeated. Two reviews were from a supervisor by the name of Jim Woods, while the last three were from Kelly Sullivan. Clearly she hadn't turned from a stand-out employee into a piece of crap in the last few weeks.

But what do I do? If he went to Mac and just tried to stop the firing, no doubt it would make Jayne's life even more miserable with Tony. No, he had to get Tony out of that position. He checked the organizational chart to see where Kelly Sullivan had moved. It was a lateral move to a supervisory position in Research and Development. He picked up the phone and dialed her extension.

"Kelly Sullivan," she answered.

"This is Gray Brandt, VP of Marketing."

"Oh, yes, Mr. Brandt. What can I do for you?"

"Is there any chance you could come to my office? There's something confidential I need to talk to you about in regard to Jayne Asher."

"Uh…sure. When?"

"I'll clear my schedule, whenever you can make it."

"Oh, well, I'll be up in a few minutes then."

When Kelly arrived at his door, she looked puzzled, to say the least. "Mr. Brandt?"

"Are you Kelly?"

"Yes sir."

He stood up, motioning her in. "Please close the door behind you. Nice to meet you." They shook hands.

"So you said this had something to do with Jayne?"

"Yes and…I'd like to ask that you keep this between the two of us."

"Certainly."

"I was made aware this morning that Tony Green has filled out termination paperwork to have her fired."

"Jayne?" Her eyes grew large. "You've got to be kidding me."

"Yeah, that was my reaction, too. So I pulled her past performance reviews, and when I saw your glowing remarks, I wanted to talk to you."

"Why in the world does he want to fire her?"

"Well," Gray swallowed, "I think it's partly because of me. She and I dated for a while—"

"Oh, you're not anymore?"

"No, we ended things a couple of weeks ago." Gray was uncomfortable with the personal nature of the discussion. "But anyway, he's not a fan of mine, and Jayne never said anything to me, but I'm finding out that her association with me pissed him off. He's been compiling any and every possible reason he can come up with to get rid of her."

"Well what did he come up with? She was by far my best employee. We used to joke that I wished I could clone her."

"I don't know…some shit about unexcused absences, one of which I know was a funeral for her friend's father. Disrespectful to authority, errors, and personal visits to the fifth floor. Which I assume is in reference to me, but that's just a lie. She only came up here once in the last two months." Gray looked away, remembering the nature of that visit, when they scheduled the meeting where they said their goodbyes.

"There is no way any of that is true. It just can't be." Kelly stood up and leaned against Gray's desk. "What can I do? Should I talk to Tony? Or Mac?"

"Well…here's the thing. If we just call off the firing, I'm sure he'll make her life a living hell down there. She doesn't deserve that. So, I was wondering…how do you like your new position?"

"It's fine, I'm still trying to get the feel for the department and learning who I can rely on and who needs a babysitter."

"Would you consider taking back your old position as supervisor for Customer Relations?"

"I loved that job, yeah, sure. But can you make that happen?" Their eyes locked. "I mean, with all due respect, do you have that much pull?"

Gray stood up, turning his back to her and looking out the window at the parking lot below. Fuck, I don't know. "If you're willing to make the switch, I'm going to find out."

"I'm on board with it. Jayne has been a wonderful employee, and I'll do whatever I can to save her. And going back to my old department would be fine by me. But what about Tony?"

He turned back around. "That's for me to worry about." He reached out to shake her hand again. "Thanks for coming to see me, and this must remain completely confidential."

"Of course." She headed to the door, then stopped and turned back around. "Does Jayne know what's going on?"

"No, and she doesn't need to."

****

Gray sat outside Mac's office, feeling nervous—an emotion he was unaccustomed to. In his hands he held a file folder with five years' worth of Jayne's hard efforts detailed on paper. He felt guilty that her association with him could potentially cost her a job she was great at and enjoyed. Guilt—another emotion he wasn't used to feeling. *I am done dating women at Nixon Pharmaceutical. Done. At least ones I give a shit about.*

"Mr. Brandt, Mac's ready for you," Scott said from his desk a few feet away. Gray couldn't decide if the conspiratorial look on Scott's face pleased or irritated him. As he walked into Mac's office, he realized Jayne was lucky to have Scott as a friend or she likely would have already been fired.

"Gray," Richard Mackenzie said, standing up and greeting Gray with a large smile and firm handshake. "How's my wonder boy doing today?"

"Fantastic, Mac," he said, exuding confidence as always. Although at the moment he certainly wasn't feeling it. Every time he walked into Mac's office, it was exhilarating to him. The rich, dark paneling, windows spanning two walls, an incredibly spacious room filled with only the finest furniture and artwork. It reeked of power, prestige, status.

Gray planned on making it his office someday.

"Sit down, sit down." Mac motioned to the plush leather chair in front of his desk. "What can I do for you?"

"Well…a situation was brought to my attention that I would like to discuss with you."

"Shoot."

"Since we instituted the latest reorganization, I think there's a real problem down in Customer Relations."

"Oh, really? What's going on?"

"Well, Kelly Sullivan used to be the supervisor down there and things were running smoothly. Now Tony Green is in that position, and apparently his managerial skills seem to be…lacking."

"In what way?"

"There's a long-time excellent employee that he's trying to fire due to…personal reasons."

"What are you getting at? And why are you getting involved in a personnel issue that's not in your department?" Exactly what Gray was worried about.

How am I going to spin this without jeopardizing my credibility with Mac? "Sir…I'm going to be absolutely candid with you."

"Okay." The look of intrigue on Mac's face was one Gray was used to, but instead of being excited about a new idea he was about to present, this time it unnerved him.

"The employee in question is Jayne Asher. We dated for about three months and just recently ended our relationship. Tony Green is aware of our connection, and he holds a grudge against me, and therefore Jayne, because it's well known I'm not a supporter of his. I turned him down for two promotions in Marketing."

"So what are you telling me? Or are you asking me something?"

"Mac, I work my ass off for Nixon Pharmaceutical. My contribution to its success is significant."

"There's no disputing that. You know how I feel about your work. But what does that have to do with this situation with some girl you messed around with?"

"I propose that you pull Tony Green out of his position in Customer Relations and put him under me in Marketing.

I don't think he can ever be objective when it comes to Jayne."

"Are you sure you aren't the one that's lost your objectivity?" His stare was laced with a subtle accusation.

"I would have never come to you if this was strictly a personal matter. I'm not asking you to help out a friend. I'm asking you to look at the five-year career of a superb employee, by everyone's account except for Tony. I would hate to think that I work for a company that would allow someone to be fired due to one individual's personal bias against them." He laid the file on Mac's desk. "It's all right here. Whether I had a relationship with her or not, her record speaks for itself. It's clear she deserves to work here. We'd be crazy to let her go."

Mac took a long look at Gray before he opened the file. He put on his glasses and it seemed to Gray like ten minutes passed before he looked up.

"Has termination paperwork been filled out?"

"Yes, I believe Scott has it."

Mac buzzed Scott. "Do you have exit paperwork for Jayne Asher?"

"Yes sir," Scott answered on speakerphone.

"Bring it in, please." Scott quickly brought in the documents and exited silently. Mac reviewed it and shook his head. "This is written as if it's about an entirely different person."

"That's my point. It makes no sense."

"Is this the woman you brought to the holiday party?"

"Yes."

"Yes, I remember Rob Schmidt mentioning that Kelly Sullivan raves about her." Gray nodded. "Well, something doesn't add up, so you could be absolutely right about his prejudice. So then Ms. Asher asked you to intervene?"

"No, not at all. She never mentioned a word to me about it. I found out from others that he's all but told her he doesn't like me and thinks she's using me to further her career."

"Is she?"

"I would think you know me better than that, Mac." Gray knew he was walking a fine line, but he also knew that Mac liked people that challenged him. "I mean, I imagine I have a bit of a reputation for dating women in the office—"

"A bit, yes," Mac chuckled.

"And have you ever, ever heard of anyone getting preferential treatment from me or anyone else due to their association with me?"

"Definitely not."

"And I'm not asking for that now, either. I'm merely asking you to not allow someone's association with me to cost them their job. She's obviously not the shitty employee that Tony claims she is…these other supervisors worked with her for years and he's only been in charge of her for six weeks."

"So if I pull Tony out, who am I supposed to put there?"

"Kelly loved that job, and I'm certain she would take it back."

"She's in R&D now, right?"

"Yes."

"I suppose we could find someone else for that slot…there's a lot of talent down there." Mac looked away for a moment before directing his stare into Gray's eyes. "So what the hell are you going to do with Tony in your department?"

"Well, I'll either whip him into shape and make him into someone productive, or I'll make sure I dot every i and cross every t before I terminate him."

"You already have a lot on your plate, Gray—"

"I can make time for more."

Mac chuckled. "Sounds like Jayne was more than just a little fling."

Gray crossed his arms. "Mac, she's a great employee, a good woman…she doesn't deserve this just because she dated me."

They looked at each other for a long spell, neither speaking. Finally Mac said, "This is a pretty big favor to ask, Gray."

"I'm not asking for a favor. I'm suggesting a solution to deal with a loose cannon supervisor that could cost this company a good, loyal employee. And if he's doing this bullshit, who knows what else he might screw up." Gray didn't back down from Mac's firm stare.

"You've got balls, Brandt," Mac said, grinning. "Well, Green has always been a bit of a problem. So you asked for it—he's your problem now. If anyone can turn him into an asset for Nixon, it's you. If not, keep me posted, and we'll make sure we cover all our bases when we let him go."

"Thank you, sir." Gray didn't realize how tense he'd been until his body relaxed.

"For what? This wasn't a favor, remember?"

Gray couldn't help but grin. "True."

Mac buzzed Scott. "Come in, Scott."

Scott appeared quickly, notebook in hand. "Yes?"

"Make two changes to the org chart and email it company-wide tomorrow. Kelly Sullivan is to be listed as supervisor over Customer Relations and Tony Green will show up under Gray as…Marketing Team Supervisor. Will that work, Gray?"

"Yeah, sure." Doesn't matter, I'll have that fucker out of this building within sixty days.

"Okay, got it," Scott said. "Anything else?"

"Yes, call Kelly Sullivan up here to meet with me now, followed by Tony Green in twenty minutes. And get me the head of R&D on the phone, Mike Gill."

"I'm on it," Scott said, leaving as fast as he'd come in.

"Well you just screwed up my afternoon, Brandt," Mac chuckled, standing up. They shook hands.

"Sorry for that."

"After all you've done for Nixon, I'm happy to do it."

Gray left the office, breezing past Scott.

"Wait," Scott said, covering the mouthpiece of his headset. Gray stopped and looked at him. "Way to go. You did a good thing today."

Gray shrugged. "I can't give her what she really wants, but this is something I can do." He started to walk away and then turned back. "You did a good thing, too. But I don't ever want her to know I was involved, okay?"

"Got it."

As he walked away, Gray looked at his watch. Quarter to four. He'd spent more than three hours dealing with this mess. Now he was even further behind on his project. He saw Kelly Sullivan getting off the elevator, and he winked at her as she headed to see Mac. She smiled broadly.

Gray was approaching his office when Katherine called out from across the hall, "Hey, stranger. You've been oddly unattached from your computer today."

"Yeah, I had some shit to deal with." He started into his office and turned back around. "Katherine, I need you to move to the empty office two doors down."

"Why?" she balked, leaning back in her chair. "Too hard seeing all of this across from you every day?" She pointed to her chest as a grin spread across her face.

He laughed. "Uh, no. But it is a lot to look at, no disputing that. I just have someone I'll need to babysit, which will be easier when I can see him from my office."

"Okay, shit. I have a lot of crap to move."

"Sorry. I'll buy you a drink as payback. How's that sound?"

"Sure. Not tonight, though—I've got plans."

"No, definitely not tonight. I'll be lucky if I get to go home at this rate." When he sat down at his desk, he felt exhausted. He picked up his smart phone, clicked on photos and scrolled through to find the one he was looking for. There it was.

It was Jayne and him, a picture they'd snapped of themselves at the top of Art Hill the day they went sledding. Her cheeks were rosy from the cold, her hair covered by the powder blue hood surrounding her. There was a twinkle in her eye that he'd never forget and a smile that got to him every time. Sure, he was used to women smiling at him. It was the norm. But hers did something different to him.

"For God's sake," he muttered to himself as he closed out the picture. "Quit being a sap."

He attacked his computer with his full attention and hunkered down for a long night. This was what mattered to him most. Not some ridiculous smile.

****

"So, kid, how are you holding up?" Karen asked Jayne as they dove into the desserts they'd ordered.

"Oh, I'm hanging in there." She knew the bags under her eyes told another story. "You know, you hear about people sleeping a lot when they're depressed."

"Yeah, I've heard that," Claudia nodded.

"Well, I'm depressed, but I can't sleep. It's like I have depression insomnia. So I've been watching old, bad reruns and crying my way through different Lifetime original movies. One night, in utter desperation, I almost bought a Shake Weight after watching the infomercial."

They all laughed, and as Jayne scooped up another mouthful of cherry-topped cheesecake, Claudia said, "Maybe we need to get you back out there."

"Where?"

"In the dating game."

Jayne shook her head vigorously back and forth.

"Jayne," Karen said, "I think Claudia may be right. It's time to get back on the horse."

"I can't. Not yet." The thought terrified her. She didn't know if she could suffer another broken heart so soon.

"Look at it this way. You said all along that Gray was too good to be true. Too hot, too charming—when he wanted to be—and he made good money. Well, maybe we just need to find you a regular, true guy."

"And where do you suppose I'll find him?"

"Well you're certainly not going to find him if you're not looking."

Jayne looked up from her cheesecake to see them both staring at her. "Now listen, I read something in Cosmo or somewhere that however long your relationship was, it will take you half that amount of time to really get over it."

"That's total bullshit," Karen muttered, polishing off her turtle brownie.

"I agree with Karen," Claudia said, a doubtful expression on her face.

"Well, if it is true, that means since I dated Gray for three months, I've got a month and a half to pine and mope."

"It's not attractive on you, trust me," Karen said, sitting back.

"What's that supposed to mean?"

"You're our eternal optimist. Our love puppy that believes everyone has a soul mate and everyone will find their true love. So when you're sulking and down on love, where the hell does that leave me?"

Jayne sighed. "Maybe there is no such thing as true love." She looked down. "Maybe I've been expecting too much. Remember Joe? He was a good guy, a nice guy, a great companion—"

"And you said kissing him felt like kissing your brother."

"But maybe that's as good as it gets. Maybe I'm setting my sights too high."

"No, you're not," Claudia said emphatically. "You just haven't found the right man yet. And you tend to waste too much time with the wrong ones, trying to make it work."

"I don't know..." Jayne shook her head. "I think I watched too many Disney movies over the years where the prince or hero swoops in and saves the girl. I've got a warped sense of reality, I'm too idealistic."

"No, you're not," Karen said. "And that's coming from me, the biggest cynic you know. Don't turn into me. Your heart believes in all of that—don't give up. If I can find happiness with someone, I know you can. Someone that's the whole package."

Jayne looked at her plate. "It's just that it's been a while since I got this hung up on a guy, and I'd forgotten how badly it hurts when things don't work out."

"Ah, that's the trick love plays on us," Karen said, sipping her glass of wine. "If you remembered all the bad stuff, no one in their right mind would give it another shot. It's like childbirth—they say women quickly forget the pain, how rough it gets. It's nature's way of making sure we fall in love and procreate."

"Speaking of procreation," Jayne said, desperate to change the subject, "is there a definite date for Project Knight Baby Making to begin?"

"Oh, no," Claudia said, beaming. "But he said summer. So I'm thinking, three or four months and it should be underway. Not that I'm counting."

"I can't wait to see you pregnant. What about you, Karen? Do you want kids?"

"Me?" Karen looked surprised. "You know, I don't know. I used to think no, but maybe."

"I can see you as a mom," Claudia said with a smile.

"You can? Really?" Karen seemed surprised but pleased. "I mean, don't get me wrong, I don't want to be that crazy Nineteen Kids and Counting broad. What an absolute masochist, right? But maybe one would be nice. I don't want to be responsible for screwing up a whole bunch of kids. So if I have an only child, I can focus all of my psychoses on just that one precious little kid."

They all laughed, and Jayne wondered if she would get the chance to be a mom. Here her friends had found what she always wanted, and she was the one still searching. Seeing them so happy made the hurt sting just a little more. She felt like a failure. Twenty-eight wasn't an old maid by any standard, but she thought by this point she'd have found the person she wanted to share her life with.

"Oh, I do have one bit of good news amid the despair of the rest of my life," Jayne said, her finger scooping up the last of the cherry sauce on her plate. "My prick of a supervisor, Tony, was transferred up to Marketing. Kelly's going to be back as my supervisor, effective tomorrow."

"Fantastic!" Claudia said. "What happened?"

"I have no idea. All I know is, today he left his office around four and when he came back down, he marched straight to my cubicle. So I was terrified I was going to get yelled at again, and I did, but all he said was, 'You conniving little bitch. I was right all along.'"

"What?" Karen said. "He talked to you like that?"

"Yeah, and I don't even know what the hell he was talking about. So I told him as much, and he just like smirked at me and said, 'You play dumb really well. I bet you're so damn happy you're getting your old supervisor back like you wanted.'"

"Well, I wonder what happened?"

"I don't know, I don't care, I'm just glad that's one less stressor on my plate."

"Yeah, that's great news," Claudia said.

"And I forgot to tell you guys who I ran into this past weekend."

"Who?" Claudia asked.

"Okay, it was Saturday, the day after I'd cried my eyes out all Valentine's Day. I wanted to get out, so I just threw on some workout clothes, put my hair in a ponytail, and left with no makeup on. I drove down to Main Street to go to that café, and guess who I saw?" She looked back and forth at her friends. "You'll never guess."

"Well then I'm not going to," Karen said.

"Gray's brother."

"No shit?" Karen asked.

"Did he see you?" Claudia asked.

"Yeah, saw me take four tries to parallel park," she said.

Karen laughed. "Real smooth, Jayne."

"Oh trust me, I know. So anyway, he bought me coffee and was sweet enough to listen to me dump on him about his brother's less-than-stellar behavior."

"So he's not a cad like Gray?"

"I don't think so…I mean, I don't know him that well, only met him twice over the holidays. But whenever I've seen him, he seems genuine, nice."

"Maybe he's adopted," Karen said, winking.

"Or Gray could be the adopted one," Claudia added.

"Well, they look a lot alike, so I'm pretty sure they're biological brothers."

Karen shook her head. "So there are two gods like Gray running around our city?"

"They look alike, but no, Josh isn't quite as drop-dead gorgeous as Gray. He's more just mild arrhythmia as opposed to heart attack good-looking."

"Oh, just arrhythmia?"

"Yeah." Jayne smiled. "He was pretty nice about the whole thing. Apologized on behalf of the Brandt family, and he completely knows what his brother is like. But I was mortified that he saw me with no makeup. Oh my God…you don't think he'd tell Gray how awful I looked, do you?"

Claudia yawned.

"Are we boring you?" Karen asked with a twinkle in her eye.

"No," she said, chuckling, "not at all. I've just been so worn out. I'm pretty much over the sinus infection, but it really kicked my butt. I've been exhausted. In fact, would you guys mind if I skip out on the movie? I'm afraid I'll just fall asleep."

"You do look a little tired," Jayne said. "Go home and get some rest. Have Sam give you one of his special massages."

"Oh, that sounds like a good idea."

"And with you gone," Karen said, "that means Jayne and I are free to talk about you all we want."

They shared a laugh, paid their bills, and Jayne hopped in Karen's car to head to the show, waving good-bye to Claudia as they pulled away.

****

Claudia was looking forward to nothing more than her plump down pillow when she walked in the door at home. She literally could hardly keep her eyes open as she kicked off her shoes.

Climbing the stairs, she thought she heard something from her bedroom. Sam's car wasn't out front, but sometimes he parked in back. Oh, it would be great to have him to snuggle with as she went to sleep. Stepping in the bedroom doorway, she froze. She couldn't move, couldn't speak. The shock of what she saw felt like a visual punch to the gut. Sam was home, all right.

And so was Rachel.

She was naked with Sam's face buried between her legs, and the shock on her face only matched Claudia's. As their eyes locked, neither spoke, and Rachel frantically shoved at Sam's head, trying to alert him to the unspoken scene he was oblivious to.

"What's the matter, babe?" he said, sitting up, his back to Claudia. "Didn't it feel good?" Rachel's eyes had grown to the size of Krispy Kreme glazed doughnuts, and Sam slowly turned around to see his wife.

"Oh! Uh…" He quickly threw a blanket over Rachel and stood up. "Claud—"

"You…you disgust me!" Claudia ran from the room, back down the stairs. Somehow, Sam managed to catch up after throwing on boxers and racing down after her.

"Claud!"

Claudia's mind had been frozen in time but was now running at a maddening pace. What is going on? How could this be happening? Rachel? Really? How long? Doesn't he love me? Ten years…ten years and this is what I get for putting my dreams on hold?

Sam grabbed her arm as she reached the bottom of the stairs.

"Let go of me, you goddamn bastard!" She was screaming at the top of her lungs.

He didn't let go, and said, "Please, can we talk?"

"You want to talk? Looks to me like you've been busy doing something else with your mouth." She glared at him, full of a fury she'd never known existed. "Oh, and your whore left a little stickiness on your face." He let go of her arm.

Just then, Rachel appeared at the top of the stairs, dressed this time. Her eyes were still huge, looking from Sam to Claudia and back to Sam.

"Well, you already fucked my husband and fucked me over. Did you want to stay and watch the fall out, too?"

"No, I—"

"Rachel, just go," Sam said quietly, his eyes never leaving Claudia.

"And to think I was trying to help you," Claudia said to Rachel, nearly spitting the words out as the girl approached them. "I felt bad that you didn't have a man. Well, joke's on me—you had my husband."

"I'm sorry, Claudia, I never meant for this to happen—"

"Shut up!" Claudia screamed. "Get out of my house."

She could see Rachel start crying as she ran out the front door. Claudia turned back to Sam.

"And you," she shook her head, trembling all over. The tears were starting. "You couldn't even be creative in who you cheated with. Your assistant? How uninspired. You make me sick—what a fucking cliché." He didn't say anything, just looked at her with the saddest expression she'd ever seen on his face. "Well, you wanted to talk…why don't you go wash your face and then talk?"

Silently, he left the hallway, and she walked into the hearth room and sat down on the couch. Well, I'm wide awake now. She felt like she was in some sad, depressing movie and she didn't want to be. She wished she had gotten a copy of the script sooner. She would have changed so much if she'd known where this was all headed.

"Claud, I'm sorry," Sam said, walking in the room wearing sweats and a freshly scrubbed face. She looked at him with different eyes now. Where once she saw only the man she loved, she now saw selfish, calculating eyes.

"Well you're a lawyer, let's hear your argument." She really wanted to hear him try to talk his way out of this one. Some ridiculous excuse or apology.

He sighed. "There's no argument. Just sadness, really."

"What?"

"Claud, you know I love you," he said, sitting next to her, and she unconsciously slid over a bit. "But who are we kidding? I was only twenty-one years old when I met you. You were only nineteen. Did you really think we could do this forever?"

He couldn't have shocked her more if he had punched her in the face. What was he saying? "Yes, yes I did. That was the whole point of our marriage vows...forever."

"It's unrealistic. We were so young. The odds were against us. Hell, nature is against us. We're not meant to be with one person for our entire lives. But I love you so much, and I'm so grateful to have spent all these years together. They've been the happiest of my life."

"Let me get this straight," she said, standing up and pacing. "Are you trying to tell me that I just caught you fucking your assistant, and instead of apologizing, you're telling me you're done with us?"

"Well I am sorry. I should have had this talk with you sooner—"

"Yes, you really fucking should have." She felt like she couldn't breathe. Like someone was sitting on her chest. "How long have you felt like this?"

"I don't know...maybe a couple of years now."

"A couple of years?" She was yelling and didn't even care. "How long have you been screwing your assistant?"

"A few months."

"Is she the only one?"

He looked at the floor. "There were a couple of others, just one time deals."

Suddenly it all made sense. "So all those nights and weekends when I thought you were toiling away, trying to make partner so we could start our family...?"

"Sometimes I was. Sometimes not." He looked into her eyes, and she did see love, but also resignation. He was done. It was over.

"But I don't understand...what went wrong? I thought we were happy."

"I am happy, Claud. You're a gorgeous woman, my best friend, a perfect wife."

"So what the hell are you saying?"

"I'm saying I don't want to spend the rest of my life with just one woman. I'm sorry I wasn't honest with you, but once we were in a few years, I didn't know what to do. I felt trapped. I wasn't sure I wanted to leave, and our marriage was so good...I just stayed. I thought my feelings would change over time, but they haven't." He stood up and touched her arm. "I had no business marrying you. But I loved you, and you're the most fabulous woman I've ever known, and I didn't want to lose you."

"But now you want to walk away?"

"We had a good run, Claud. But I can't be faithful to anyone. I don't want a family. I want to focus on my career, have fun."

"So you basically want to act like some adolescent boy?"

He shrugged his shoulders. "I don't think I'm good husband material. I'm sorry, Claud, I tried. I really tried. I'm sorry I let you down."

The tears which had stopped now came out at full force. "You made me wait all those years to start a family, and now I won't have one—"

"I was putting it off because I wasn't sure that's what I wanted. I didn't want to leave kids behind."

"But it's okay to leave me? You told me we could start trying this summer. Why on earth did you tease me that way?"

"I planned on being gone by then."

She smacked him. The action shocked both of them, and she pulled her hand away, trembling. "You are a coward. You've wasted years of my life because you didn't have the balls to tell me you wanted out."

"I was still weighing things in my mind—"

"Well, while you were weighing things, I was planning our future. I'm twenty-nine years old. I have to start over, and in five years my fertility starts to drop rapidly. I hate you!"

"You don't mean that."

"Oh, but I do. If you would have just been truthful, it would have hurt, but we wouldn't have wasted all these years—"

"These years weren't a waste. They've been filled with love and joy and great memories. All of that was real. Don't degrade what we had just because I want something different now."

"Don't you fucking tell me what to do. Ever. Again."

They stared at each other, and Claudia felt the overwhelming urge to vomit. The vision of him with Rachel, the impossible words he was saying...it was all too much.

"I think you should leave, Sam," she said quietly.

"I understand." He looked so sad, she almost felt bad for him. Which made her even angrier. He didn't deserve any pity, any compassion. But somewhere inside her, it was there. "I'm going to say one more thing, and then I'll leave you alone. I do love you. That's why I couldn't decide for so long what I wanted to do. You are an amazing woman and very hard to walk away from. So don't think for one second that you did something wrong or I didn't love you enough. Because that couldn't be farther from the truth. And the hardest thing of all is that I feel like I'm losing my wife and my best friend. I had hoped we could still be friends...but I see that's probably not possible."

Claudia chuckled. "Not even remotely."

He left the room, and Claudia sat back on the couch. She watched the pendulum on the grandfather clock in the corner, as it lulled her into a detached, calm state. A few minutes later Sam appeared, a bag over his shoulder.

"I'll be at the Courtyard Marriott if you need me. And if you're thinking that I'm a lawyer, so I'm going to use my buddies to screw you over—you're wrong. I wouldn't do that to you. You can have whatever you want, honestly. I don't want to fight you. You can have the house, furniture, whatever. Just pick a good attorney, I'll pay for it, and let me know what you want. It's yours."

She looked up at him, tears spilling from her eyes, wondering how this morning they had a future and now he was no longer hers. There was no more them. Just Sam. And Claudia. Separate.

"Okay," she nodded, wiping her eyes.

"You know, I'm sure you and Jayne and Karen all think that Gray is such an asshole, but he's a better man than me. He was honest about what he wants, what he's looking for. I owed you that, and for the rest of my life, I'll regret misleading you." He was crying now. "I will always, always love you, Claud. I hope you believe that, and I hope that, in time, maybe you'll remember that you loved me, too."

He held their stare for a moment longer and then turned to walk out the door. The fact was, she knew she did love him. Sure, the feelings were conflicted and tainted now, but there was still love. And she hated that even now, as he was walking away, she still loved him.

According to that poll Jayne talked about at dinner, it would take her five years to get over him.

At that moment, she was sure it would be a whole lifetime.

Chapter Ten

As Jayne waited for Josh at the entrance to the restaurant, she was glad she hadn't canceled their lunch. She'd considered it, after the horrible turn that Claudia's life had taken in the past few days. It was Saturday, and Jayne felt like she should spend the day with Claudia, but the three girls were getting together for a grown-up slumber party that night, so Claudia urged Jayne to not waste the entire day on her.

Jayne hadn't told them who she was meeting today. She wasn't sure why; maybe because it seemed a little weird, even to her. Hanging out with her ex-boyfriend's brother. But he'd really made her laugh when they ran into each other last weekend and was such a great listener that she was looking forward to seeing him again. Maybe he could make her laugh some more—because there certainly hadn't been much reason to for the last couple of weeks.

Never in her wildest dreams did Jayne think that Karen would be the only one of them in a relationship, and a solid one at that. She was thrilled for Karen but utterly disappointed for Claudia. And, yeah, for herself too. It looked like Gray wasn't the only guy hanging on through the holidays...unbeknownst to any of them, Sam had been biding his time, too. A poorly timed rendezvous meant they didn't make it to St. Patrick's Day, either. But almost.

Her mind was cluttered with those depressing thoughts when she felt a gentle tap on her shoulder.

"Waiting for someone?" asked a familiar, warm, masculine voice.

Jayne turned to see Josh smiling at her. "Actually, I am. This great guy with a rather unscrupulous younger brother."

"I'm afraid, miss, that would be me."

They embraced in a quick hug.

"You look great," he said to her as they approached the hostess to be seated.

"Oh, thanks," she said, smiling. She wasn't wearing anything special, just leggings, boots and a sweater. But this time she'd at least put some effort into it. "Of course anything would be an improvement over the way I looked last weekend when we ran into each other. No makeup, swollen eyes."

"You looked fine to me." As their eyes caught, she noticed that whereas his brother's eyes were that intense blue, Josh's were a vibrant green. Not so much hazel, they were an actual green. Rather striking.

They took their time ordering, chatting and laughing. After they finally decided and the waitress walked away, Josh said, "The patio here is really nice...I like coming here in the spring."

"Yeah, I ate on the patio once. Nice for people watching on Main Street. Do you come down here a lot?"

"Actually, almost daily. I live about five minutes down the road."

"Really? Do you live in one of the older homes with lots of character?"

He chuckled. "Character, yes. Lots of work to upkeep, yes. But I love it. It's small, but cozy and perfect for me. It's got a fenced in yard so Atticus can run around, full of big old trees. And I love being down here in the historic district. Always something going on—festivals, art shows, ice sculpture exhibits...it's all here. And the pub to person ratio is pretty high in this part of town." They both laughed.

"I've always thought it would be neat to live in an older home. I grew up in your typical suburban home...it was a nice house, still is, but nothing unique about it."

"Well I bought my place for a steal, and I've spent the past three years working on it, fixing it up. Eventually I'll finish. I just recently redid the whole kitchen—put in granite countertops, ceramic tile floors, new cabinets. I'm pretty proud of it."

"You should be. Did you do all the work yourself?"

"A lot of it. When it got too tricky, I'd call in a professional, but I did quite a bit. My dad helped, too. He's a really handy guy."

"My friends Claudia and Sam have an historic home…" Her voice trailed off, her thoughts turning to Claudia. There was no longer a Claudia and Sam. It broke her heart to think about it.

"Is something wrong?" His face was so expressive, and he had a way of really looking at you that Jayne found refreshing and open.

"Oh, it's just…one of my two best friends in the world, Claudia, caught her husband cheating on her a few days ago. And he left, it's over…and I'm just so upset about it."

"That's tough, trust me, I know." He nodded his head, but looked away, his eyes with a faraway look. "So did she actually walk in on them?"

Jayne sighed. "Yeah, she did. He was…you know…going down on the girl."

"Oh, shit. That must have been awful."

"It was, from what I hear. Did…did you walk in on your fiancée?"

He crossed his arms. "Not exactly. I had just finished the school day and was supposed to be working late with the book club, when I got a call from her sister. She was hysterical. I could hardly understand her. I finally made out that she was saying she thought her husband, Pat, was with Amber—my fiancée. At our house." Josh looked down at the table, playing with the wrapper from his straw. Wadding it up, unrolling it, wadding it up again. "So I cancelled book club, ran out of the building and raced over there. I parked down the street, so they wouldn't see my car, and quietly snuck in the back door." He looked right at Jayne. "They were done, but still lying naked in our bed together."

"I can't even imagine." She touched his hand, and he looked at her with grateful eyes.

"You know, you always think you know what you're going to do at a time like that, but when it hits you…you're not you. You go into some weird alternative reality mindset, and it's hard to even comprehend what you're seeing."

"So what did you do?"

He chuckled, looking embarrassed. "I guess I could say something macho like I beat him up. But really, I cried. I grabbed a suitcase from the basement, tears pouring the whole time like some teenage girl, and threw some clothes and essentials in the bag and left. I never said a word to her."

"Nothing?"

"Nothing." He sat back in his seat and sighed. "I think it's because I wasn't really shocked. Deep down, I knew. I didn't want to believe it, so I ignored all the signs. But when Ashley, her sister, called me that day…I knew in my gut that she was right. So instead of being mad or shocked, I was just heartbroken, honestly."

"Well, I'm sorry that happened to you." Jayne offered a smile. He smiled back.

"Thank you. It's been three years though, I've moved on, and I really am over her. Took a while, but I realized she wasn't worth the pain or regret. Onward and upward."

"That's what I'm working on right now with…well, you know. That kid you grew up with." She grinned.

"You seem a little less melancholy today than the last time I saw you." He gave her a lopsided grin.

"Yeah, well, when your friend's ten-year relationship falls apart—it kind of puts your three-month relationship into perspective."

"There's a lot to be said for perspective, that's for sure. But it doesn't mean that what you're feeling isn't real or valid. It is. But hopefully it will be easier to move past it."

"I'm sure it will be." The waitress brought their food. "Oh, wow, this looks delicious."

"It is," Josh said, nodding his head, food already in his mouth.

"So where do you like to go here on Main Street?"

"There are some great pubs with live music and good food that I frequent," he said, smiling. "But I also love shopping in all the stores around here."

"A man...likes shopping?"

"Oh great," Josh said, looking sheepish. "First I admitted that I cried like a baby and now I'm admitting that I like to shop. No wonder I'm single." They both laughed. "I also watch a lot of football, if that helps."

Jayne was still chuckling. "There's nothing wrong with a guy enjoying shopping. It's just not the norm."

"Well, you're not going to catch me browsing at the mall or shopping the sales racks or anything like that. But down here, there are so many unique little places—antiques shops, gift stores, art galleries, book stores, you name it. They know me by name at Main Street Books. I just love browsing down here—I never know what I might find. And I love giving gifts, so it's a great place to find just the perfect, special thing for whoever you're shopping for."

Jayne started laughing and couldn't stop. "I'm sorry," she said, covering her mouth, afraid she was going to spit her food out.

"What?" Josh asked, looking confused.

Still laughing but starting to calm down, she tried to explain. "Oh my God, just hearing you talk about finding the perfect thing and finding something special...wow. You couldn't be more different from your brother." She was shaking her head, still with the giggles.

"Oh shit, why am I afraid to hear what you're talking about?"

"The single worst gift I ever received from a man came from Gray."

"Yeah, Gray's not exactly a sentimental kind of guy." He smiled at Jayne, and for a moment, he looked a lot like Gray. But softer, fewer edges. "So what gem did he bestow on you?"

"A Best Buy gift card."

"You've got to be kidding me," Josh said, laughing now. "Was this for Christmas?"

"Yes. I mean, we'd been together for two months. I thought I rated more than a gift card."

Josh shrugged. "You would think. Was it at least for a good amount?"

"Fifty bucks."

"Oh, damn, that is bad. Every woman's dream…fifty dollars to spend at an electronics superstore."

"Well, his intention was because I love music so much, I could buy CDs. So he put a little thought into it."

"Little being the operative word there."

"Exactly. Especially since I don't own a CD player. I have an MP3 player and that's it."

"In two months he never noticed that?"

"Guess not."

"On behalf of the Brandt family, hell, on behalf of all men—I apologize for his lack of gift-giving talent."

"Wanna know what made it even worse?" She took a big gulp of iced tea.

"Probably not, but I'm game."

"I bought him a five-hundred-dollar watch."

"Holy shit," he muttered. Then he started laughing. "He must have looked like a complete ass."

"Yeah, well, he was gracious enough to say he couldn't accept it." She sighed. "That was my first really big sign that we were not on the same page when it came to our relationship. He bought me a gift card probably while he was there buying something else."

"He did pick up Mom and Dad's computer from Best Buy that we gave them for Christmas," Josh said quietly.

"Yeah, I figured it was something like that. I, on the other hand, shopped half a dozen stores to try to get the Movado watch I wanted for him at the best price."

"I'm sorry, Jayne."

"Nah, no big deal. Onward and upward, right?"

"Right." He winked at her as he dove back into his sandwich.

****

Despite the cold temperatures, they decided to hit the shops. Josh was going that night to his parents' thirty-fifth wedding anniversary party and wanted to find something meaningful to give them. He and Gray had gone in on a large spa gift certificate so they could have massages, sauna, the works. But unlike his brother, Josh wanted something a little more personal to give, too.

They'd been in and out of several stores, Josh making her laugh with his silliness and wisecracks. As he held up about the fifteenth thing he'd come across that he was considering, he asked, "What do you think of this?"

"Well, do you like it?" she asked, being non-committal on purpose. She didn't like it, but didn't want to disagree with him. They were having fun, and she didn't want it to end.

He cocked his head at her, grinning. "Why do you do that?"

"What?"

"You never say what you want, what you think."

"What are you talking about?" She scrunched up her face. I don't do that. Do I?

"When I asked if you wanted to get together, you wouldn't tell me what you liked or where you wanted to go. I picked the place. When I asked if you were ready to leave the restaurant a while ago, you said you'd leave whenever I was ready. And now instead of giving your opinion, you ask what mine is." He was looking very intently at her. "Jayne, I want to know what you think, not what you think I want to hear."

The intensity in his gaze became a bit uncomfortable, and she looked away. "I'm sorry. I didn't realize I was doing that." But she knew exactly why. Gray. She pretended to look at some figurines while she spoke, but really, she didn't want to look at Josh. "I think I know why. Recently, I got into the habit of just going along with whatever a certain guy wanted, because we always did what he wanted. Usually, he never even asked me. And if I disagreed, it was pretty much then okay, see you later, I've got other stuff to do." She looked at Josh out of the corner of her eyes. "So I hoped if I just complied, he would stay."

Josh put his hand on her shoulder. "You don't have to do that with me. I'm not him, Jayne. I want to know you—you can be yourself with me."

She looked up at him, and when their eyes met, they shared a connection it sometimes took years to feel with another person. His words, though small, nearly brought her to tears. She'd forgotten what it felt like to be valued, for her words and thoughts to matter. His face lit up with a smile, a special smile just for her. She felt it to her very soul.

"Well in that case, I don't like it," she said, pointing to the sculpture he was holding. "I don't think it says enough about the occasion."

"Okay," he grinned at her, promptly putting it down.

"What is the traditional gift for a thirty-fifth anniversary?"

"I have no idea."

"Well, hang on, let me look it up." She pulled out her phone and within a minute she said, "Jade. We need to find something made from jade or incorporating jade."

"Yes, ma'am."

"I mean, if that sounds good to you," she said with a grin.

"It sounds perfect."

"Or I know where you can get a deal on a Movado watch."

He laughed out loud. "I bet you do."

After checking a few more shops, they found the perfect gift. A sculpture of two lovebirds, beak to beak, carved from jade. The lines were delicate and it was sentimental without being too hokey.

As they walked back toward the restaurant, Jayne felt far different about Josh than she had when the day began. They had made a real connection, and she could tell he felt it too. What started out as just a lunch between friends felt more like a date. A date with an old friend, someone you already trust.

He stopped when they reached her car, a smile at his lips. "I'm so glad we did this today."

"Me too, Josh." She couldn't resist smiling back. His stunning green eyes set off by his dark, messy locks were captivating. No, he wasn't Gray.

He was better.

She realized he was the charming parts of Gray, minus the hard, cold, driven parts of him. He was sensitive and open and giving. Funny without being biting. Smart and well read. And his body, although smaller in frame, was almost as toned and built as his younger brother's. As they were shopping, she'd caught some glances when he didn't see, and she saw his firm stomach and broad shoulders, even through his fitted sweater and coat.

Oh crap. I can't seriously be falling for the brother of a man I've slept with, can I? That is so wrong. So messed up. And how do I know that, deep down, all Brandt men aren't selfish pricks?

"Well I hope you've gotten to know me enough to find out that all the men in the Brandt family aren't complete pricks."

Can he read my mind? She panicked inside.

"So far," she said, smiling. The palpable attraction between them was obvious to anyone passing by. The attraction was unspoken but acknowledged with the smile they shared.

"Well, you have your adult slumber party to attend, and I have to change into a suit and uncomfortable shoes." He chuckled as he explained, "I'm not a suit kind of guy, although I will say I look pretty damn nice in one."

I bet you do, she thought, images of him dressed up coming to mind. "So what kind of a guy are you?"

Arms outstretched, showing off his ensemble, he said, "What you see is what you get. I'm a jeans and sweater kind of guy."

"You wear it well, Mr. Brandt." She knew she was using her flirty voice now. She couldn't stop it.

"Why thank you, Ms. Asher." There was an awkward silence...they weren't sure how to part. "Well, have fun with the girls. And please tell your friend Claudia that it will get better. From someone that's been there, let her know that if she can just make it out of bed every morning, suddenly one morning she'll realize it's not so hard to get up anymore."

"I will let her know." Jayne didn't look away from his stare. "And you have fun doing that suit justice."

He chuckled, then reached forward and kissed her on the cheek. "Thanks for the great afternoon. Maybe I'll call you this week?"

"I look forward to it." She unlocked her car with her key fob, and Josh rushed to open the door for her. "Thanks."

He stayed on the sidewalk, in the cold, his hair growing messier in the wind. He waved as she pulled onto the street, and in her rearview mirror, she could still see him watching her as she drove away.

****

Josh knew exactly what he wanted to say to his brother. The more he got to know Jayne, the more he knew he wanted a shot with her. And the angrier he became at Gray for the way he'd treated her.

As he walked into the restaurant where they'd reserved a large private room for their parents' thirty-fifth wedding anniversary, Gray was easy to spot. Generally one of the tallest guys in the room, his was a commanding presence. Ever since Gray was born, there was something special about him. That "it" factor that could never be explained, but everyone sensed. He had a magnetic charm. No one was really immune to it completely, and certainly not Josh.

He remembered them being the best of friends when they were kids, but by their teenage years, their differences became more glaring. Gray was all about show, impressing, being seen. Josh was about close friends, sweats, and a good book. He remembered coming home after his first year of college and realizing that he hardly seemed to know

183

Gray any more. Since then, the gap between them seemed to grow wider.

Gray's loud laughter rang out at something one of their cousins had said to him, and then he saw Josh. He waved, displaying a broad smile for his brother. Some of the anger Josh was harboring seemed to dissipate. But it didn't completely go away.

Josh waved back and as he reached Gray, he asked, "Are Mom and Dad here yet?"

"No, not yet. So what's shakin', big bro? You look pissed."

"Well, I am kind of pissed. Come here." He was glad his parents hadn't arrived yet, so he could confront Gray before their party got underway. He didn't want to turn their night into being about an argument between their sons.

Wearing a quizzical expression on his face, Gray followed Josh to the corner of the room. "What's going on, Josh?"

"I ran into a friend of yours the other day," Josh said, his mind flashing to the image of Jayne crying on the sidewalk, the pain so raw on her face.

"Who?"

"Jayne."

Gray's face registered shock, and he swallowed. "So how is she?"

"Well, let's see, at the mention of your name, she started crying in the middle of the sidewalk on Main Street in St. Charles. So, I'd say, not great."

"Yeah, well, breakups can be hard."

"Especially when someone's not a part of your 'master plan,' huh?" Josh saw Gray's face harden.

"Listen, I don't know what she told you, but I was just honest with her. I was good to her."

"That's not what I heard—"

"Well then she's either got it wrong or she's got selective memory. What difference does it make to you?"

"Because the poor girl was distraught, and we had coffee, and she had an awful lot of stories to tell me that certainly didn't sound like you were good to her. I heard even more from her today—"

"Wait a minute. How did you see her again today?"

"We met for lunch."

"Oh, I get it now," Gray said, grinning. "She gave you a sob story about how awful I was to her, so you decided you'd be a shoulder to cry on so you can get my sloppy seconds, huh?"

Josh exploded with rage, shoving Gray up against the wall, pinning his chest. "Fuck you, Gray! Jayne is nobody's sloppy seconds." Everyone turned to stare at them.

Gray said quietly, through clenched teeth, "Hold on, Joe Frazier. If this is what you want to do, you know I'm much bigger and much stronger than you. If you want to fight, I'll fight, but I'll win."

Pushing Gray harder up against the wall, Josh said, "But I'm really fucking pissed, and that counts for something."

"What are you boys doing?" Their mother's voice rang out as she and their dad rushed over from the doorway.

"Josh, let go," Bob Brandt said, tugging on his son. He was a big guy himself, still in great shape.

"What's wrong?" Sara asked, and Josh felt bad about the worry he heard in his mom's voice. He let Gray go.

"Your son is an asshole that treats women like shit, that's what's wrong," Josh said, glaring at his brother.

"Is someone going to tell me what's going on?" Sara asked, looking from Gray to Josh.

"It's about Jayne," Gray said, adjusting his blazer. "We broke up and now Josh seems to be her protector or something."

Sara and Bob looked at Josh. "Mom, Dad, he was a complete jerk to her. I ran into her last week and heard an earful about the things he did and said."

"And now I think Josh has his eye on her, because they met for lunch today."

"I did meet her for lunch—she's a great girl," Josh defended himself. "And then ladies' man here, Gray, said I was going after his sloppy seconds."

"Oh, Gray," Sara said, looking with such disappointment at her youngest son. "That's such a degrading thing to say."

"Well, Mom, out of all the women out there, why can't he find someone else?"

"I didn't go after her, Gray," Josh said, shaking his head. "I just ran into her."

"And then asked her out for lunch."

"So what are you saying? Are you saying you don't want me to pursue anything with her?"

The two brothers stared at each other. Josh's palms began to sweat; he'd never thought Gray would care. What would he do if Gray said he didn't want Josh to see her?

"Let's step outside for a minute, okay?" Gray said, looking at Josh. His eyes looked intense.

"Mom, Dad, I'm sorry," Josh said.

"We'll be right back," Gray said as he preceded Josh out of the room and into the hallway. "So are you done with acting like you're going to kick my ass?"

"I think so," Josh said, having calmed down a bit.

"I'm sorry about the seconds comment, okay?"

"Okay." Josh crossed his arms.

"So here's the thing." Gray looked directly in Josh's eyes. "I don't know what she told you, but I'm not a complete asshole. I was always honest with her about where things stood. I told her I couldn't give her any more than I was, I told her I have huge ambitions and I couldn't be distracted from that." Josh could usually read Gray pretty well; he seemed sincere. "But I have to say, I've been with a lot of women, and Jayne was the first one that made me think—every now and then—that maybe I should rethink the whole ambition thing."

"I can see how Jayne could do that to a guy."

"But at the end of the day, I am who I am. I know that. And as I could see her falling more and more for me, and

186

wanting more from me—I had to pull back. I couldn't tease her or give her the wrong idea. Do you know how many nights I wanted to just fall asleep in her arms? But that would have just made those big doe eyes look at me with even more emotion. There were a few moments I almost caved, gave in to my feelings, but I couldn't play her like that. I didn't play her like that." Gray looked down, sighing. "So I always left right after, and never told her I loved her, and tried to see her a little less when it was obvious where her head was."

"Did you love her?"

Gray looked away for a minute. "What do I know, Josh? I think maybe I did. She really means something to me. She's great, she's sexy…but I love my career more. I would have just broken her heart over and over again."

Neither of them spoke, they just stood facing each other, arms crossed. Finally Josh dropped his arms and said, "So if you don't want me to date her, I won't." Please say I can, he screamed inside. Being with Jayne earlier that day was the first time in years that Josh felt like there might really be a woman out there for him.

Gray looked at Josh, with more caring than Josh remembered seeing on his face in a long time. There seemed to be a trace of sadness, too. "Josh…Jayne deserves someone who can put her first. Who cares more about her than his career or his ambition." He patted Josh on the arm. "You're that kind of guy. I'm not gonna say I'm thrilled about the thought of you dating her, but I know you'll treat her right and give her what she's looking for. So yeah, I'll be okay with it."

Josh didn't realize how tense he'd become until he felt his whole body relax. "Are you sure? I mean, I really feel something with her, for the first time in years. But you're my brother, and that's more important."

"Really?" Gray asked, looking pleased.

"Really." Josh hoped Gray wasn't about to change his mind.

"Well that means a lot to me. Come here." Gray opened his arms, and they embraced in a quick hug. "She's all yours, big brother. That is, if she wants you."

"I might not be Gray the Magnificent, but I'm no slouch," Josh said, laughing.

"No, you're definitely no slouch," Gray said as they headed back into the ballroom. "Actually, the more I think about it, you two are probably a good fit for each other. And she likes your big beast of a dog."

"Everyone likes Atticus." Josh grinned. "Except you."

As they walked in together, all heads turned their way, questioning looks on their faces.

"It's all good, folks," Gray said, flashing his most charming smile. "We just wanted to remind our parents, on the occasion of their thirty-fifth wedding anniversary, that their parenting duties are never done. You never know when you might have to break up a fight between the Brandt brothers." Everyone laughed, and Josh looked at his brother with admiration. Something he didn't do a lot, but tonight he was proud of Gray.

He was comforted to learn that although Gray might not have gone about it the right way, his little brother had actually tried to be careful with Jayne's heart. He wasn't as much of an asshole as Josh had believed him to be. But he also knew that Gray could never truly love someone like Josh could. He just didn't have it in him.

As they walked toward their parents' table at the head of the room, Josh whispered to Gray, "By the way, you can't ever tell a woman she needs breast augmentation. Especially right after you've had sex with her."

Gray grinned. "Shit, she really did tell you everything, didn't she?"

"Well, you know what they say—hell hath no fury like a woman scorned."

"True." Gray shrugged. "Maybe when you look like me, you get used to saying whatever you want and getting away with it."

"It's such a rough life, looking like a movie star, huh?" Josh elbowed his brother.

"Yeah, but I'm not complaining."

They reached their parents' table and sat down.

"So are you boys done fighting?" Sara asked, searching both of their faces.

"Yeah, Mom, I'm really sorry," Josh said, kissing her cheek. "This is your night."

"It's fine," she said, smiling at him. "All's well that ends well."

"It would be nice, though," Bob said, looking with disapproval at his boys, "if my sons wouldn't still be having physical fights with each other now that they're grown men."

"Sorry, Dad," Gray said.

"Well," Sara said, "I always thought that by the time we'd been married for thirty-five years, I would have some grandchildren. So I hope all this fighting over Jayne results in some babies for me to cuddle." She looked with hope at her sons.

"And that is why I'm stepping aside," Gray said, shaking his head with a grin.

I can only hope I'm that lucky, Josh thought to himself as he smiled at his mom.

****

They were all polishing their toenails and snacking on popcorn and chips with queso dip. There was wine, and for Jayne's benefit, a bottle of blackberry wine. Karen teased her about the ultra-sweet wine but was thoughtful enough to have bought it for her.

Poor Claudia was trying to keep a stiff upper lip but kept having moments where she'd break down. It was unsettling for Jayne to see her that way; Claudia was everyone's rock. Seeing her rock reduced to a crying mess made Jayne feel helpless. Claudia had relayed the story in detail, and of course Karen and Jayne had weighed in.

"I can't believe he was so fucking calm about it," Karen said, shaking her head. "It's obvious that son of a bitch had been planning it for a while."

Jayne still had trouble reconciling Sam as a bad guy. "Well, I know what he did was awful, unforgivable. But it's not like he said he didn't love you. In fact, he told you just the opposite. It's just that he realized he doesn't want to be married." Jayne looked at Claudia, and her tear-stained face. "He didn't reject you. He still loves you. It's just marriage that he's rejecting."

"But he was married to me," Claudia said with obvious hurt.

"Claud, I know, I'm not trying at all to diminish what he did or how this completely changes your life. I'm just saying that it has nothing to do with you. He's screwed up, that's all. So you can walk away knowing you gave your all to the relationship, you did good. He just decided he wants to be an immature whore."

Claudia giggled, and Karen joined in. Soon they were all laughing, and Karen held up her glass in a toast. "To us, friends that will never screw around on each other!"

They all cheered, drank, and went back to their pedicures.

It was only ten-thirty, but as they popped in one of their collective favorites, When Harry Met Sally, Claudia was already yawning.

"You know, I doubt if I'll make it through the movie," she said, rubbing her eyes. "Some slumber party, huh? I'm so freakin' old."

"Watch it, sister," Karen said, jabbing her with her elbow. "I'm the same age. Watch who you're calling old."

"Ha. You're both older than me," Jayne said, laughing.

"By one year. And you're gonna hold that over our heads forever, aren't you?"

"Pretty much."

They were all snuggled together on Claudia's bed, watching the flat screen in front of them. It didn't take long before Claudia's quiet snoring began while Karen and Jayne continued to watch and eat and talk.

As the movie was coming to a close, Jayne grew emotional at the part when Harry runs in the rain on New Year's Eve to tell Sally how he really feels about her. Tears filled Jayne's eyes, and Karen handed her the box of Kleenex, causing them both to laugh.

"You know that shit doesn't really happen, right?" Karen said, staring at Jayne. "I mean, has the past two weeks taught you nothing? Sam's an asshole, Gray's an asshole…for all I know, Rick's an asshole and I just don't know it yet. But it seems to me that love is a giant fucking crapshoot. And quite frankly, the odds suck."

"Well that's a little harsh." Jayne blew her nose.

"Just realistic."

"I still believe in love. I still believe there are good men and that I will find one of them. I think you already have one. And I think that someday, Claudia will find one, too."

"You seem pretty optimistic for a girl who just had her heart broken."

"You said the other night that I'm an eternal optimist and it was scary for you that I wasn't being so optimistic. Now you're complaining because I have hope?"

Karen looked at Jayne with distrust. "No, there's more to it than that. You're holding out on me. Spill."

Jayne wasn't sure if she should. But she had to. It was Karen, after all. "I kinda met somebody." She grinned, a nervous, uh-oh-you-caught-me grin.

"Oh Christ. Here we go."

"It gets better. Or maybe worse." Jayne sighed. "It depends how you look at it."

"Okay, curiosity piqued. So?" Karen looked like a tiger about to pounce on her prey.

"It's Josh Brandt." A look of utter alarm clouded Karen's face. "Yes, Gray's brother."

"No!" She said it so loudly that Claudia stirred, and they both looked at her. Snoring soon resumed. Claudia was in between them, so Karen climbed over her to sit next to Jayne. "You're not serious, are you?"

"Well, I mean, we're not dating yet or anything—"

"Yet? You mean you're actually considering it?"

"He is nothing like Gray. Sure, they share DNA, and look similar...but that's where it ends."

"Jayne, there are so many guys out there...why him?"

"Well, I certainly wasn't looking. I did not want to jump back in, like you suggested." Jayne shrugged her shoulders. "But he invited me to lunch, and it started out just friendly but then...I don't know. There was this crazy chemistry, pheromones flying...I could tell he sensed it too."

"Please tell me he's not a right-wing snob like Gray."

"Oh, God, he's not a snob at all. He's a schoolteacher. Messy hair, casual, fun."

"He already sounds a hell of a lot better than Gray." Karen grabbed Jayne's hands. "But...can you imagine having sex with him after having had sex with his brother? I mean, think this through. The comparisons in everything will be inevitable. And Gray would be hard for anyone to stack up to, physically."

"On paper, Gray was fantastic. But on an emotional level...there was no intimacy. Not much, anyway. And he was obviously insensitive."

"What if Josh is the same way? What if it's how they were raised?"

"In one coffee date and one lunch, Josh has shown me more compassion and sensitivity than Gray ever did." Jayne's face lit up. "He's pretty amazing."

"Oh, Jayne..." Karen shook her head, but smiled at her friend. "You're impossible. You know that, right?"

"Yeah." She chuckled. "But who knows? Maybe even though there was a spark, maybe he'll think it would be too weird to date one of his brother's exes."

"Maybe. So how was it left?"

"He said he might call me this week. Then I saw him standing on the sidewalk, still watching me drive away two blocks down the street."

"Then he's in. Just please promise me I'll like this Brandt. Because none of us liked the last one."

"I promise."

Chapter Eleven

Jayne was driving home from Claudia's slumber party the next morning when her phone rang. Glancing at it, the name that flashed on the screen said, Brandt, Joshua.

"Good morning," she answered, a grin spreading across her face.

"Good morning, Jayne," he said, and she could hear the smile in his voice, too. "Did I call too early? Are you still having pillow fights and talking about boys?"

"No, we did all that last night. I'm on my way home."

"Wish I could have been a fly on those walls."

"Actually, it was more like pedicures, When Harry Met Sally, and blackberry wine."

"Oh, so you're into the hard liquor, eh?" He laughed.

"You caught me. So how was the anniversary party?"

"It was...interesting. But good, it was touching and memorable, everything it should have been. It's quite an accomplishment, thirty-five years...don't hear that a lot anymore."

"No, you really don't. My parents are at thirty-three years, though, so maybe there's hope for the rest of us."

"Maybe." He cleared his throat. "I know it's really last minute, but I thought I'd see if you had plans today."

"Just laundry and hanging around. Why?"

"Well, a friend of mine from work does photography and has an exhibit at a gallery. I've been meaning to go by and see it but haven't yet, and today is the last day. I'm going to go, and I wondered if you might want to join me."

"Sure," she said, trying not to sound too enthusiastic but pretty sure she was failing, "that would be great."

"Well I'm glad I asked," Josh said, and she noticed that although his voice was very similar to Gray's, his cadence and tone were much different. Gray always spoke quickly and often sounded preoccupied, like he was probably staring at his laptop while talking. Josh, however, spoke at a slower, more deliberate pace. And always sounded as if you had his undivided attention. "I can pick you up. Let's see…it's eleven o'clock now…would two o'clock be okay?"

"Perfect." She gave him directions to her place and as they hung up, she pulled into her condo complex. The familiar tingling in her stomach, the one that always seemed to accompany a first date, began.

Of course, he hadn't said it was a date, but she was sure it was. A date with Gray's brother. Here we go, she thought to herself as she climbed out of her car, grinning ear to ear.

****

When Jayne opened her door and saw the lopsided grin, striking green eyes, and untamed dark locks standing before her, she knew she was done for. She certainly hoped this was a date, because she desperately wanted it to be.

"Hello," he said, and the mere sound of his voice started the tingling in her stomach.

"Hi," she said, grinning back at him. "I just need to grab my coat."

"Would you mind if I use your restroom? Too much coffee this morning."

"Sure." She ushered him in. "Down the hall, first door on the right."

She threw on her coat and tossed a scarf around her neck.

"Hey, did you know your faucet is dripping?" he asked, coming out of the bathroom.

"Yeah, it's been doing that for months."

"Do you have any tools?"

"Yeah…" She walked into the kitchen and he followed. She opened up her junk drawer that had some small tools scattered about, and he grabbed a couple of them.

"I'll be right back," he said, heading for the bathroom.

Jayne was in shock. She sat on the couch, and a couple of minutes later, Josh came walking in holding a small washer.

"We'll pick one of these up on our way home. It'll just take a couple of minutes to put it in."

"Really? And then no more drip, drip, drip?"

"No more," he said with a chuckle.

"You are officially my hero, Josh Brandt." She threw her arms around him in a big hug.

"Well in that case, what else needs fixing around here? If I get that for a leaky faucet, I'd love to see what I'd get for some drywall patching or electrical work."

They both laughed as she pulled away. "I'll be sure and make a list."

"Nice place, by the way," he said, looking around. "It's got your personality."

"Is that a good thing?"

"There's never anything wrong with warm and cheerful." They shared a smile. "Ready for the gallery, Madame?" he asked in a highbrow British accent.

I'm ready to go anywhere with you. "Indeed, sir." They headed out the door.

"Your chariot awaits." He motioned to his car. Resuming his normal voice, he said, "Otherwise known as a Toyota RAV4. Sorry, I know it may be a step down from what you're used to, but there's no BMW on my budget."

"Oh, please, I drive a Honda Accord. This is just my speed." I'm thinking you're just my speed, too. They climbed in the car. "I just figured it out!"

"What?" he asked with a laugh, smiling at her.

"Your hair. It kept reminding me of something, and I just figured it out. McDreamy—Patrick Dempsey. Your hair is a lot like his."

"Is that good or bad?"

"Oh, good. Very good. You're rocking that look."

"Well, thank you," he said with a chuckle as he backed out.

Twenty minutes and plenty of great conversation later, they were walking into the art gallery. As they walked in, Josh placed his hand on the small of her back.

The exhibit was stunning. Most of it was in black and white, but some photographs were in color. His friend had obvious talent. Strolling through the gallery with Josh just felt right. She felt like herself, like she didn't have to watch what she said or worry that her actions might make him want to leave. She knew he wanted to be there with her. His smile, his attentiveness, his glances when he thought she wasn't looking—all these things told her so. For the first time in a long time, she felt like the interesting, fun, strong woman she knew she was.

As they walked in front of a large color print, it took her breath away. Entitled simply "Teamwork," it was quiet but powerful. It portrayed a snowy scene in a field with the sun starting to set. Brilliant oranges and intense pinks lit up the sky in a glorious display. The remaining rays of sun illuminated a man in profile with a teenage boy putting the head on a snowman. Behind them was an empty wheelchair, explaining why the smiling teenage boy was riding piggyback on the man's broad back. The man's shaggy locks were dark against the snowy background.

"It's you," she whispered, tearing her eyes from the photo and looking at Josh. He only nodded, looking moved and unable to speak. "Did you know?"

"No," he said, swallowing. "She told me I was in one of the pictures, but she's always wandering around with her camera, so I had no idea she'd taken this one."

"It's beautiful."

"Yeah, she's a really great photographer." He looked at Jayne, and she could see his eyes were a bit misty as he smiled with tenderness at her.

"Who's the boy?"

"He's one of my students, Trey. It was our first day back from a snow day, and everyone was talking about sledding and messing around in the snow. I asked him what he did on his day off, and he said he just stayed inside playing video games. After talking a little bit, it came up that he'd never made a snowman. I'm not certain what his disability is, but his parents are apparently pretty over-protective. So I promised him that after school, I'd take him out to build a snowman." Josh wiped his eyes. "I mean, fifteen years old and never made a snowman. I had to do something about that. So we went back out in the field behind the school. He helped me get the snowballs started and then when they got too big, I'd take them, finish and roll them into place. When it came time for the head, he made it and I threw him on my back so he could put it on the snowman himself."

"You did a good thing." Jayne knew then that he was exactly the kind of guy she'd been waiting for. Sensitive, caring, unselfish—not always easy to find. Josh just shrugged, and she could tell he didn't like the spotlight. He moved to the next print, then grabbed her hand and pulled her away to the corner of the room.

"Jayne, I can't hold this in anymore." He stared into her eyes, his gaze intense. "Last night when I saw Gray, I lit into him. I was so angry with the way he treated you, the way he broke you down. We got into a fight—"

"Like, a physical fight?"

"I might have shoved him up against a wall and pinned him there for a minute," Josh said sheepishly. "But I also found out something. I know he completely went about it the wrong way, but I think he actually really cared for you. All the hopping out of bed right after...sex..." He looked uncomfortable as he said it. "And the cheap gift and dwindling time spent together...it was all his way of trying to protect you. I think he fell for you, but his ambitions are so much bigger than his heart, unfortunately for him. And he could see that you had fallen for him, and he was afraid to hurt you even more, so he pulled away."

"So what are you saying?" Jayne looked right into those green eyes, so confused. She thought Josh wanted her...so why was he defending Gray?

"I'm saying that my brother, although a narcissistic, selfish guy, didn't mean to hurt you. He actually was trying to keep you from getting too attached."

"Why are you telling me this?"

"Because…because I wanted you to know the whole truth before I tell you this." He took both her hands in his. "I know you feel so hurt and burned by my brother. And I don't know if you can ever imagine giving another Brandt guy a shot, but I would love nothing more than to be with you. You make me feel, for the first time in years, like I could maybe fall in love again. The first time I ever met you, you took my breath away, and I just knew Gray would screw up what was clearly the best thing that ever happened to him. Well, he did. And unless you think it's too bizarre to date the brother of your ex, or you just don't find me attractive—I want a chance with you."

Josh exhaled loudly, with obvious relief to have just said it. Then worry crept onto his face. Jayne squeezed his hands, and her smile was so broad it nearly hurt.

"I was hoping you'd want that, because that's what I want, too."

Josh put his hands on the sides of her face and kissed her. A kiss full of joy, full of passion. The chemistry that Jayne had sensed was alive and well.

"Ahem," said another patron, shooting them a disapproving glare.

Jayne felt her cheeks flush, and Josh said, "Let's get out of here."

When they hit the pavement of the sidewalk outside, he embraced her and they kissed again. Longer this time, finally pulling away just to come up for air.

"So," he said, looking worried again, "does what I told you, about Gray maybe not being as careless as you thought…does that change anything for you? The way you feel about him?"

"If you're asking if that makes me want to be with him, no. But there is some comfort in knowing that I meant something to him, even if it wasn't what I wanted. I know now that he is absolutely not the right person for me."

"And the whole dating brothers thing…that doesn't scare you away?"

"Well, I'd rather it wasn't that way," she admitted, sighing, "but I'm not about to pass on my dream man because of a technicality like that."

"I'm your dream man?" His smile was adorable.

"Well…yeah." She felt her cheeks grow warm. "Hot, smart, funny, sensitive. Check, check, check, check. You've got it all."

He chuckled. "If you say so."

"Does it…does it bother you, knowing I was…intimate with your brother?"

"Yeah, it really fucking bothers me." He held her tighter. "Just that he's been with you that way…yeah, I hate it. But like you said, it's not enough to scare me away. You're the whole package, Jayne."

"Do you think your parents…how do you think they'll feel about it?" She looked down. "I couldn't stand the thought of them thinking I was…some kind of loose girl—"

"Stop it, okay?" He touched her cheek. "My mom raved about you after she met you. And she loves Gray, but she knows who he is. We all knew it wouldn't last because he doesn't want any relationship to last. But she saw enough of you that after we got into it last night, she said she hoped that all this fighting over you resulted in some grandchildren for her." Josh winked at Jayne, and she laughed.

"So, Josh," she swallowed, her brows furrowed, "if we're really going to do this…I need to know you're not going to play games. I mean, I know from what you said, Gray was well intentioned, but I need someone that's not going to hold back. I don't want to do this unless I'm going to get all of you." She smiled, full of the strength that grows from adversity. "If I learned nothing else from being with Gray, it's that I deserve more. I deserve better. And I won't settle for less."

"I would never ask you to." He kissed her cheek. "But being with me will be nothing like being with him. If you like his lifestyle, I'm sorry, that's not me. I'm the kind of guy that thinks a fun night is crawling into bed with a good book, not a stack of market analysis reports. I'm not a rich guy and won't ever be, but I love what I do. I'm passionate about being a teacher." He kissed her gently. "I'm passionate about you."

"Well that will be a refreshing change," she said, initiating their kiss this time. "You know, I'm actually glad I dated Gray."

"Really? After everything?"

"Yeah, after everything. Because that's how I met you."

Josh took her hand, kissed it, and as both of them beamed with delirious smiles, he said, "I need to go fix that faucet."

But Jayne knew he was fixing so much more.

****

Maybe all the recent turmoil in Claudia and Jayne's love lives was making Karen paranoid. But now that she was settling in good with Rick, and she actually, for the first time in her life, could see a future with someone…she had the feeling he was hiding something.

He was normally such an open book, so transparent, no agenda. But the last couple of weeks, she'd noticed a couple of phone calls that seemed cryptic or hushed. And he worked late two nights, which was very unusual for him. Then a few times there seemed to be something different in his eyes, but she couldn't quite put her finger on it.

She was in the kitchen, making a big bowl of soup to help warm them from the cold February chill. February was her least favorite month in St. Louis. Still bitingly cold, with no hint yet of the impending spring. It was late in the month and after an entire season of cold and ice and snow—she was done with it. Rick was the only warmth she had through the cold winter.

And what was going on with him?

She'd be damned if she'd put up with less than full disclosure. If he was cheating on her, that was it. She'd be done with men other than to use them and abuse them. All this time, she believed he was the one man that could convince her they weren't all selfish and living by their dicks like her father. So if he betrayed her—

Well, she didn't know what she would do.

He was in the bedroom, changing the sheets on their bed. What guy does the laundry and changes the sheets? My guy. What a catch. She was about to put a loaf of Italian bread in the oven when she heard his phone ring, and his hushed voice say, "Hello?"

Feeling completely ashamed of herself, she snuck over to the bedroom anyway, standing just outside of his line of sight. She strained to hear him; it was obvious he was trying to keep his voice down.

"Tonight? Okay, yeah, I don't want to wait any longer if I don't have to. I just didn't think you'd be available today." He sounded excited. "No, she doesn't know… It's not easy hiding it from her, but it's definitely worth it… I can't wait to see you, sweetie. I'll come up with an excuse and be there as soon as I can. Please wait for me."

Oh my God. He's cheating on me. After I finally made myself vulnerable, this is what I get. Fuck it, I'll move in with Claudia and become a lesbian. I'm so done with men.

He walked out of the bedroom, and the sight of him both sickened and titillated her. Why does he have to look so damn sexy? Why did he make me love him if he was just going to do this? He looked startled to see her standing so close to the bedroom.

"Hey, baby," he said, smiling at her. "Whatcha doin'?"

"Listening to you arrange your booty call, apparently." She stared at him with angry, hurt eyes. She didn't know if she wanted to punch him or cry.

"You heard that?" Fear and worry registered on his face. "Karen, it's not what you think—"

"Oh, really? How stupid do you think I am, Rick?"

"Karen, I know you're not stupid, but you're just way off base. Tell you what, this is not the way I wanted to do this, but considering your history and what just happened with Claudia…I want you to come with me. I have to show you something."

"What?" Karen couldn't decide if she should be relieved or not. There was no other way that conversation could have been interpreted. Did he want a threesome? Not a chance in hell.

"Come on, grab your coat and let's go. And I promise, we're not going to see Christmas lights this time."

Completely baffled, she put on her coat and took the hand that he offered as they walked out the door. Please be wrong, please be wrong, was her internal mantra.

As Rick steered his Jeep onto the highway, he looked over at Karen. "Please stop looking like that. I love you. You know that." He grabbed her hand. "I am not your dad, I am not Sam." He chuckled. "And if I was, do you think I'd really bring you along?"

Karen laughed, although her heart was still racing. "Well what is going on? You've been secretive lately. I know you've been hiding something from me."

"You're right. I'm a terrible liar—let that be of comfort to you." His dark eyes twinkled at her. "You'll see in a bit. But I wish you weren't so damn inquisitive…I can never surprise you."

He turned on some music, and as a Barenaked Ladies song coursed through his speakers, her mind was as numb as her butt on the cold seat. She didn't know what to think.

As they pulled off the highway, he said, "Now since you've ruined my surprise, at least let me have a little fun. We're almost there, but you need to close your eyes now."

"What?"

"Dammit, Karen, help me out here. Humor me and close your eyes."

Shooting him an irritated look, she complied.

"No peeking, either. I know how you are."

She sighed and crossed her arms. "Since you know how I am, you know that I hate this."

He laughed. "Well if you weren't so damn distrusting and nosy, we wouldn't be doing this. Trust me, I had something completely different planned. But now we're onto Plan B, and that means no peeking."

The Jeep stopped and he said, "Wait there, don't look, I'm coming around to get you."

He helped her inside…where, she didn't know.

"Hello, Rick," a woman's voice said, sounding surprised.

"I know you weren't expecting me to bring Karen, but she overheard me so I had to improvise. Her eyes are shut."

"Well then, follow me."

They walked through a doorway and Rick said, "Sit here and please, don't open your eyes yet. I'll be back in thirty seconds."

Karen sat there, feeling like a complete idiot with her eyes shut and some strange woman with her boyfriend. This better be good.

Very soon, Rick said, "Almost time to open your eyes." She heard him moving around, he grabbed her hand and said, "You can open them."

He was down on one knee in front of her, in someone's office. On the wall was the logo of a local jeweler. Her heart seemed to stop beating.

"Karen, I know you're not the sentimental type, but I have to tell you that I knew when I met you that you were meant for me. I'm sure you're thinking that's complete bullshit, but I knew. I could feel it." He smiled at her, his eyes more tender than she'd ever seen. "That's why I waited until you were ready to open your heart to me. I've been with you for almost two years, but I've only had all of you for a couple of months. I want nothing more than to spend the rest of my life giving you the love and the security and the happiness that you deserve. Karen, now that you know how it feels to truly give yourself to someone—I want that someone to be me, forever. You're the most amazing woman I've ever known. Will you marry me?"

He opened up the ring box he held in his hand, to display the most unique, beautiful engagement ring she had ever seen.

For once in her life, she didn't have a smart-ass comment or snide remark. All she had was love and tears in her eyes.

"Of course I'll marry you," she said, crying. She threw her arms around him, and they kissed, her tears dampening his face.

"All the secrecy lately was about this ring. I was working with Chelsea to design this. You remember Chelsea, my old friend from high school?" Chelsea peeked in, waving.

"Hi, Karen. Congratulations!"

"Thank you," she said, embarrassed to be crying in front of someone. She wiped her eyes.

"I know a thing or two about design," he said, grinning, "so this is mainly my creation, but Chelsea gave a lot of input to really make it work. I didn't think it would be ready for a couple of days, and I was going to take you out for a nice dinner and propose to you properly. But you kind of screwed that up, kid."

Karen laughed. "I'm sorry, I was so worried—"

"I know, baby, that's why I didn't want to leave you with doubts in your mind."

"But you don't deserve that. I should have trusted you—"

"It's okay. You've got half a lifetime's worth of distrust in men to rebuild. But that's all right, because we're going to spend our lives together."

"I can't believe it," she said as he slipped the ring on her finger. "It's the most beautiful ring I've ever seen."

"Well, you're no ordinary woman, Karen. It had to be an extraordinary ring."

****

It was midway through the workweek, and Jayne was excited as she left work because she was meeting Josh for a quick bite. They hadn't seen each other since Sunday but had talked and texted every day. This was the first night they had time to see each other, but it would be brief because he had promised one of his colleagues, the school's drama teacher, that he would supervise the box office and ushers at that night's showing of Twelve Angry Jurors. So it would be a quick meal before he went back to school. He had promised her a proper date on Saturday, though—nice dinner out and everything. She hoped everything meant, well...everything.

As she climbed into her car, her phone rang. A picture of her mom flashed onto the screen.

"Hi, Mom," she answered, starting up the car and silently begging the seat heater to kick in. It was freezing after sitting out in the cold all day.

"Hi, kiddo," she said, sounding pleasant as usual on the other end of the line. "I haven't heard from you since Saturday, so I just thought I'd check in and see how you're doing."

"Oh, I'm great." Jayne wasn't able to suppress the grin that spread across her face.

"Well I'm glad to hear that. I've been worried about you, ever since the break-up with Gray." If she only knew, Jayne thought. Should I tell her?

"No need to worry. I'm getting over it."

"We haven't done a game night in a while—why don't you come over Saturday night? Your dad and I will be here, and maybe we could see if your brother can come, too."

"I can't, Mom," she said, turning onto the main road. "I'm busy."

"Are you going out with the girls?"

"Not exactly."

"Well what are you doing that's better than game night?" Game night was actually a lot of fun—the Ashers always made it fun. But Josh was even better.

"Um...I've got a date."

"A date? Well that's news. With who?"

Jayne took a deep breath. She might as well get it over with. "His name is Josh. Brandt."

"It sounded like you said his last name is Brandt."

"It is." Dead silence for at least twenty seconds. The sound of the car's blinker seemed more like a ticking time bomb to Jayne.

"Is he related to the infamous Gray Brandt?"

"Yeah, Mom. It's his brother."

"Oh, Jayne." Her mother's disappointment was about as subtle as bagpipes playing in a corner café.

"Now, Mom, before you start lecturing me—"

"Well of course I have to say something. Isn't getting worked over by one self-centered member of that family enough?"

"Mom, Josh is nothing like Gray. I mean, he's good looking, no doubt, but he's all the good parts of Gray with none of the bad. And lots of extra good thrown in."

Her mother sighed. "But two brothers? Isn't that a little...awkward?"

"Yeah, it is. I mean, I haven't seen Gray since I've been dating Josh, so that will definitely be weird when it happens. But for now, I'm just enjoying falling for a guy that's as into me as I am into him. And he's such a good guy, Mom. He's a high school English teacher—you're going to love him."

"Hmmm...so he's not a money hungry status seeker like his brother?"

"No," Jayne said, chuckling. "He's just sweet, and sensitive, and funny...and it's very very new, but so far he's been really good to me."

"So no game night?"

"No, not this time. But soon, I promise."

"Okay, Jayne. Please be careful with your heart, okay?"

Jayne smiled, loving her mom so much. "I will, Mom. I love you."

"I love you too, sweetie."

She hung up just as she pulled into the St. Louis Bread Company parking lot. Josh was already there, waving at her from the front door. After she parked, she practically ran to greet him.

"Hi, you," he said, grinning, his breath visible in the chilled air. As soon as she reached him, he gave her a big kiss.

"Hi back." Their eyes met as they smiled at each other.

"It's cold out here. Let me stare at you inside," he said with a chuckle.

****

It was finally date night. She was ready for a nice meal; since she and Gray had broken up, she avoided the work cafeteria at all costs. So she was brown bagging it every day or would sometimes run out for some McDonald's. At home, she didn't cook much just for herself, so she was looking forward to real food. Josh had actually asked her where she wanted to eat, and although her first inclination was to say she didn't care, she asserted herself and picked Sqwire's because she craved their crab cakes.

She'd gone out earlier in the day and picked up a new outfit. Not because she needed it, but because she felt like the occasion warranted it. There was something different about this man. Whereas with Gray, she was so excited to be going out with a guy like him—seemingly perfect in every way—with Josh, she was excited to be going out with the man. With Josh.

When he rang her doorbell, she glanced in the mirror one more time before running to the door.

"Wow," Josh said, wearing a stunned expression. "Just...wow."

She grinned at the dopey look on his handsome face. His messy hair was tamed into a sleeker style and he was wearing a nice overcoat. She could see dress pants and dress shoes peeking out underneath.

"Thank you," she said, leaning forward to give him a kiss. "You clean up pretty good yourself. I'll just grab my coat."

Jayne was glad he liked her outfit, since she'd picked it out just for him. She wore high peep-toe pumps with an ankle strap for a little extra va-va-voom. Her black fitted skirt was long, hitting her at mid-calf, but had a suggestive slit all the way to her thigh. The deep-V cowl neck sweater hid what Gray obviously saw as a flaw—her less than ample chest—but showed off the cleavage her push up bra was engineered to create. She had pulled her hair up in a sparkly rhinestone clip, and wore long drop earrings that added an extra layer of sexiness.

When they walked into the restaurant, she noticed a few heads turn. Together, they made a striking pair. She liked how he gently rested his hand in the small of her back as they walked to their table, as if to say, Yes, I'm right here with you.

Dinner was delicious, and the company was even better. They found out they liked a lot of the same music and books, too. She loved hearing him talk about his students and was inspired by his passion. Listening to him talk, she could tell he was one of those teachers that the students would always remember and cite as one of their favorites. The kind that taught so much more than what was in the textbook. He was making a difference in the lives of his students. Lucky kids. Lucky her.

They were just contemplating what they wanted to do next when her phone started ringing from her purse. It was Claudia's ringtone.

"Oh, Josh, I'm sorry. I should really get this—it's my friend, Claudia, the one whose husband—"

"Go ahead," he nodded.

"Hi Claudia," she answered, smiling at Josh. He played with her foot under the table. She thought he looked especially yummy in the striped button down shirt and thin sweater he was wearing.

"I have a big favor to ask," Claudia said, sounding frantic.

"Anything. What?"

"Sam is coming over tonight—I agreed to let him come get more of his things. And I thought I would be okay with it, but he's going to be here in about twenty minutes, and I'm starting to freak out." She was babbling. "So could you come over here, just for a little bit? I just don't want to be alone with him. I'm not ready for that. I need reinforcement."

"Sure, you bet," Jayne said, biting her lip. I hope Josh doesn't mind.

"I mean, I would call Karen, but I'm afraid she'll just be really nasty to him out of loyalty to me, and I don't want that, either. I just want him to get in and out quickly without a bunch of drama."

"I completely understand. We can be there in about ten minutes, we're nearby." She shot Josh an apologetic look as he paid the bill.

"We? Who are you with?"

"Oh...Josh."

"Josh? Who's Josh? Oh, I'm so sorry, are you out on a date?"

"Yeah—"

"Never mind, I'm sorry. Forget about it, I'm a big girl, you don't need to come."

"Claudia, we're coming over, okay? It's no big deal. We'll just hang out there with you until Sam leaves. We'll be there soon. Bye." She hung up the phone, and looked pleadingly at Josh. "Please don't be upset with me, but Claudia really needs us to stop by."

"Why would that upset me?"

"Well, it's kind of our first real date—"

"And you want to help your friend in need. That just shows me what a good-hearted person you are." He took her hand in his, smiling.

"She's been there for me, whenever I needed her."

"Sounds like you've got a pretty good friend. So what's going on?"

"Her husband is stopping by to get some of his things, and she thought she could handle being there alone, but she's kind of flipping out and wants some support."

"Let's go then." His smile was genuine.

Within fifteen minutes they had pulled up in front of Claudia's house. "Oh, I haven't had a chance to tell her about you yet, what with her whole life falling apart. Karen knows, but not Claudia."

"So is she going to do a double take when she sees me? I mean, I have a pretty strong resemblance to someone whose name I'm guessing is mud with your friends."

"Yeah, pretty much," she said, opening her car door. "But maybe the shock will distract her from the stress of seeing Sam."

"I hope so."

Claudia opened the door before they even reached it.

"Oh, you look so pretty, Jayne," she said, motioning them inside. "And you are...oh, my gosh..." Her eyes nearly bulged out of her head. She was staring at Josh. Then she looked at Jayne with questions in her eyes as she closed the door behind them.

"Claudia, this is Josh Brandt," Jayne said, her arm around him. "And yes, he is Gray's brother. Long story, but please know that Josh is not Gray. It's weird, I know. But just push your eyeballs back into your head and say hello."

Josh's smile was nervous, but he worked his charm. "Nice to meet you, Claudia," he said, holding out his hand. They shook, and Claudia continued to stare at him.

"Nice to meet you, too. Surprised, but nice." She motioned them into the living room. "I'm so sorry to tear you away from your date."

"No problem," Josh assured, and she visibly relaxed a bit. "I've been where you are—I know what you're going through, and I understand completely why you'd want someone here with you."

"Thank you," she said, smiling back. "I'm sure I'll get used to it, but it's been just a little over a week and it's all so new and scary."

Just then, there was a knock at the door. Claudia took a deep breath and went to open it.

"Hi, Claud," Jayne heard Sam say. "Can I come in?"

"Sure." Claudia's voice sounded strained.

"Whose car is that out front?"

"Jayne and her friend Josh are here."

"Oh...I didn't know anyone would be here."

"They just stopped by." Their footsteps approached the living room, and then Jayne saw him. It was hard to look at him differently—everything about him looked the same. Same good looks, toned body, friendly expression on his face. But everything else had changed. He had walked out on one of her best friends. Betrayed her. He didn't look like a bad guy, but he fit the bill. Even knowing that, it was hard for Jayne to completely forget the man she'd grown to care for over the last decade.

"Hi, Jayne," he said quietly, and she then noticed a gaunt look about him, an emptiness in his eyes that had never been there before. Serves you right, she thought to herself. Their eyes locked for a moment, and his seemed to apologize. He glanced at Josh, and she saw surprise register on his face. "Wow, for a minute, I thought you were someone else. I'm Sam Knight."

He extended his hand, and it was awkward for everyone in the room. Josh stood up, shook his hand, and without smiling said, "I'm Josh Brandt."

Sam grinned with mischief on his face. "Are you—"

"Yes, Gray's older brother. But I don't think you're in a position to make any moral judgments, now are you?"

Jayne wanted to cheer for Josh, but instead, she squeezed his hand.

"No, I wasn't judging, just surprised, that's all." Sam looked deflated. "Sorry to interrupt your visit, I'll be out of your hair soon."

"I'll be in here with them," Claudia said before he left the room. "Please show me what you're taking before you leave, just so I know."

"I'm only taking clothes and stuff like that," he said, looking at her, but she wouldn't turn to face him. "And I'd rather not talk about this in front of everyone, but I don't really have a choice. It's been over a week...have you hired a lawyer yet? I haven't received word, and I want to talk to whoever it is."

"No, I haven't hired one yet." Her voice sounded tired.

"Well, I told you I'd pay for it. I just want to make sure your lawyer understands that I'm not going to contest anything. You just need to draw up a list of what you want and it's yours." She didn't respond. "And I just signed a lease on an apartment, so please let me know soon if you want to keep all the furniture, or if there are some pieces you don't want." He walked back in front of her. "If you want every piece of it, I told you, it's yours. I just don't want to buy new stuff and then find out you wanted to get rid of some things."

"You can have the bed." She cleared her throat. "I don't really want it anymore."

He nodded. "Okay."

"And you can have the rest of the furniture that goes with it."

"Claud—"

"What, Sam?" She practically hissed at him.

"Are you getting enough sleep? You look tired. Your color's not good."

Her stare directed at him, she said, "It's hard to sleep when you're crying all night." He stepped back, as if her words were a physical blow to him.

"I never meant to hurt you—"

"Sam," Jayne said in a gentle tone, seeing the anguish on her friend's face, "why don't you just get your things? It would be easier for everyone."

"Jayne, I'm still the same guy, you know. I'm not some monster."

"I know that."

"We were always good friends—"

"Sam, you broke my best friend's heart. I don't hate you, but I can't possibly feel the same way about you anymore. You have to understand that."

"Yeah, yeah, I do." He looked down at the floor. "Take care of her, would you, Jayne? I know I caused this, but it doesn't mean I don't care what happens."

"I will always be here for Claudia."

Claudia smiled faintly at Jayne.

"Okay," he said, giving Claudia a long, tortured look before he left the room.

Within fifteen minutes, he was gone. Claudia urged them to leave, too, thanking them profusely for coming over. When they climbed back in the car, Josh asked, "So now where to?"

"Well," Jayne said, chuckling, "that little interruption kind of put a damper on our evening. So as long as we're making this first date an unusual one...I have an idea." She glanced at her watch: eight-thirty.

"Shoot."

"You'll probably hate it, so feel free to say no way."

"Well I can't say yes or no if you don't tell me what you have in mind." He smiled at her, his face full of adoration.

"My mom wanted me to go over and play games with them tonight. I told her I had plans, but now that everything is screwed up..."

"What kind of games?"

"Well, we're into some old classics...Scrabble, Boggle, and a newer one, Bananagrams."

He chuckled. "You want to play word games with an English teacher?" His bravado made her laugh. "Bring it on, baby. I warn you, though, I have no problem taking your whole family down."

"Oh, really?" She smiled. "So are you sure you don't mind?"

"No, sounds like fun. Besides, didn't you say something last week about Gray really pissing off your parents because he kept taking you away on the holidays?"

"Yeah, my mom is still mad."

"All the more reason to head over there. I have to show her that this Brandt doesn't get between his girl and her family."

"I was kind of hoping you'd say that. Let me call Mom and let her know we're coming." She smiled at him and then kissed him with passion.

"I can play games all night if that's my reward," he quipped.

Oh, I'll give you more than that, Joshua.

Chapter Twelve

When they walked out of her parents' house at eleven-thirty that night, Jayne decided the evening had been the best foreplay ever. How many men would willingly and happily go help rescue a friend and play games with a woman's family on a first date? Not many. And not only did he play games, he won over her parents, who were reasonably gun shy. He was charming, no doubt, but his charm was layered with sincerity and goodness. The way he bonded with her dad and admired her mother...well, that was the greatest aphrodisiac ever.

They climbed in the car, her mom standing at the door, waving goodbye.

"Your parents are great," Josh said, looking at Jayne with tenderness.

"You are great. I mean, Josh, this was the craziest date ever."

"But it was fun. Well, not the part with Sam, but the rest was a blast. And sorry about clobbering everyone at Boggle. I'm competitive, what can I say?"

She laughed. "It's fine. You are the Boggle Master. Impressive."

"Well, that's how I usually court the pretty ladies," he said with a chuckle, leaning over and kissing her.

Glancing at her mom in the doorway, Jayne said, "You better pull this car away soon, because my mom will not leave that doorway until we're halfway down the street." They both laughed, and he started up the car. Waving at her mom as Josh backed down the driveway, she said in a suggestive tone, "Do you want to go back to my place?"

"Uh...yeah!" His smile melted her heart. He was so sexy and fun and kind. Truly kind, she was starting to see that. "Oh, wait...can we go to mine?"

"Sure."

"Well, it's just...I don't know how late you want me to stay, and Atticus is in his crate."

"Oh, so you think there might be reason to stay late?" She teased him.

"I don't know. I was kind of hoping..." His grin was almost more than she could bear.

"Well so was I, so off to the Brandt Chalet." She giggled, and he put his hand on her thigh, pulling up her skirt. Jayne was glad his part of town was only fifteen minutes away.

As soon as they set foot in his house, she could see that the differences between the Brandt brothers could not be greater. Whereas Gray's condo was cold, modern, minimal...Josh's was warm, cozy, and full of character. Not the typical bachelor pad. Built-in honey-colored bookshelves in two rooms, full of books. Books that looked like they were actually read. Warm throw rugs tossed about on the refinished original hardwood floors. Overstuffed, inviting furniture that made you want to snuggle in with one of those books. Neat and tidy, but touches of Josh everywhere—pictures of family, friends, him rock climbing, with his students on a field trip, a bust of Shakespeare, another of Mark Twain, stacks of students' papers littering the enormous old oak desk in his office, and best of all—the happy, loving dog that bounded her way as soon as Josh opened his crate.

"Atticus, off!" he hollered as the dog exuberantly cleaned Jayne's face. She was pretty sure her makeup was all gone, but her face wore the biggest smile.

"It's okay," she tried to say in between tongue baths. "I love dogs. You're such a sweet boy, aren't you?" The more she talked to him, the more rapid his tail wagging became and the more he couldn't resist licking her face. Laughing, Josh pulled him off.

"I think he likes you. I'm not sure, he's rather subtle sometimes, but I've just got a feeling." They both laughed as Jayne petted the dog's silky ears. "And I don't think it's fair that Atticus here has gotten more action with you than I have."

"We should really do something about that," she said, batting her eyes at him. "I'm going to go wash my face."

He pointed eagerly. "Bathroom's right there."

Turning on the light, she saw an elaborate pedestal sink, which perfectly suited the age of the home and the small quarters of the bathroom. After she washed her face, she looked in the small, decorative mirror, noticing that her makeup, for the most part, was gone. If she'd been with Gray, she'd have panicked. But with Josh, she knew he wouldn't care. He'd already seen her without makeup, puffy-eyed and vulnerable.

Josh had already given so much of himself, so soon. She wanted to give him everything.

When she stepped out of the bathroom, he was standing in front of his bedroom door, his silhouette illuminated only by a small night light in the hallway. He had unbuttoned his shirt, exposing his tight abs and sculptured chest. She wanted him physically but mentally, too. She wanted to lose herself in this man that she already felt safe with. For the first time in her life, she didn't feel insecure or nervous with a man.

She felt like she was finally home.

As they made love, she tried not to make comparisons, but it was inevitable. Whereas sex with Gray seemed technical, routine, albeit pleasurable...with Josh it was all emotion, tenderness, exploration—passion. Pure passion, for both of them. Like his younger brother, he knew what he was doing, but he did it with feeling. They shared themselves.

Afterward, she waited nervously, hoping that he wouldn't urge her out of bed like Gray always had. Their lovemaking had been the most sensual experience of her life. There was chemistry between them...animalistic, almost. As he snuggled into her, he ran his fingers up and down the graceful curves of her body.

"That," he whispered, "was perfect."

She could only nod, her emotions so raw, she was afraid if she spoke that tears would surface. She looked at him with big eyes, completely vulnerable, hoping with all of her heart that he was the man she believed him to be. Please don't break my heart, she said to herself as she stared into his green eyes that seemed to see into her very soul. She felt more naked, more exposed then ever in her life. But she sensed that with Josh, her heart was safe.

"Do you want to stay here with me tonight?" he whispered, kissing her head that was nestled in the crook of his shoulder.

Then the tears began. "I'd love to," she whispered, pulling him even closer. Soon the wetness of her tears trickled down his side.

"Are you crying?" he asked, sitting up to look at her. Alarm clouded his face. "Jayne, did I do something wrong?"

"No." She smiled at him through her tears. "You did everything exactly right. Come back here." She pulled him back to her.

"I'm sorry for what he did," he whispered. "I want you to feel safe with me. I hope, in time, that you will."

"I already do," she said, wiping her eyes. "And it wasn't just him…it's been a lifetime of careless men."

"I won't be one of those men." The way he said it as he cradled her in his strong arms, she knew it was true.

****

When Jayne woke up the next morning, there was no empty pillow with a note on the nightstand. She awoke to the sight of Josh looking down at her as he sat next to her on the bed. The stubble on his face made him look irresistible, his hair was a crazy mop, and his eyes seemed greener in the morning sunlight.

"Good morning, sleepyhead," he said with a smile.

"It is a good morning," she said, stretching. "I get to wake up and see you." They kissed and the tenderness of his lips sent shivers through her.

"Are you hungry?"

"You'll learn that I'm always hungry. Should we go grab something?"

"Definitely not. I made you breakfast." He smiled, obviously happy with himself.

"Okay, you better stop being so wonderful or my friends will tell me you're too good to be true and insist that I get rid of you."

"Well, then I'll just have to prove to them that I, Joshua Allen Brandt, am really this fucking good." He laughed, and she loved the beautiful, throaty sound.

She playfully hit him with a pillow, completely overwhelmed by her good fortune. He stood up, moving out of the way. "So, Joshua Allen Brandt, what did you make for me?"

"Since I wasn't sure what you like, I made you pancakes, eggs, sausage and hash browns." She giggled, and he smiled. "I know, too much. But I woke up early with all this energy...it's been a while since, well, you know. And I've never had sex like what we had last night."

"Me neither."

He hesitated a moment, then asked, "So was it strange for you...was the whole Gray thing in the back of your mind?"

"Well, I couldn't help but compare, sorry." She looked at him with an embarrassed grin. "I don't want to take anything away from your brother, he's good, he knows what he's doing. But he approaches it like he's competing in an athletic event—all technical moves, no heart." She stood up, putting her arms around him. "You, however...well, you're all heart. There really was no comparison."

Josh grinned. "Ah, come on, I bet you say that to all the brothers you've done."

She slapped his boxer-clad bottom as he started laughing at her. "Don't you ever say anything like that again." She was laughing too.

"I'm sorry, that was wrong." He was still laughing, and she thought he'd never looked sexier. "It was just too good to pass up."

"Well, don't you have a cousin or something that I could move on to—"

"Okay, now that's not funny," he said, tousling her hair. "I'm glad we got past that. All sexual awkwardness gone."

"Yeah, I'm just dreading seeing your parents and Gray again."

"Don't you ever see him at work?"

"He's up on the fifth floor with the big boys. I, however, am with the lowly people on the second floor. We met in the cafeteria, so now I just bring my lunch."

"Well, you can't hide from him forever. He is my brother."

"Yeah, I know. I think now that I have you, it will be easier to face him. Just awkward at first."

"Maybe we should get that out of the way soon."

"Probably."

He kissed her. "So come with me…breakfast is served."

As they feasted on the delicious spread he'd made, she couldn't stop staring at the wonderful man across from her. Their toes played together under the table, and they were both full of smiles.

"So, Ms. Asher, what are you doing today?"

"I don't know. There's nothing on my agenda. Did you have something in mind?"

"Well, it might be boring, but I'm supposed to be going over to Shawn's house today for a Daytona 500 party. He's a friend from work—super fun guy. NASCAR's not really my thing, but some of the other people from work will be there, so it could maybe be fun."

"You're everybody's friend from work, aren't you?" She liked the embarrassed look on his face. Humble guy.

"I don't know…probably." He grinned, shrugging his shoulders. "I'm a pretty friendly guy, I guess. So anyway, if you want to come with me, I'm sure you'd make it a lot more fun."

"There won't be any old girlfriends there or anything, will there?"

"No," he said with a chuckle. "The only good looking teachers in my building are married."

"I bet your female students are hot for teacher, aren't they?"

A smile crept up, and he shrugged again. "Some, yes. I have to be very, very careful not to be too friendly. Teenage girls are a mess—they can misconstrue the simplest gesture or comment."

"I bet. Especially from a hot teacher like you."

"We could head back in the bedroom for a lesson…"

"I'm not opposed to that at all," she said. "I am definitely hot for teacher."

"Good," he said, leaning across the table and kissing her. "So do you want to go there with me today?"

"Yes. I'd go pretty much anywhere with you today." Or every day.

****

There were a dozen or so people at the Daytona 500 party. Mainly guys that Josh worked with, many with their wives or dates. They all seemed pretty friendly, and the host, Shawn, was a funny guy. His place was the quintessential bachelor's pad with all the guy essentials: huge flat screen TV—probably too large for the room— black leather sectional with cup holders and recliners, not one but two gaming systems, and very large speakers for the best in surround sound, or so Jayne was told.

Josh was attentive and stuck by her side, not leaving her alone like someone else with the last name Brandt. She liked the way he casually stayed connected—arm around her, or hand on her leg, or fingers intertwined.

Shawn had a nice food spread on the island in his kitchen, and Jayne was getting bored with watching the race, so she leaned over and said to Josh, "I'm going to grab a plate of food. Do you want anything?"

"Uh…can I just nibble off of yours?"

"You bet." Their eyes locked, and they shared a smile.

When she walked in the kitchen, one of Josh's colleagues was there, pouring chips into a bowl. He turned around and Jayne immediately noticed the long white cane in his hand. She'd forgotten Josh mentioned that one of his friends, a history teacher, was blind. They'd been introduced earlier, but his cane wasn't out then, and she hadn't realized he couldn't see.

"Hi," she said, smiling. "Jason, right?"

"Yeah. And you are…?"

"Jayne. I came with Josh."

"That's right." He smiled, nodding. "Thought you looked familiar."

Jayne giggled. "I get that a lot."

He laughed. "So, are you enjoying watching cars drive around in a circle?" He walked toward Jayne and leaned against the counter next to her.

"Uh…not exactly." Looking at Jason, her heart went out to him. She couldn't imagine living without her eyesight. He was a very good-looking guy; it was obvious he worked out a lot. His body was great, and his smile was fantastic. Even his blue eyes were pretty.

"You know, when I was a kid and could see, I didn't get watching racing then, and I certainly don't get it now."

"I'm with you. That's why I'm at the food spread. This stuff is amazing."

"Glad you like it. You're looking at the chef." He smiled with pride.

"Really?"

"You sound surprised," he said with a chuckle. "Is it because I'm a guy or because I'm blind?"

"Actually, both."

"Yeah, well," Jason leaned in, adding suggestively, "I'm really good with my hands."

"Jason, back off," Josh said as he approached, laughing. Jason quickly stepped back, looking surprised that Josh was there.

"Oh, hey, Josh." Jason blushed.

"In case you don't remember, Jayne's here with me. Turn off the charm machine."

"You know, I don't see a ring on her finger. That means she's fair game."

"Jason, you couldn't see a ring on her finger even if it was there."

"Ouch," he said, showing off a broad smile. "I know she's yours, Josh. I was just shamelessly flirting. She's the only other person here not glued to the scintillating action on the TV."

"Yeah, well, NASCAR's not exactly my thing, either, but I like a good gathering."

"Me too. And Shawn paid me in beer to cook the food for him. I can't pass on free booze." They all laughed. "So, where did you two meet?"

Josh and Jayne looked at each other, grinning, not sure what to say.

"Uh…you guys still there?" Jason asked.

"Yeah, we're here," Josh said, chuckling.

"Sorry, didn't mean it to be a trick question."

"It's not," Jayne said. "We met over the holidays—I was actually dating his brother at the time."

Jason nodded, grinning. "Now I get the uncomfortable pause. So now my only question is, since you like to keep it in the family—do you have a sister?"

Jayne chuckled. "No, sorry."

"Me neither," Josh said, laughing.

"Well, Josh," Jason said, "I guess you get bragging rights at the next family dinner, huh? You won."

"I hope I did. Let's see how long she puts up with me." He smiled at Jayne, rubbing her back.

"Well I hear you're not bad on the eyes, and I know you're a good guy, so here's to Jayne sticking around." He held up his beer bottle to toast.

"Jason, we don't have our drinks with us—you're toasting on your own."

He shrugged. "I'm okay with that." He took a swig.

"Okay, well I'm going back in the living room. Stand down, Scharp, got it?"

"Got it."

"I'll be there in a minute," Jayne said, thinking how cute Josh's butt looked as he walked away.

"Is he gone?" Jason asked.

"Yes."

"I didn't want to say too much in front of him. Didn't want him to get a big head. But he's a really, really great guy. I don't know anything about his brother, but I know you can't lose with Josh. A loyal and big-hearted guy."

Jayne smiled. "I'm starting to figure that out. And for the record, his brother—not so much."

"Oh, really? Well, I'm glad you found the better brother. Josh deserves a good woman like you."

"Thank you," she said, touching his arm. "So will you share any of these recipes with me?"

"You bet."

"Especially for this dip."

"I'll email them to Josh for you."

"Awesome," she said, looking at Jason. "A man that cooks this great should definitely have a girlfriend."

"I completely agree. If you have any friends that you wouldn't mind setting up on a literal blind date, let me know."

He laughed, and Jayne wondered if there was any sadness behind his self-deprecating humor. She also wondered how he lost his sight, but didn't want to ask such a personal question. "I will keep that in mind. Well, I've loaded up my plate with lots of goodies, so I'm going to go try to stay awake in front of the TV."

"Okay, I'll be in there in a minute. It was nice talking with you."

"Same here. Oh, and thanks for flirting—always makes a girl feel good."

"My pleasure." He flashed a big smile as she walked out of the room, and Josh was grinning at her as she approached. He patted the spot next to him on the couch, looking eager to be with her. Feeling scared but exhilarated, Jayne knew without a doubt that she was a goner. She was already falling in love.

March

Chapter Thirteen

Daylight again. If it wasn't for needing a job to pay her bills, Claudia would never even get out of bed. Sleep was easier...no pain, no questions, no despair. But work forced her, at least five days a week, to go to the effort of showering, putting on some clothes, and engaging with the rest of the world.

It was Saturday, though, so she didn't really have to get up. She thought that maybe she wouldn't. But then she glanced at the clock: nine-thirty. She'd gone to bed at nine o'clock last night. Twelve and half hours—probably long enough.

As she sat up, she realized that she felt nauseous. Fantastic. Straight from a sinus infection, to the breakup of her marriage, to the flu. She ran to the bathroom and made it just in time. When she finished throwing up, she washed her hands and splashed cold water on her face. She felt a little better.

Walking into the kitchen, she turned on the coffee pot and grabbed a couple of Saltine crackers. Looking around the room, she realized the demise of her marriage even tainted the house that she loved. They had worked so hard together, picking everything out, rehabbing it, decorating...all in an effort to make the perfect place to raise their family and grow old together. What once gave her so much pleasure was now just a reminder of all she'd lost.

She glanced at the little magnetic dry erase board that hung on the fridge. All she had written on it was bananas, milk, Call Sam.

He'd been leaving her messages for two days, and she had been avoiding calling him back. She'd found a lawyer a friend recommended and had her first appointment with him. Just as Sam had requested, she told the lawyer that he wasn't going to contest anything and gave the lawyer Sam's card. In the meantime, she'd filed for divorce. It was officially underway.

So now Sam started calling her, and she just didn't feel like calling him back. It was actually nice to hear his voice on the messages he'd left. She'd replayed them several times. As much as Claudia hated to admit it, she missed him. Despite what he'd done and the fact that he'd left her…she still missed him. Hearing his voice was nice. Talking to him, however, was another thing.

Her stomach seemed a little calmer as she poured a cup of coffee. She suddenly put the coffee pot down and ran to look at the calendar she kept on the back of the pantry door.

Sighing, she closed the pantry door, then picked up her phone and sent a text message to Sam: I have to meet with you today. Are you free for lunch?

Within two minutes, he replied, Yes. Just tell me when and where.

She typed back: Noon. California Pizza Kitchen at The Galleria.

It was always noisy in there; she wanted lots of people and plenty of distractions. She headed upstairs to take a shower and go to the drug store before she met with him.

****

Claudia was sitting at a table in the crowded restaurant, her stomach still a bit unsettled, when she saw Sam walk in the door. He looked so handsome in his T-shirt, fitted sweater, and blue jeans, with a scarf tossed around his neck. He almost never wore a coat. He scanned the restaurant, and Claudia thought it was odd that he was her husband and yet she was nervous to see him. How did they go from being completely intimate to feeling like strangers in just a matter of weeks?

Sam spotted her, nodded, and headed her way. She noticed he had a yellow legal pad with him; always the lawyer.

He smiled as he approached, though it was not the smile she remembered. This was a new smile, a cautious one. "Thanks for meeting with me," he said, taking his seat across from her. "I was starting to think you weren't going to call me back."

"Well it's sometimes easier to deal with all of this by just ignoring it. Ignoring you," she said, looking away.

"I understand." His voice was quiet.

"So I wasn't tearing you away from anything today? Or anyone?" She didn't say it with anger, more of resigned sadness.

"No, Claud," he answered, looking right at her. "You know, I may be the one that decided to end our marriage, but it doesn't mean that it's easy on me, either. I love you. I miss you, I miss hearing you laugh, seeing you smile, talking things over with you." He looked down at his menu. "So I'm not partying it up, having orgies. I'm pretty depressed, too."

"I'm glad. You should be hurting. I was good to you. I was there for you. No more."

The waitress came and took their orders. A long silence followed. Claudia folded her napkin meticulously. Finally, Sam said, "I'm glad you picked Steven to be your lawyer. He's nice to work with, and he'll do a good job for you. I'll make it as painless as possible." He took a drink. "He said you don't want maintenance—"

"No, I don't," she said, looking up at him. "But something has changed that will complicate the proceedings quite a bit."

"What?" He stared at her, surprise on his face. She pulled a brown paper bag out of her purse and handed it to him. Confused, he opened the bag and pulled out an e.p.t. pregnancy test with a deep blue plus sign in the window. He stared at it for a minute and then looked up at her, his face ashen. "You're pregnant?"

"Yes," she nodded, sickened at the thought that the thing she wanted most in life and had waited to happen for years...was now bringing pain and not joy. She was so upset that Sam's selfishness had tainted the most precious thing.

"I don't understand…you're on the pill…how could this happen?"

"The antibiotics I took for a sinus infection. I forgot all about it, but antibiotics decrease the effectiveness of the pill. That night you drew me a bath…."

Sam looked at her, worry in his eyes, fear on his face. He said nothing.

Finally, Claudia said, "I know you thought this would be a clean and easy break. But it looks like we're not going to get off that easy. So I still don't want maintenance, but I obviously want child support. And I was going to suggest we sell the house because I don't need a place that big by myself. But, with a baby…well, I do want the house. That house is a place that was once filled with our love. Well, at least I think it was."

"It was, Claudia," he said, taking her hand.

"So I thought it might be good for a child to grow up in a place that holds some happy memories, some history of its family."

"That's fine, the house is half paid for, and we got it for such a good price. Can you afford it if we refinance it in your name for the remaining balance? With a thirty year mortgage, that would put your payments at probably only nine hundred dollars a month."

"Sam, I don't make a lot of money, and I'm not asking for maintenance."

"Okay, then why don't I pay half of whatever the remaining balance is, so your payment will be closer to five hundred dollars?"

"I can handle that, yes." She finally looked at him, really looked at him, and their eyes met. "Thank you."

"I ruined our marriage, the least I can do is make it easier for you to move on."

She knew Sam enough to know he was being truthful. At least she thought so. "So…there will be child support."

"Of course. There's a calculation the state has for that, but I don't care about their calculation. I want to make sure our baby has everything he or she could ever want." He took a deep breath. "I'll pay for any daycare, schooling, whatever. Only the best. And then whatever you decide you need monthly on top of that—a thousand dollars, two thousand, just tell me. I know you'll be fair."

She exhaled, relieved that she wasn't going to have to deal with fighting Sam while going through a pregnancy alone. Deep down, she knew he was basically a good man. It was like Jayne had said, he wasn't rejecting her. He was rejecting marriage and spending the rest of his life with just one person. She knew too, that in his way, he did love and care for her. She just wished she had known years ago that he was having doubts. It would have made parting so much easier.

But now there was a baby. Although the situation was definitely not what she'd ever imagined, she still was thrilled at the thought of finally having what she'd always dreamed of—a baby. Going it alone was never what she imagined, but she knew she could do it. She was strong. And she had something to look forward to now.

Their food came, and as she gingerly picked at her BBQ chopped chicken salad, Sam said, "So now I know why you were looking so pale and tired. I knew something was wrong. But you weren't sick—you were pregnant."

She smiled at him. "Yes, I didn't realize it until this morning when I threw up. I'd been so preoccupied with everything going on that I hadn't even noticed I'd missed my period. I looked at the calendar, and I just knew."

Sam took a bite of his pizza and looked at her with intensity. "What...what role do you want me to play in the child's life?"

She didn't answer right away, and sighed. "I don't know, Sam. I guess that's up to you. I mean, as long as you support the child financially—"

"Of course I will."

"I know, I know you will. Then the rest is up to you. If you want to do weekends or share custody, or whatever, we can work that out. I won't keep you from your child. I would never do that. But the day you left, you said you didn't want a family. So if you want to just support the baby but not have a relationship…that's up to you."

"Claud, I don't know what I want. I have no idea." The look of absolute shock on his face almost made her feel sorry for him. But not quite.

"Well, you don't have to decide right now. You can think about it."

"But raising a baby on your own would be tough."

"I'm sure it will be. But if you're financially supporting the baby, I can hire a nanny if it gets too crazy. And I've got great friends."

"Yeah, you do have great friends." He looked down at his plate. "I suppose they all hate me now."

"Well, Karen despises you. You know how protective she is of the people she loves. And I think Jayne is just hurt by it all. She loved you like a brother, always did. So she probably feels somewhat like I do…torn. Between caring about the man we thought you were and dealing with the fact that you aren't him."

"But I'm not a bad guy, I'm really not. I just want something different."

"Something other than me."

"Something other than a lifetime spent with one person. It's not about you. I wouldn't have stuck around for ten years with anyone else, trust me."

"Well, so now you'll be stuck dealing with me financially for the next eighteen years."

"At least twenty-two. Our baby will go to college."

"Of course." She nibbled on some salad, still not sure about her stomach. "As far as our investments go, you can have them. I'm young enough I can start socking away for my retirement now, no problem."

"Claudia, no, we invested that while we were married. You're entitled to half—"

"Sam, as long as you take care of the house like we talked about, and support this child—I won't need your investments. I'll be fine. Just put a good chunk of it in the baby's name so college will be taken care of."

"I'll definitely do that." He started jotting down notes on his legal pad.

The salad tasted good to Claudia; her stomach seemed to be settled. She wondered what stage of development the baby was at; she'd have to get online when she got home and start researching. A baby. I'm going to be a mom, she thought to herself, and unknowingly, a smile crept on her face.

"Why the smile?" Sam asked.

She shrugged her shoulders, her smile broadening. "I don't know, it's just...I'm having a baby. I never in a million years would have guessed this would happen, but...thank you, Sam. It wasn't your intention, or even mine, but you've given me the greatest gift. Even though you've left, your parting gift is the one thing I wanted most in the world."

He smiled back at her, and for a moment, it felt like old times. "I guess I owed you that."

Tears came to her eyes. "Yes, you did."

"Claud, I need to think about this...this completely threw me for a loop."

"Yeah, me too. I understand."

"So...I'll work with Steven to draw up everything that we discussed. I don't want you to have to worry about all of this anymore than necessary. Once we get something drawn up that I think you'll be happy with, Steven will go over it with you."

"Okay, thank you."

"And as far as our baby..." He looked away. "Our baby. Holy shit."

"Yeah," she said, seeing the fear on his face. "Sam, take some time to think about things. I'll let you be as much a part of this pregnancy and this baby as you want. If you don't want to be involved, I'll go it alone. It will be okay."

He seemed to relax a bit. "I'll just let you know what's going on, when my appointments are, and all of that. I'll keep you in the loop. You can decide where you want to take it from there."

"Okay, thank you. Thank you for being so great about all of this. I'm sorry for ruining everything, I really am." His eyes were begging her to forgive. She wasn't there yet, but this new development was a step toward moving on.

"I guess I'd rather be alone than be in a marriage that only one of us wanted." A sudden sob caught in her throat, and he looked at her with pain in his eyes. "Was it all just an act for you? Was any of it real?"

"Claud, my love, our intimacy, our friendship—it was all real. Every bit of it. This baby inside of you, it was created out of our love for each other. Just because I decided I don't want the things out of life that I once thought I might doesn't mean I was faking it all those years. I'm not an actor. I always loved you. I'm just selfish, I guess. I want to be a bachelor."

"You are selfish," she said, wiping away tears. "And I want to believe it when you say all those years weren't bullshit, but I just don't know if I can."

"Believe it, Claud. I still love you. I always will."

Maybe it was the hormones, or the earnest look on the face she had loved for so many years, but she did believe him.

****

Karen couldn't keep herself from staring at the fantastic ring on her finger. She caught herself looking at it all the time. While driving, sitting at her desk at work, in a boring sales meeting. It was spectacular. And so was the man that gave it to her.

With the engagement came an extra breath of excitement and anticipation to their relationship. Forever. It sounded perfect to Karen, something she never thought she'd want, but now craved.

Rick's laughter made her look away from the dazzling ring. She was at the kitchen sink and he was staring at her from the living room where he'd been watching TV.

"What?" she asked, grinning.

"You're doing it again. Staring at your ring."

"I know," she said, feeling her cheeks flush. "I can't help it."

"Well I'm glad you like it so much," he said, coming into the kitchen, putting his arms around her from behind. "I can't believe you're keeping this a secret from the girls."

"I know, neither can I. But it's only been a week, and we're all getting together in a couple of days for St. Patrick's Day. I want to surprise them."

"Okay, fiancée," he said, kissing her neck. "Why don't we grab dinner out tonight? Someplace fun. How about Fast Eddie's? We haven't been there in ages."

"That sounds perfect, fiancé." She chuckled. "I just made myself sick. Like, vomit in the back of my mouth."

"Why?"

"Because I sound so…happy."

He laughed. "And that makes you sick because…?"

"Because it's so not me. I'm cynical and don't believe in all that happily ever after crap."

"You don't?"

"Well…I do with you now. You've screwed up my whole persona, dammit." She laughed, too, and he kissed her with tenderness.

"I am so sorry to taint your otherwise sinister mind with happiness." His dark eyes looked right into hers, and she couldn't believe how good it felt.

"You should be sorry. You're a cruel man, Rick Gordon." As they kissed, she stole another glance at her ring.

****

Jayne practically had to pinch herself as she walked into Josh's house after work on Friday night. She could smell the meal he was cooking as soon as she hit the door. Her hot boyfriend was cooking her dinner. How could she have gotten so lucky?

They had been dating now for almost a month, and things were fabulous. No red flags, no mixed signals, no apprehension. Just comfortable, fulfilling, and intimate. None of which she'd had with Gray.

"Is that my gorgeous girlfriend I hear, or a robber?" Josh hollered from the kitchen.

She grinned as she walked into the kitchen, carrying an overnight bag. He already had on his sweats and there was red sauce simmering on the stove, pasta boiling, and salad on the table. He had never looked more adorable to her.

"The only thing I would consider stealing is you," she said, giving him a tender kiss.

"Well, I've got news for you. You already stole my heart."

"Likewise." She put her arms around him. "Did you have a good day?"

"Yeah, it was good," he said, pulling away and returning his attention to the stove. "I've got some great kids this semester. How about your day?"

"Interesting." She put her bag in the hallway.

"How so?"

She thought back to the day's events and was still trying to piece everything together. She had gone to lunch with Scott and at some point in the conversation he asked, "So are things back to normal for you, now that's Kelly's back?"

"Yeah, things are great," she'd answered. "Do you see much of that bastard Tony Green since he's on your floor?"

Scott chuckled. "No, I think Gray pretty much keeps him chained to his desk. He's on a pretty short leash."

"He works directly for Gray?"

"Yeah, I bet Gray's regretting that now."

"Regretting what?" She noticed an odd look come over Scott's face. "What would he regret?"

"Well, I just meant that he's probably wishing Tony hadn't been put under him." He looked very uncomfortable.

"You're acting weird," she said, looking at him closely. "Like you're hiding something."

"What the hell would I have to hide? I'm just a lowly assistant." He smiled, but Jayne didn't believe it.

"What's going on?"

"Nothing is going on. I think working for Tony made you paranoid."

Maybe. But something was weird. Did Gray have something to do with Tony being transferred?

Scott changed the conversation, and she let it slide. But when she got back from lunch, she walked into Kelly's office, trying to be casual. "Do you have a minute?"

"Sure, for you, anything. What's up?"

"I was just wondering, do you know what went down when Tony was transferred and you came back here?"

"Oh, I'm not sure," Kelly said, looking a little nervous. "All I know is Mac called me into his office, asked if I wanted my old job back, and I jumped at the chance. Those R&D people are a different breed."

"Hmmm." Jayne scrutinized Kelly. She'd known her for years. She was acting strange, Jayne was sure of it. "How did Gray end up supervising Tony?"

"Don't know. He's under Mac, I guess Mac thought Gray could whip him into shape."

"But why was he transferred? Was he in some kind of trouble or something?"

"What's with all the questions, Jayne? I don't know. I'm just glad it all worked out—it was close."

"What was close?" Jayne saw fear register on Kelly's face.

"I mean…"

"What is going on?" Jayne closed Kelly's door. "I'm friends with one of Mac's assistants, Scott, and he was acting weird about it today and now you are, too. Scott was the only one that knew I was having troubles with Tony…did Scott talk to Mac about it or something?"

Kelly looked away. "I don't know anything about Scott's involvement. The only thing I will tell you was that Tony was transferred out of here specifically because he had filled out your termination paperwork."

Those words took Jayne's breath away. Nearly brought tears to her eyes. "Are you serious?"

"Yes. But you can't ever let on that you know about any of that. Mac had the paperwork expunged from your record so it's not in your file. I have to report to him weekly now on your performance."

"Well, are you pleased with my work?"

"Of course I am. You know that. You have nothing to worry about."

"But I don't understand why I wasn't fired, if Tony had done the termination paperwork."

"Jayne, stop wondering how it all went down and just be happy with the outcome." Jayne could tell by the look on Kelly's face that she was done talking about it.

"Yeah, okay," she said quietly. "Thank you for taking your old job back."

"It was a blessing for me, trust me."

Jayne walked out of the office, her mind still spinning. If Tony had filled out termination papers, who had stopped it? Kelly was hiding something. But why?

Jayne called one of the people she'd worked with before in HR, Christy. "Hey Christy, it's Jayne Asher in Customer Relations."

"Hi, Jayne. What's up, girl?"

"Well, I just had a question. If a supervisor fills out termination paperwork on someone, does that go straight to HR?"

"No, it has to be signed off by the head of the department, and then it comes to us. Why?"

"So if someone in Customer Relations is going to be fired, does it go to Mac?"

"Yeah, he signs off on all terminations for Customer Relations and Marketing. Why?"

"Oh, I'm just checking on some procedures for Kelly, that's all." Jayne knew enough to know that nobody ever just handed paperwork to Mac. Everything went through one of his assistants—either Leslie or Scott. So Scott must have known about it.

"You know, Jayne, I was going to tell you something, but I really shouldn't…"

"What's that?" Jayne asked, her heart beating faster.

"You have to swear not to tell anyone because it's confidential."

"I swear."

"I mean, it's not critical information or anything, but I'm really not supposed to tell you."

"Tell me what?" Just spit it out, Christy!

"That hot Marketing VP, Gray Brandt, you know the one that looks like a freakin' Greek god?"

You have no idea how well I know who he is. "Yeah, I know him."

"Well he came down here one day, asking to see all of your performance appraisals for the past five years. Which I thought was strange, because only department heads can see those, and they normally send their assistants or shoot me an email."

"When was this?"

"A couple of weeks ago, I guess. And I wasn't going to give it to him, but he said Mac wanted it, and when I called Scott Hickman, he said Mac was waiting for it. The whole thing seemed a little weird, though. Scott could have just emailed the request. I don't know why Gray was involved." She giggled. "But on the plus side, Gray said we could get a drink together sometime, so it worked out for me."

"Good for you. Well thanks for letting me know. That is a little weird."

"I'm sure it was nothing."

"Probably not." She hung up the phone, and sat back, trying to process everything she'd heard.

Scott knew something, because he vouched for Gray to get Jayne's records.

Gray was no doubt involved, because he was the one getting the reviews.

Kelly knew Jayne was about to be fired, but how else was she involved?

Then she remembered Scott's words at lunch about Gray supervising Tony: "I bet Gray's regretting that now." Regret involves something you've done, not something someone else has done. What did Gray regret?

Then Tony's parting words suddenly made sense. "You conniving little bitch. I was right all along." All along, he'd insisted Gray was somehow boosting her career. Gray must have been involved, and Tony must have known as much but assumed that she had gone to Gray about him. The only person that knew about his treatment of her was Scott, so had he gone to Gray? And did Gray really take care of this for her?

She couldn't just let it go. She had to know. So she picked up the phone and called Scott.

"Richard Mackenzie's office," he answered.

"It's Jayne."

"Hey Jayne. What's up?"

"I almost got fired, and you knew about it." Dead silence on the other end.

He finally said, "I see an awful lot of stuff that comes across this desk that's confidential."

"I know you do, but I think when you saw that, you helped me. You're the only one that knew about Tony treating me the way he did."

"Jayne..."

"Why won't you just tell me what happened?"

"Because I was asked not to."

"By who? Gray?"

"Jayne, I admit I saw the paperwork and there was no way I was going to let you go down when I knew you'd done nothing wrong. The only problem was that I couldn't do anything about it. So let's just say I gave the information to people that could do something."

"It was Gray, wasn't it?"

"I'm not saying another word about it."

"Well I am," she said, getting a little teary eyed. "Thank you. Whatever it was you did, whoever helped you out—you started the ball rolling to save my job. That's unbelievable. I will never forget that, and I owe you one."

He chuckled. "Well you're very welcome."

"Are you sure you don't want to tell me what happened?"

"Positive. I don't want to be on anyone's bad side around here."

"I understand. But if I can ever repay you, let me know."

"I will. I gotta go, Mac's buzzing me."

"Okay, bye."

Jayne felt overwhelmed by the kindness of her friend, and she was fairly certain it was Gray that had taken care of everything. Why didn't he want her to know? Why not take credit for helping her out?

When she relayed the day's events to Josh, he said, "I know Gray can be very selfish, but deep down, there's a good guy inside." He looked proud.

"But why wouldn't he want me to know?"

"Maybe he didn't want you to feel indebted to him or something. Either way, you'll see him tomorrow at our cousin's wedding—why don't you ask him?"

"Yeah, I think I will."

"Dinner is served," Josh said, bringing a heaping bowl of spaghetti and meatballs to the table.

Looking at Josh, she could see the traces of his younger brother Gray in the shape of his eyes, the bone structure of his face, the contours of his nose. But the similarities ended there. In his heart, Josh was capable of giving so much more than Gray ever could. Had already given so much more.

After what she'd learned today, though, she hoped that maybe the two brothers shared more than just a physical resemblance. She hoped that maybe Gray had some of Josh's goodness. Gray would never be the kind of man she needed or the kind of man that Josh was. But she was hopeful that there was more to him than she'd thought.

Because if she was lucky, she'd be hanging around with the Brandt clan for years to come. And it would be nice to know that maybe despite everything, she could believe in Gray.

****

"This is going to be strange," Jayne said, keeping a tight grip on Josh's hand as they headed up the church steps.

"It will be fine, I promise." He grinned as he added, "And if not, we'll just sneak out the back." They both laughed, and Josh stopped at the top of the stairs. He took both of her hands. "You are with me now, and I intend to keep it that way. My parents already like you, and they know about us, so it will be okay. And Gray gave his okay to me pursuing you, so it's all good, Jayne."

"You asked him?"

"Well, yeah…once I found out he did care for you, I couldn't destroy my relationship with him. But he said he could actually see us together."

"And here we are."

"Yes, so let's go inside, enjoy my cousin's wedding and the free food at the reception, okay?"

"Okay, Josh." Although nervous, she felt better holding onto him. This would be the first time she'd be around his family since their relationship began. The first time she'd be seeing Gray.

When they walked inside, Jayne remembered a lot of the faces she saw. Various relatives that had been at his parents' for Thanksgiving. *What on earth are they going to think of me being here with a different brother?*

Josh, ever perceptive, whispered, "It's okay, really. Please don't look so scared. There have been far worse scandals with this clan, trust me."

She giggled. "Cousins dating cousins?"

"Not exactly, but don't even ask, okay?" He winked at her.

Just then, she saw Sara Brandt, Josh's mom, waving at them from a pew near the front. Josh waved back and picked up the pace. As they approached the pew, she could see Gray with a blonde, sitting on the other side of his parents.

"Josh, Jayne!" Sara said, standing up to kiss Josh and hug Jayne. The smile on her face bore no hidden agenda, just warmth.

"Hello, Mrs. Brandt," Jayne said, returning the smile. "Mr. Brandt."

"Oh, don't be silly, call us Sara and Bob."

"All right, I will." Josh squeezed her hand as Gray stood up.

"Hey, brother," Gray said as they gave each other a quick man hug. Gray looked right at Jayne, offered a dimpled smile, and said, "It's nice to see you, Jayne."

"Good to see you, too," she said, her heart pounding in her ears. He looked the same but somehow not as attractive to her anymore. There were too many hurt feelings wrapped into her memories of him, and although he was undeniably good looking, he looked a little too polished to her now, a little too slick. But the previous day's revelations had her looking at him with fresh eyes.

"How about a hug for old time's sake?" He offered his arms, and she hugged him back.

"And who's your date?" Jayne asked, desperately wanting the focus off her.

"Oh, Josh, Jayne—this is Alexis." They all greeted her and sat down in their seats.

Jayne was trying to get her heart to slow down; a lot had just happened in one minute. Josh put his hand on her thigh and leaned over, whispering in her ear, "You're still alive."

She grinned and looked into those green eyes she'd grown so enraptured by. Taking his hand, she said, "I'm glad we got that over with."

"Me too."

Just then, a lovely string quartet began playing, and bridesmaids started walking down the aisle on the arms of groomsmen. When the bride entered, everyone stood up, and Jayne thought Josh's cousin looked stunning. Instead of looking at the bride, Jayne felt Josh's stare on her. She looked at him, a smile on her lips, and he put his arm around her to pull her closer.

In her ear he whispered words he'd never spoken to her before. "I love you, Jayne."

Without a moment of hesitation, she said, "I love you, too."

****

At the reception later, the Brandt family filled up their own table with the six of them. About midway through dinner, the awkwardness had dissipated; it seemed to Jayne like she'd known Gray in some other life, some other place. She felt like she'd never been his—like she'd always belonged with Josh.

Sometime after dinner, Gray's date excused herself to go to the bathroom, Josh was at the bar getting drinks for him and Jayne, and Sara and Bob were on the dance floor. That left just Jayne and Gray. He was sitting a few seats away but got up and sat down next to her.

For the first time all night, she felt a little uncomfortable, but also glad they had a moment alone.

"Hey, Jaynie," he said as he sat down.

"Hello, Gray," she said, offering a small smile.

"A little weird, huh?" he asked, chuckling.

"Yeah, a little." Neither one spoke, and Jayne fixed her eyes on the dance floor.

"Jayne?" She turned to look at him. "I'm sorry for the way things turned out with us. I know I hurt you, and I never wanted to do that. Really, I didn't. I should have cut you loose sooner, but to be honest with you, I wasn't ready to see you go. I wanted to spend more time with you, as long I could get away with it." He swallowed. "But I realize now that wasn't fair to you, because I could never give you what you want, what you need."

Even though she was so beyond Gray, and Josh had told her some of those things...hearing it come from Gray felt good. It made the pain from their relationship hurt a little less.

"Thanks, Gray," she said, looking at him with gratitude. "It's nice to hear that."

"And I have to say...I didn't like the idea at first of you and Josh together. But seeing you tonight—wow. I mean...it's like you were meant for each other. You guys are perfect together."

Her smile grew larger and she said, "Yeah, I think we really are." Their gaze lingered for a moment. "What about Alexis? How are things with her?"

"Oh...." Gray shrugged. "It's nothing." He added quietly, "She's no Jaynie, that's for sure."

There seemed to be a sadness in his eyes that she didn't remember. Taking a deep breath, she said, "I have to ask you something."

"What?"

"I know I was almost fired, and someone intervened to save my job and get Tony off my back." Gray looked down. "It was you, wasn't it?"

Without looking up, he nodded.

"Thank you, thank you so much," she said, touching his arm. He looked up.

"You're welcome, Jaynie."

"I can never repay you—"

"You don't owe me anything. You weren't even supposed to know. Did Scott say something to you? I told him to keep his mouth shut."

"No, I just started putting the pieces together. But why did you do that for me? And why didn't you want me to know?"

He sighed. "I know you think I'm an asshole, that I was a total jerk to you. But the truth is I had real feelings for you. We just want different things from life, and I'm not the kind of guy you're looking for, anyway. So when Scott came to me with those termination papers...I realized I had a chance to do something important for someone that means a lot to me." He chuckled. "For a guy that usually just looks out for himself, it felt good knowing I could maybe do something to help you. And help me get rid of some of the guilt. Besides, it was my fault Tony was all over your ass, anyway."

"How was it your fault?"

"Because I was responsible for him being turned down for two promotions, and he clearly holds a grudge. Our relationship was his chance to get back at me." Gray nudged her. "And why didn't you tell me what was going on? I could have intervened before it got that far—"

"I didn't want to complicate our relationship further. Things were already kind of precarious by then."

"Well I'm sorry you were in that position because of me."

"But you saved my job, Gray. That's...amazing."

Gray smiled, his dimples peeking out. "So don't say I never gave you anything."

"I never will. And you know I owe you an apology."

"For what?"

"I really underestimated you. You aren't the heartless cad I tried to tell myself you were."

"Well, I'm not going to sit here and pretend that I'm not an overall selfish guy, because we both know I am." He smiled.

"There's some good stuff in you, too, Gray Brandt. But don't worry, I won't tell anyone." They both laughed. "So I hope there wasn't any fallout for you in taking care of me. And how did you do it?"

"Well, Ms. Asher, it wasn't easy," he admitted. "But the only fallout is having to babysit that prick Tony until I have enough ammunition to fire him. And he's so worthless, it shouldn't be much longer now."

"I'm sorry. How did you get stuck with him?"

"That was the deal I struck. To get him off your back, I had to take him." He looked into Jayne's eyes. "Your job was on the line, which was my fault in part. And after everything…it was the right thing to do. I'd done so much wrong when it came to you, but I knew that was right."

"If I can ever repay you—"

"Seeing you make Josh this happy is more than enough. I know I'm never going to have what you and Josh have together, but that's not what I want from life. I'm married to my career."

Josh was approaching them, and Jayne looked at Gray. She felt sad for him. It was like Josh said, Gray wasn't capable of real love—his ambition was his one true love. He was going to live a lonely life.

"Am I interrupting something?" Josh asked, sitting down on the other side of Jayne, handing her the fuzzy navel she'd requested. He was smiling, but there seemed to be a bit of tension on his face.

"I was just apologizing to your girlfriend here for being such an ass," Gray said, his face lighting up. "And I told her it seems like you two were made for each other. Like this is how it was always supposed to be."

"I think you're right," Josh said, grinning as he held up his glass. "To Gray, for screwing up his shot with the best woman in the world." They all laughed, clinked their glasses together, and took a drink.

They chatted for a bit, then when the band began to play "The Way You Look Tonight," Josh said to Jayne, "May I have the honor of this dance?"

"Of course." He pulled her up and led her to the dance floor.

As he began leading her across the floor, he said, "You are the most beautiful woman in this room. You look stunning tonight."

"Thank you," she said, beaming at him. "And I think you should wear suits more often, because all I can think about is tearing it off of you when we get home."

He threw his head back, laughing. "I like the way you think, Ms. Asher." He kissed her. "So, are you all right? Is everything okay between you and Gray?"

"Yeah, he said some really nice things, things that help me finally shut that door and feel not so damaged by it all. And it was him that saved my job. He actually had to agree to take Tony in his department to get him out of mine."

"Wow," Josh said, looking surprised. "I didn't think he had that kind of selflessness in him."

"Me neither. He did some hurtful things to me, but I really was too harsh in my assessment of him."

"I probably was, too. But then again, I think you brought out something in Gray I haven't seen since we were kids. Kindness."

"Well then we both got something out of the relationship. His heart maybe grew a little bit, and I got you."

They kissed again, and when he pulled away, he had a mysterious look on his face. "You mentioned earlier about tearing off my clothes when we go home…and maybe this is way too soon, and if I'm scaring you, just let me know. But…would you like to move in with me?"

It sounded crazy so early in their relationship, she knew, but it also sounded perfect. "I would love to," she said, unable to stop the smile that was taking over her face. "I know it's only been a month, but they say when it's the one—"

"You'll just know," he answered for her.

"Exactly."

"If you want, I can come over this week after work and help you start packing things up. And then next weekend we can rent a U-Haul and move you in."

"I'm so excited!" she said, her enthusiasm bubbling over.

"Me too," he said, chuckling. "Every night you're not there in bed with me, just seems…wrong."

"I know what you mean."

"And Atticus misses you. He's never had a mommy before, and it's not fair to him that you keep leaving."

She smiled. "That's the whole reason I'm doing this. For Atticus."

"Well, of course, you have to think of the children in a situation like this." They laughed as they swayed together on the dance floor and Jayne knew what she'd been looking for her entire life.

Josh.

****

It was St. Patrick's Day and Claudia was sure to wear her forest green turtleneck sweater. As was the case most days as of late, she felt sick in the morning, but armed with Seven-Up and crackers by her bedside, she managed it. She was still tired all the time but was happy to be. At least she had a reason for it.

She was heading out of the office early because she had an appointment with the doctor for her first ultrasound. She'd sent a text to Sam two days ago that said, Ultrasound w/dr on 17th. U r welcome to come if u want, but don't have to. He had replied right away: Thanx for letting me know.

When she arrived at the doctor's office, she was glad to see there was only one other person in the waiting room. A very pregnant woman. Looked like she was about to burst. Claudia smiled at her, thinking, That will be me in just a few months. Wow.

Within fifteen minutes, Claudia was in a lovely paper gown, her feet in the stirrups with a huge dose of anticipation. Just as the doctor was about to start the vaginal ultrasound, there was a knock at the door and the receptionist poked her head in.

"Um, Mr. Knight is here. He'd like to join you if that's okay, Claudia."

She wasn't sure why, but it made her happy that he'd come. She didn't feel like she needed his support, but it felt like confirmation that maybe he would care for their baby. She didn't want her child to grow up without a father around. Maybe this meant he'd stay in the picture.

"Of course," Claudia said, smiling.

Sam walked in the room, looking a little nervous. He gave Claudia a small smile.

"I'm sorry I'm late."

"You're just in time, Mr. Knight," the doctor said. "Stand up there by Claudia. You'll get a better view." He did, and it felt odd to Claudia to have him so close to her now. She could smell his cologne, feel his breath on her. "Now, we won't hear a heartbeat at this point, but what we're really looking for is the yolk sack. And there it is."

Looking at the screen, against a sea of fuzzy whiteness was a black circle with a white yolk sack inside.

"So that's our baby?" Claudia whispered.

"Yes, it is," the doctor smiled with reassurance. "Next month we can expect to hear a heartbeat."

"This is real," Sam said quietly. Claudia looked at him as he stared at the screen.

"Let me print out a picture for you," the doctor said.

"Can you please print two?" Sam asked.

"Of course."

After the exam was done, Sam left the room and said he'd wait for her in the lobby while she got dressed. When she came out a few minutes later, he was sitting there, looking uncomfortable, staring at the picture in his hand.

They walked outside together, and Claudia was relieved that the weather was finally warming up. Sixty degrees was sure a nice reprieve from the cold winter months they were trying to leave behind.

"I'm glad you came," Claudia said as they stopped outside the doors. "What made you decide to come?"

Sam looked away for a moment and then looked back at Claudia. "Because I am a complete failure at being a husband, and I decided I didn't want to fail at being a parent, too."

"Well, if you decide you want to be a father to this child, you will be great at it, I'm sure. Just don't think that you can pop in and out of its life. You're either in or you're out. I don't want our child to grow up always wondering when he might see his father again."

Sam nodded his head. "I understand, and I agree." He smiled. "You said he...do you think it's a boy?"

She shrugged her shoulders. "I have no idea."

"Do you want to find out the sex when the time comes or be surprised?"

"You know, I think I've had enough surprises lately to last quite a while. I don't need another one."

"Yeah, I can see that." They looked at each other for a moment, neither knowing what to say. Sam cleared his throat. "I've been working pretty closely with Steven since we talked, and he should have something for you to look at in a day or two. If there's anything in it at all that you're not happy with, let me know."

"Okay, I will."

"And Claud...I know you said I could keep the investments, that you don't want them. So I'm going to set up an account in the baby's name, whenever we know what that name is. And then, I want you to have this." He pulled an envelope out of his pocket and handed it her.

She opened it, and saw it was a check for seventy five thousand dollars. "It's for you, to do whatever you want with. Set it aside for retirement, buy a new car, take some trips...whatever you want. We invested money when we were together, and you deserve a portion of it. Your whole life is changing, between us and the baby, so I hope you can find something special to do with it, just for you."

Maybe she would take a trip. Take the girls along with her, before she was a mom and taking a trip would be difficult. The beach, an all-inclusive resort...she could use some relaxation. Then sock away the rest, save it for whatever else life throws at her.

"Thank you, Sam," she said, giving him a smile. "You don't have to do this."

"It's the least I could do."

"If this is a payoff for what you did, it's grossly inadequate."

"No, there's no way I can ever make up for that," he said, looking sad. "It's…it's more of a peace offering."

"It's a start, then," she said. "I gotta go. I'm meeting the girls and their guys for St. Patrick's Day." For once, I'll be the odd man out, she thought to herself. Well, I might as well get used to it.

"What did they say about the pregnancy?"

"They don't know yet. I'm going to surprise them today."

"That will be a pretty big surprise. I know it was for me."

"Me too, trust me. But it's the best surprise I've ever had." She leaned in and gave him a hug. "Thanks for coming. I'll be in touch soon."

"I guess it's too much to tell the girls I said hello?"

"Uh…yeah. Don't think that would go over too well. Bye."

She hurried to her car, glancing at her watch. She would be a few minutes late, which was very unusual for her. But she had a fantastic reason for it.

Chapter Fourteen

Karen could see a green hue from all the St. Patrick's Day decorations reflected in her sparkling diamond ring. Yes, she was staring at it again. A smile played at her lips as she turned her attention back to her laptop. She was holding a table at McGurk's, finishing up some work while she waited for others to arrive. McGurk's was the perfect place to hang out on St. Patrick's Day. Nestled in an historic building in the western St. Louis suburb of O'Fallon, complete with exposed brick walls, massive bar and beautiful patio, it was always popular but never so much as on St. Patrick's Day. To ensure they got a table for their party of five, Karen arrived there at four-thirty, ordered herself a salad and opened up her laptop. By the time the rest of them were scheduled to arrive at six o'clock, the place was brimming with Irish and those declaring themselves Irish for the day.

Rick had texted her a few minutes before, saying he was almost there. So she anxiously kept her eye on the door and waved at him when she saw his handsome frame filling the doorway. He smiled broadly and greeted her with a small kiss on the cheek. She knew he would have rather kissed her on the lips, but she also knew he was sensitive to how uncomfortable she was showing affection in public. She was getting better, trying to loosen up, but it was baby steps.

"You look cute," she said to him as he cozied up next to her in the large booth.

"So do you, my Irish lass."

She laughed. "So are you drinking Guinness Stout tonight?"

"Is there any other drink on this day?"

"Not that I know of." She spotted Jayne near the door, holding hands with a man that looked an awful lot like a guy Karen despised. Please let her judgment be better this time around, she silently begged the universe. I don't know if I can deal with another Brandt if he's a jackass. Karen stood up, waving at Jayne until she saw her.

Jayne's face lit up, and she practically dragged Josh with her. Karen hid her left hand under the table; she wanted to reveal the engagement after everyone was there. As they approached, Karen inspected him with a watchful eye. Well, he did seem a little...less. Not so in-your-face gorgeous, although he was very good looking. But whereas Gray looked like a brunette Ken doll, Josh looked more like a regular guy. Instead of the fancy designer duds that she'd seen Gray in, Josh was wearing jeans and a nice green sweater. As they reached the table, she could see that the sweater matched his eyes. And unlike his brother's perfectly coifed hairdo, Josh's hair was longer on top, wavy and untamed.

"Hey you guys," Jayne said, grinning from ear to ear. "Rick, Karen, this is Josh."

Rick stood up, and shook hands, "Nice to meet you, Josh."

"Nice to meet you," Josh said, offering a nervous but sincere smile. He shook Karen's hand, too. "So good to finally put a face to the names. I've heard a lot about you guys...I feel like I already know you." He and Jayne sat across from them on the other side of the booth.

"I've heard an earful about you, too," Karen said, smiling, yet checking him out all the while.

"Well, I'm sure your guard is up with me, after everything with Gray," he said, and Karen was impressed that he jumped right in to address the elephant in the room. He's got balls. I like that.

"Oh," Rick said, chuckling, "we're big fans of your brother." Rick winked at Jayne.

Josh smiled. "I know better. I mean, we're brothers, we get each other, but we're about as different as…corned beef and cabbage."

They all laughed. "Actually," Jayne said, "Gray's a better guy than I gave him credit for. I found out that he's the one that got that horrible boss, Tony, transferred out of my department."

"Gray did that?" Karen asked, surprised.

"Yes, and he didn't want me to know about it. Apparently Tony was trying to get me fired, and Gray went to the head of the department and agreed to have Tony work for him in exchange for saving my job."

"Wow," Rick said. "Didn't see that coming."

"Yeah, me neither."

"So is he having problems with Tony?" Karen asked.

"Yeah, he's gathering ammo to fire him." They all laughed.

"Well I'm glad to hear your brother isn't the complete douche I chalked him up to being," Karen said to Josh.

"I'm not going to sit here and tell you he's a saint," Josh said with a chuckle, "because he's not, and he did do some things that hurt Jayne. But it's nice to know he's not a total loss for the Brandt family."

Karen glanced at her watch; it was ten minutes after six. Claudia was meticulous about being on time, all the time.

"Claudia's late," Karen said to Jayne, who then looked concerned. "I wonder what's going on. She's never late."

"Let me call her," Jayne said, pulling out her phone. The others chatted, and when Jayne hung up the phone she said, "She's almost here. She had a late appointment or something."

As they talked, Karen got a good feeling about Josh. She liked the way she saw him gently holding Jayne's hand, and the look on his face when she was talking was nothing short of adoration. The thing was Jayne looked at him the same way. It was mutual. When Jayne had been with Gray, Karen always got the impression that she felt lucky just to be in his presence, and he felt she was lucky, too. Such bullshit.

Josh was certainly no Gray Brandt. Thank God.

"Claudia!" Jayne exclaimed as she neared their table. Karen was happy to see Claudia looking good; the last time she'd seen her, she was practically despondent. Today she looked more like her normal self.

"Hello," Claudia said. "Where can I squeeze in?"

"Right here," Jayne said, urging Josh closer to the wall, making room for Claudia.

"Hi, Josh," Claudia said, smiling at him. "Nice to see you again."

"Oh, you've met?" Karen asked, surprised.

"Unfortunately for Josh, yes," Claudia said, chuckling. "The poor guy had to come over with Jayne on their first date because I was in a panic. Sam was on his way over to get some of his things, and I wasn't quite ready to be alone with him."

"And not only did he do that on our first real date," Jayne said, grinning, "we followed that up with game night at the Asher household."

"Impressive," Karen said, nodding her head in approval.

"It was no big deal," Josh said, looking at Jayne. "Doesn't matter what we do, as long as I get to hang out with you." Jayne's face lit up, and she kissed him.

"Oh, for God's sake," Karen said, rolling her eyes. "I'm all for love, blah blah blah, but can we tone down the ick factor just a bit?"

They all laughed. "Don't mind her," Rick said, grinning at Karen. "She just recently got a heart. It's not fully functioning yet."

"Speaking of getting a heart," Karen said, her face displaying the biggest smile they'd ever seen, "somehow I've conned this gorgeous man into thinking I'm a keeper." With that, she pulled her hand out from under the table, ceremoniously flashing her ring.

"Oh my God!" Jayne squealed, grabbing Karen's hand and taking a closer look at the ring. "First of all, this ring is exquisite."

"Thank you, I designed it," Rick said with obvious pride.

"Rick, it's stunning," Claudia said.

"And second of all," Jayne continued, "I never thought you'd ever get married."

"I know." Karen shrugged, looking at Rick. "But how could I ever leave a guy like this? I mean, look at him—look at that hair."

They all laughed and Josh said, "This calls for a toast. To Rick and Karen, at the risk of grossing Karen out, may this be the beginning of a beautiful life together."

"To Rick and Karen," they all said. Karen had never been happier.

"Wow, Rick," Josh said, "you've set the bar kind of high there when it comes to engagement rings, haven't you? I can't do that on a teacher's salary."

"Sorry, man," Rick said as they both laughed.

"Wait a minute," Karen said, eyeing them both. "It's only been a few weeks, hasn't it? A little too early to be talking engagement rings."

"You're right, it's too soon to have a serious talk about it," Jayne said, looking at Josh. She looked back at Karen. "But we are moving in together."

"Oh, Jayne, that's wonderful," Claudia said, giving her a hug. "That's a huge step."

"Yeah, it is. I'm so excited. Josh has a great place right by Main Street in St. Charles, and he's got the most lovable dog I've ever met."

"I think she likes my dog more than me," Josh quipped.

"No, sweetie, but I do like him just as much."

"Thanks," he groaned. "So, Rick, you did such a great job designing that ring—I guess your experience with graphic design came in handy."

"Oh, yeah, you bet. I also dabble in painting, sometimes sculpting. But this was my most important work, for sure."

"I'd love to see some of your stuff. Do you ever show your work?"

They all kind of looked at each other, each of them remembering Gray's comments about Rick's interest in art. How he had dismissed it since Rick wasn't in it to make a buck.

"No, I don't," Rick said, keeping his eye on Josh. "I just do it as a form of expression."

"I know exactly what you mean. I mean, I'm an English teacher, and most of us are closet writers. So I've got a couple of novels under my belt and more in me. I don't know if I'll ever try to publish them, but they're floating around in my head, so I just have to get the words out."

The entire table seemed to breathe a collective sigh of relief. Josh looked around him, confused, as Rick said, "Thank God you're not like your brother. No offense, but he's a pompous prick."

"None taken," Josh chuckled. "I don't think he's as bad as he comes across. He's harmless, actually. But I know where you're coming from."

"Well, you are light years away from him," Rick said. "I propose a toast to Josh, the clear winner in a battle of brothers." They all laughed as they toasted Josh.

Afterward, Karen looked at Claudia. Despite everything she was going through with Sam, she seemed pretty good. Karen wondered if it was all just a good act. She did look tired.

"Hey, Claud," Karen said, touching her friend's hand. "How are you hanging in there? We're all gushing about what's going on with us...I guess we were being a little insensitive. I'm sorry."

"Oh no, don't be sorry, it's wonderful news for both of you," she said, smiling at her friends. "Really. I've never seen either one of you happier, and I'm thrilled."

"Well how are you?" Jayne asked.

"You know, I'm doing well, all things considered. It's starting to get easier, I'm starting to come to terms with everything." She looked down at her glass of tea, running her finger around the rim. "The more I think about things, I realize what Sam and I had was good. Ultimately, it wasn't what he wanted forever, but it was good while it lasted. I don't regret any of it, and I'm moving past the anger. He's not my favorite person on the planet right now, but I certainly don't hate him or anything like that."

"You're a better woman than me," Karen said, shaking her head.

"Well don't get me wrong—I'm not exactly ready to trust someone any time soon. But I'm in a good place. Our time together had meaning. It led me to this..." She reached in her purse and pulled out the ultrasound picture.

There was stunned silence at the table.

"Does that mean...?" Jayne's whispered words hung around them, afraid to hope too much.

"I'm pregnant." Claudia's eyes welled with tears as she spoke the words aloud to the people that she loved. Karen leapt out of her seat and threw her arms around Claudia. Jayne's eyes filled with tears as she kissed Claudia on the cheek.

After words of congratulations and many tears, Karen finally asked, "But how? You were always so careful about being on the pill."

"Remember when I had a sinus infection? I was on antibiotics."

"Oh, and antibiotics can decrease the effectiveness of birth control pills," Jayne said, nodding her head.

"I'm making a note of that," Rick said as Karen elbowed him.

"So...yeah. I'm having a baby. That's what I've always wanted."

"Did you tell Sam?" Josh asked.

"Yeah, and he's been pretty great about it, really. I think he's in shock, sure. He's taking care of everything financially, giving me much more than I asked for. This baby will want for nothing. And in return, I've told him it's up to him how much he wants to be involved in the child's life."

"And what does he say about that?" Jayne asked.

"Well, he showed up for the ultrasound today, even though I told him it was completely optional. But he said he'd failed at being a husband, and he didn't want to fail as a father, too."

"We should give him a little credit for that," Rick said, finishing his beer and motioning to the waitress.

"Just a little," Karen said, still filled with anger about what Sam had done.

"Since this baby means Sam will still be around, we'll all have to move on. The past is the past and you can't be mean to the father of my child. No matter how much you want to, Karen." Claudia chuckled.

"Maybe just glare at him?"

"Okay, I'll concede to a glare."

From the speakers overhead, John Mayer's smoky voice sang the chorus of St. Patrick's Day.

"Do you guys remember last fall, talking about this song?" Jayne asked, looking with fascination at all her friends.

"Yes, I do," Karen said, nodding.

"Me too," Claudia said.

"Well, ladies, here we are." Jayne sighed. "Absolutely nothing turned out the way we thought it would."

"That's for damn sure," Karen said. "Sorry, Rick, I told them back then that I'd stay with you through the holidays but probably not much more."

"Oh, really?" he asked, giving her a strange look.

"Well, yeah. I was getting too attached, and the old Karen didn't like how that felt. But the new improved Karen can't get enough of you." She kissed him in front of everyone, and jaws at the table dropped.

"That is something I wish I had a picture of," Jayne said, giggling.

"Me too!" Rick laughed.

"And back then," Claudia said, looking at Jayne, "you were just hoping that you and Gray would last until at least St. Patty's Day."

"Yeah…and we didn't quite make it to Valentine's Day." Jayne squeezed Josh's hand. "But he did lead me to Josh."

"True," Claudia said. "And I was foolish enough to think I had nothing to worry about. I thought I had it all. Now look who's alone?"

They were all quiet for a moment. Then Jayne said, "No you're not. You've got that baby with you, wherever you go."

Claudia smiled with gratitude at Jayne. "You're right. Thank you."

"You're welcome. A toast to St. Patrick's Day."

As they raised their glasses, faces smiling, full of hope—even Karen could feel optimism about the future. The winter months had been difficult for all of them, but as the temperature outside was starting to creep up and flowers were beginning to bloom…the spring looked brighter than ever.

THE END

ABOUT HOLLY GILLIATT

When she's not busy daydreaming of someday spending her life writing from a cozy house in the woods, Holly Gilliatt has a hectic life in the suburbs as a wife and mom to three glorious—and crazy—kids. Working full-time selling packaging supplies and equipment in St. Louis, Missouri pays the bills (most months). A hopeless romantic and music addict, she finds time to pursue her passion for writing by avoiding housework. Her biggest ambition is to someday be caught up with the laundry.

If you enjoyed Holly Gilliatt's *'Til St. Patrick's Day,*
you might also enjoy these women's fiction authors
published by Turquoise Morning Press:

Margaret Ethridge, author of *Commitment*
Karen Stivali, author of *Meant To Be*
Grace Greene, author of *Kincaid's Hope*

Thank you!

for purchasing this book from
Turquoise Morning Press.

We invite you to visit our Web site to learn more about our
quality Trade Paperback and eBook selections.

As a gift to you for purchasing this book, please use
COUPON CODE Ebook15 during your visit to receive
15% off any digital title in our Turquoise Morning Press
Bookstore.

www.turquoisemorningpressbookstore.com

Turquoise Morning Press
Because every good beach deserves a book.
www.turquoisemorningpress.com
~~~~